# ELLE HARTFORD

# Death Pulls the Strings

*The Alchemical Tales #6*

*To all the wonderful people in my life
who have helped me untangle myself—
and patiently helped me figure out this friendship thing.*

# Contents

# Preface

Long, long ago, a coven of witches created a world just
beyond ours—
a realm of fairy tales.
In Beyond, humans rub shoulders with mythical creatures,
and magic mixes with science.

There are only three rules:

**Happily**
accept that we share the same home

**Ever**
remember that what you take, you must also give

**After**
struggle will always lead to new beginnings

So, if you are ready . . . you are welcome here.

* * *

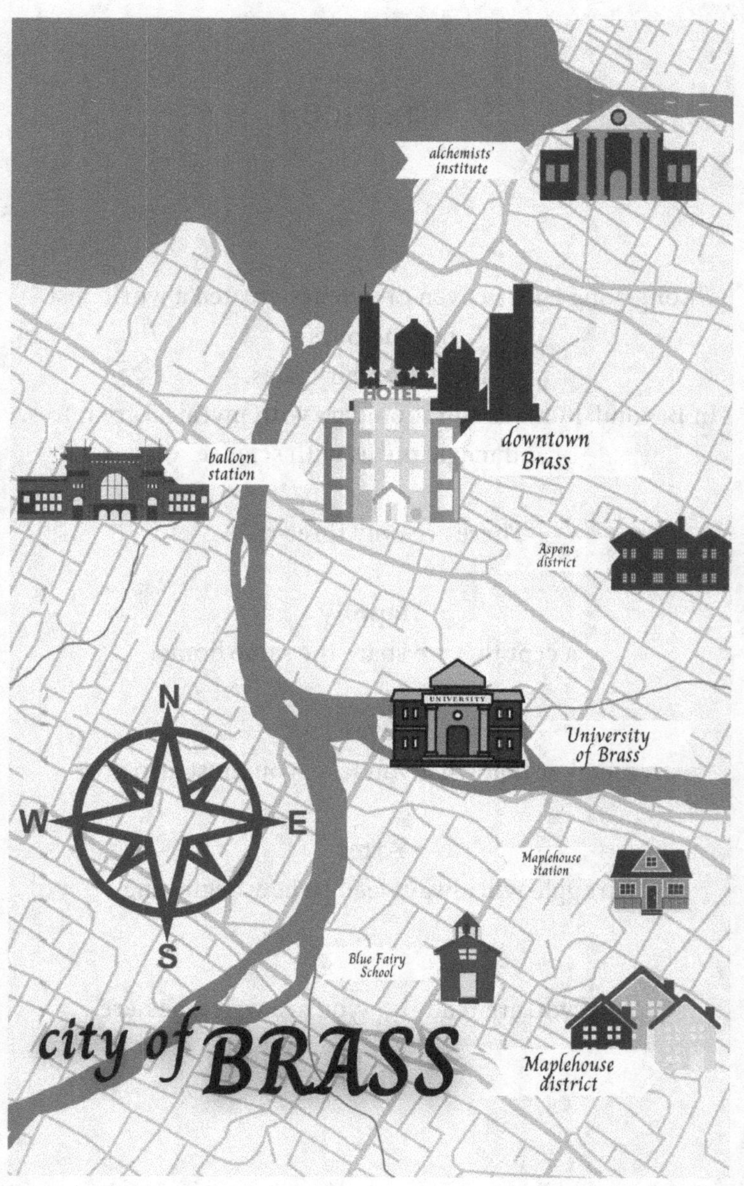

alchemists' institute
balloon station
downtown Brass
HOTEL
Aspens district
UNIVERSITY
University of Brass
Maplehouse station
Blue Fairy School
Maplehouse district
N
W
E
S
city of BRASS

# Cast of Characters

*Top thirteen, in alphabetical order*

Adam: headmaster of The Blue Fairy's School for Magical Children

Bakis, Chief: chief of police in Brass; friend of Officer Thorn; first name Koda

Boa: friendly member of the Lost Rabbit Supper Club; carpenter

Bryn: acting secretary of the Lost Rabbit Supper Club

Katerina: vice president of the Lost Rabbit Supper Club

Luca: bookseller and scholar, headed to a conference; dating Red

Meteor: miraculous child of Mix and Shades; uncle, Bricky, victim of murder

Orlix: mysterious sorcerer who lives in Brass

Paracelsus: legendary alchemist; mentor to Red

Red: alchemist and child of Seers, full name Cinnabar Sunset; dating Luca

Sweep: a broom familiar known to accompany Bricky; both murdered

Thorn, Officer: half-orc policewoman in charge of keeping law in Belville

William: canine familiar, capable of protection magic and plenty of sass

1

# No Strings Attached

"This is your last chance," I warned William. "Want to relive the glory days?"

"It's hardly 'reliving' anything when your *boyfriend* will be there," he snorted.

I stood at the door to our small apartment and settled my traveling bags at my feet. The early morning light streaming in through the bank of windows facing Market Square gave the cozy studio a warm glow, and for a moment I regretted leaving—a strange new feeling.

"You don't miss the traveling days at all?" I asked William, more gently.

He shifted in his spot on the couch, turning his head so he looked away from me. A magical being—a "familiar" with just as much attitude as magic—William looked like a big black sheepdog, but he could be as expressive as an actress on stage. "That isn't the point. Someone has to watch the shop. *One* of us should be responsible, after all."

"Neither one of us has to watch the shop," I reminded him, a little exasperated. We—well, *I*—had been preparing for this

1

trip for weeks. The shop had been William's main objection all along, but it made no sense. Red's Alchemy and Potions was *mine*, and if anyone should be worried about keeping the business going, it'd be me. "Rhys has things under control. This isn't the first time he's held down the fort, remember?" My employee and one of William's good friends, Rhys, was a former knight with an eye for detail and a penchant for writing daily reports. He was probably more responsible than William and me put together. I leaned my shoulder against the door frame, staring across the little kitchen at my best friend. "What is it *really*, William? You know you don't have to come if you don't want to. I'm not going to force you to do anything. I just don't see why you're being so . . . *weird* about it."

"*You're* being weird," he grumped.

I hesitated. Normally I would ignore this attitude as a fit of pique. Though he was intelligent and protective, William could be petty sometimes, too. But I couldn't help but wonder, now, if he really meant it . . .

. . . *But what is weird about me going on a trip?* I fiddled with the edges of my embroidered traveling cloak, my tan skin standing out against the dark red border. When William and I met years ago, I'd been starting out as a traveling alchemist, going from town to town selling potions and doodads. Just as I'd left my magical Seer heritage behind, he'd left behind his former life and was looking for new adventures. We'd spent years on the road before settling down in Belville to open a shop. I'd worked hard to get the store and my lab up and running; we'd only been on a handful of vacations since settling down. *Does William really prefer it that way? Does he feel so strongly about staying in Belville?*

"Well, either way, it's only five days," I said uncertainly. "The conference itself is only three, but Luca wanted to get there a day early, and we don't want to rush on the way back." I'd told William all this before, of course, but something about this strange goodbye made me cling to the facts. "The city should be pretty windy and cold this time of year, so I don't want to stay any longer. Not to mention it'll be full of tourists for the holidays. But I thought it'd be neat to show Luca a few of the sights while we're there. It's his first time, you know."

Actually, that was why I was going. It was Luca's first time for a lot of things: first time attending a conference, first time in Brass, first time in a big city, first time traveling so far from Belville (aside from a few memorable trips to Seaside). The conference itself was an event for scholars and booksellers, like Luca; I wouldn't have any part in it at all. But Luca had been nervous about going, almost determined to stay home, and I hated to see him like that. Besides, a trip to Brass was a good excuse to stock up on rare alchemical tools and supplies.

None of that reasoning, spoken or unspoken, made any impact on William. His large black nose was turned resolutely from me. I sighed.

"Well, you know how to reach me, I guess. Let me know if you decide you want a souvenir. We're going by balloon from Pine, so I've got to head out soon if we're going to get there in time. I guess I'll . . . I'll see you in a few days, then."

William said nothing, so reluctantly, I gathered up my bags and turned to go.

It was actually a relief when, instead of walking through the open door, I ran right into something solid and warm.

I stumbled backward into my kitchen, reeling, and got an eyeful of black hair as the incoming Officer Thorn tossed her head. Her half-orc heritage gave her mossy green skin, impossibly broad shoulders, pointed ears, and a toothy, no-nonsense smile. She was, as always, perfectly made up in her guild-issue uniform, boots sparkling, long hair swaying like she'd just emerged from Gloria's salon next door. My five-foot-nine barely reached her chin.

"Oh, Red, I caught you," she declared unnecessarily. "Good. Gather round, both of you. This is big."

"Bigger than the balloon I need to catch?" I demanded, fully distracted from the pain of leaving.

"You mean the balloon *we* need to catch," my friend the police officer corrected me. Impervious to the look on my face, she pressed her way farther into the kitchen, opening cabinet doors and peering into the icebox as if she owned the place. Sugar, a tiny sparkling pixie, shot out from her little nest above the kitchen window and began chittering angrily, circling Officer Thorn's head. I shook my head again, trying to make sense of my morning. Thorn demanded, "Don't you have any food?"

"Luca and I are meeting at the café," I said, doing my best to organize my thoughts. "In about five minutes. So can you please tell me what's going on?"

Officer Thorn freed a roll from the breadbox on the counter—one of the rolls I'd intended for William, to keep him fed and happy while I was gone—and devoured half of it in one bite before explaining herself. "I've been called in to a special case in Brass. Timing couldn't be better. I need your help on this one."

"Why?" I asked suspiciously as I tried to calm Sugar down.

"There's a question of partiality among the local force," Thorn said, through the remaining half of her roll. "That's why they're calling in an outside investigator. As to why I need *you,* I have a feeling this one will be magical. And not in a good way. The primary witness so far is a rock child named Meteor."

"A *child?*" I asked.

"A *rock* child?" Across the room, William's ears perked up. "In Brass?"

"That's the whole problem," Officer Thorn said, licking her fingers. "Some big political dispute going on in the city right now about 'em. The official name is 'magical near-life forms.'"

"'*Near*-life'? That's a terrible thing to call someone," I said indignantly. "Why, that could include automata, magical puppets or animations, or even—"

*Familiars, like William.* It didn't need to be said. At least, *I* didn't feel the need to say it . . . But Thorn was oblivious.

"Rumor has it a familiar is one of the victims," she informed us, looking hard across the room at William. "Some kind of magic broom, if my intel is right. Why aren't you ready to go?"

I cleared my throat. "Oh, he isn't com—"

"I *am* ready," said William, hopping down from the sofa. Ignoring me and focusing on Thorn, he added, "You can explain what happened along the way."

# 2

# A Friendly Conscience

Before I could ponder William's sudden change of heart or Officer Thorn's perpetual hunger, they'd swept out of my kitchen and down the stairs like an exiting plague of locusts. The lid of the breadbox clattered in their wake.

"Okay, well, it looks like it might be just you in charge for the next few days, Sugar," I told the little winged fairy hovering by my shoulder. Despite my efforts to reassure her, my voice shook. "You'll be alright? You can always hitch a ride up to Daisy with Rhys, if you want to."

The pixie shimmered at me. She'd been haunting my kitchen for two years now, and rarely chose to speak. Instead, she communicated in aerial gestures and little bits of light. Most pixies in Belville lived either high on the mountain with the reclusive Daisy, or in a hidden headquarters in town . . . and in the sudden silence of my soon-to-be-abandoned studio, I found myself relating more to Sugar than ever.

"Alright, if you're sure," I said, interpreting her shimmer as an encouraging *go on, I'm fine, Red.* Her moods, like William's apparently, could change on a dime. But she was always honest about them. I smiled. "In that case no raiding the pantry. Stick to the bread box. And if anything happens, get Rhys or Gloria—she's promised to look in each evening after she closes up the salon."

Rather than hear about our neighbor's plans to check in, Sugar had begun ineffectually pushing me toward the door, her tiny hands tangling in the black hair of my ponytail as she struggled against the weight of my head. She usually liked playing with my hair and its intermittent iridescent strands, marks of magic I'd never known what to do with. Sugar could always be relied upon to see half-hidden truths. I laughed. "Okay, so I'm stalling. I'll go now, promise. Be good, okay?"

The pixie was a warm ball of light, illuminating the kitchen as I slung my duffel bag over one shoulder and tucked my lab case under my arm. I glanced around once more—just long enough to see that the sun had fully risen over Market Square, and the winter morning had begun—before stepping outside and locking up behind me.

Outside my kitchen door was a little landing, and from there a staircase took me down to the back of my shop. Red's Alchemy & Potions was my pride and joy, my anchor; now that William had so gleefully abandoned it, I felt a little pang. I locked my outer door and resisted the urge to head into my lab. I'd already made all the potions for the week and cleaned everything up yesterday. There was nothing more to be done. In a few hours, Rhys would come into work—he'd long since been trusted with a key to the shop—and he'd run the sales floor, leaving the lab behind it safely undisturbed. Though I would have trusted him with my equipment in a pinch, he seemed to prefer selling and tidying to brewing potions or distilling fools' gold. "My days of experimenting are over," he liked to say. In many ways, it made him a perfect assistant, because I loved to lock myself in my lab and get lost in alchemical processes. Experiments and science were where I felt safe.

However I knew that if I poked back into my lab now, I'd just lose more time. So I cut across my back patio, its potted plants covered and tucked in for the winter, and made my way into the street.

Belville's streets were quiet this time of morning, especially on such a chilly day. I came around the corner of my shop and was faced with a misty, empty Market Square. The trees stood watch quietly, a lingering smell of frost in the air. *Thorn and William must have gone ahead to Saki's,* I thought with a sigh.

The Pomegranate Café was the one lively storefront along the Square, its dark pink siding and prim white trim hardly containing all the bustle and brightness of Belville's early-morning coffee drinkers. It was immediately to my right, on the same corner as my own store. My friend Saki, or Sakura, had opened the café nearly a year ago now and had quickly seen success—as much because of her tea and coffee as because of her match-making ways. Rumor on the street had it that because Sakura was a shadow witch, her advice about love and relationships was *certain* to be true. If a little blunt and sometimes dark. Fortunately, Luca and I had not needed to turn to her for match-making services . . .

The moment I crossed the front porch and entered the café, I was met with not only my boyfriend but the errant William and Officer Thorn as well. The three of them stood at the end of the sales counter, tucked away to the left, staring at me over a sea of tables and sofas.

"Hi, Red!" Luca, unsurprisingly, was the first to speak. Even in a café full of early risers and go-getters picking up orders or working at tables, he was the brightest presence in the room. Like all scholars in Beyond, he wore floor-length black robes; but today his hood was thrown back over his shoulders, exposing dark brown skin and deep green tattoos peeking out from beneath closely cropped black hair. He also sported an old-fashioned aviator's cap, no doubt in honor of the balloon ride we'd soon be taking. Beneath the leather cap with its fluffy white lining, his green eyes shone. The moment I made it within arms' reach, he pulled me into a hug.

Our bags slung and knocked into each other awkwardly, but I didn't care. Luca's hug was the highlight of my morning so far.

"I ordered you a spinach, sweet potato, and egg pasty and chai with almond cream and extra cinnamon syrup," Luca said, still talking as he let me go. "It should be ready any minute. Saki said we can take the mugs with us as long as we bring them back. Actually she threatened me with a rather serious anti-theft spell. I'm not sure how it will work given that Brass is a full five-hour ride away from Belville—"

"Rest assured, it will," said the shadow witch in question. Perhaps five foot tall, capped with a bright white bob and youthful blue eyes, she smirked at me from behind her counter. Today, her Pomegranate apron was burgundy red, layered over a hot pink sweater and under a white fuzzy scarf. As she passed two tall ceramic to-go mugs to us, she added, "Here's your order. Just give me a minute for the officer's mocha and William's peppermint bun. Glacial's warming up the pastries in the kitchen. Why are there so many of you? I thought it was just you lovebirds going," she teased over her shoulder as she returned to her machines.

"I don't suppose they've explained it to you yet?" I asked Luca, still ignoring Officer Thorn and William hovering nearby.

"They haven't, they just showed up behind me in line," he told me. Turning to William specifically, he asked, "Did you decide to come with us after all?"

There was so much joy in Luca's question that I couldn't bear to look at him. It made my heart, hidden under cloak and thick winter tunic, feel like it might overflow. Luca is and always will be a complete sweetheart, but he was genuinely excited and accepting of William. Everyone in Belville accepted William; he didn't give them much other choice, after all. But still, in this particular instance, Luca's sweetness made me just want to burst.

Naturally, though, Officer Thorn barreled her way right over the moment. "We're both coming," she informed Luca. "There's been a murder."

Sakura's well-run café ground to a halt for just an instant. Officer Thorn was many things—many of them good—but discreet was not one of them. Fortunately, most of the citizens of Belville were polite enough to pretend to return to their own business.

For his part, Luca looked stricken. I found myself inwardly cursing Thorn—Luca was really excited about this, his first in-person conference of scholars, and I hated to think anything could ruin it. "Someone in Brass, you mean?" he asked. "I mean, it must be, otherwise why would you be going there, right?"

"We haven't heard the details yet," I told him.

"We'll talk it all over on the way there," Officer Thorn agreed, suddenly becoming aware of how the entire two-story café was leaning in to listen.

"Mocha and food," Saki announced, returning to the counter across from us. "And don't worry about leaving your new recruits in charge of the station, Officer. We'll make sure they're well taken care of."

***

I doubted Officer Thorn was the type to worry. But *I* was, and all my friends knew it.

As we piled out of the café, hands full of breakfast, Luca still brimming with questions, William leaned into my leg. "See? Everything's going to be fine."

"Big words from someone who didn't want to leave in the first place!" I hissed back. "We are talking about that later. Just because we suddenly have a million things to talk about doesn't mean I'm going to forget."

"I knew she'd say that," Officer Thorn was saying meanwhile. "I knew it'd be fine. Ruff and Tuff are nearly up to snuff."

*"Nearly" being the operative word,* I thought, re-shouldering my bag as we made our way across the Square. "Ruff" and "Tuff" were mostly-affectionate nicknames that the town had developed for Officer Thorn's latest trainees, a pair of centaurs who seemed to do everything together. They'd arrived at the beginning of fall and so far their most remarkable feat had been putting on a wild dancing display at the town Halloween party on the Square. Between the two of them they had four times as many legs as Thorn, but about half the confidence. Their hearts were in the right place, though. And if Saki said she would help keep the peace, she meant it.

But I had other things to worry about.

"Red and I made arrangements with the boat club for someone to ferry us over to Pine," Luca was telling Thorn. Despite any misgivings he may have had, his voice was upbeat. "We're supposed to meet them at the dock. I think they said they'd take the old fishing boat, so there should be plenty of room. Don't you have any luggage?"

"They'll have everything I need at the station in Brass," Officer Thorn said confidently. "Besides, I have my go bag."

She did, indeed, have a slim black bag hanging from one shoulder, like she was the cool kid in school. I hadn't noticed it before, but now that William and I walked behind her and Luca, it swung in front of my nose like a mesmerist's watch.

"Exactly how much notice did you have about this case?" I asked, doing my best to keep my voice down as we passed businesses and apartments lining the street.

"The request came over the wire half an hour ago," Officer Thorn said. "I would've been on my way already if all your dithering hadn't slowed me down."

She said it affectionately enough that I didn't suppose she minded too much. Besides, it was *our* travel plans she was crashing.

"Say bye to Frank," Luca said whimsically as we passed the bookshop on the corner. Though the lights were on, it was doubtful that Frank—an ancient mink who worked as the bookstore's assistant—was actually watching for us. He had promised to watch the bookstore in Luca's absence, but he really wasn't a very social creature. "Anyway, Officer, were you hoping to get there faster than balloon travel? Because maybe you could go ask Trent—"

"No Witches needed," Thorn interrupted. "The incident

happened last night. With this kind of situation, a few more hours won't hurt."

"We still haven't heard anything about the situation," I muttered.

As we started down the hill to the lake, Officer Thorn turned and grinned over her shoulder at me. "Oh, Red. Don't you know that patience is a virtue?"

3

# A Tall Tale

Officer Thorn seemed to enjoy making me wait. The four of us huddled in silence on the boat ride across the lake, eating our pastries and turning our backs to the damp breeze. Once we got to Pine, the local county seat, all we could focus on was how to find the balloon station in time. Though I had been to Pine before, it had been years since I'd ridden in a magitech balloon.

The station, as might have been expected, was on the outskirts of town. Pine sprawled out across the hillside above the lake, bigger and busier than Belville, but still not so large that we couldn't cross it on foot. We huffed and puffed our way up the steep cobblestone roads until we came upon an old stone building, big enough to be a castle. It was wide and impressive and just the sight of it made Luca perk up further . . . but I couldn't help thinking to myself, *I bet it's stone because they tried building a wood one first and it burned down!*

It's not that I am, by nature, a pessimist. Not exactly. It's just that, in Beyond, sometimes there's a little competition between *magic* and *science*. On one side you have Witches and spells and familiars, and on the other you have botany and geology and alchemy and . . . well, magitech. Most of what folks call "magitech" is actually steam-powered technology, so intricately designed that it seems like magic. It tends to be elaborate and showy and, frankly, unreliable. It also tends to give more *serious* science a bad name.

Let it not be said that I am prejudiced—after all, I adore William, and the local Witch, Trent, is basically a younger brother to me. But I *do* usually avoid magitech when possible. And out in the wild backwoods of Belville, it is extremely possible. But when in, or going to, Brass, it would be more difficult.

"Come on, Red," William muttered as we joined the throngs filing through the station to board the balloon. "They never explode any more. Usually."

I knew he was being negative on purpose, so I didn't dignify his comment with a response. I had to focus on buying our tickets, anyway. Full fare for me, half for William . . . it was common practice, so I usually didn't give the matter another thought, but this time it did give me pause. I remembered what Officer Thorn had said the new term in Brass was: *magical near-life forms*. Technically, it was true. As a created, magical being, William wasn't considered "alive" in the same sense that I was, and that was why he got half fare.

For the first time, I realized that maybe this didn't sit very well with me.

But in the surge of the crowd and the stress of making sure we didn't lose Luca, I soon set that particular worry aside. Actually, it turned out to be quite convenient that Officer Thorn came along—not that I'd admit as much out loud. Her confidence and bulk was enough to cut a path for us through the throng; all I had to do was hang on to Luca, keep one eye on William, and follow in her wake.

Because of the confusion and slight delay in our morning plan, we ended up in perfect time to walk right on to the balloon. After buying our tickets, we went up and up a series of stairs and magical lifts until we got to the dock, spanning the roof of the building. The balloon itself was massive—not the largest I'd ever seen, but as large as the building, easily. It stretched out like a sleeping whale, bullet-shaped, a patchwork of blue and green canvas. Beneath it, the passenger cabin was slung like a baby calf clinging to its mother.

We made our way up a gangplank and into the cabin. The main hall was just that, a long hall with windows on either side, and beneath each window, tables framed by plush booths. Concessions stands sold overpriced popcorn and all kinds of drinks; puzzles and games and toys were available for rent or sale, too. But Officer Thorn was all business. She led the way to an empty table and claimed it like an explorer in unsettled land, slinging her backpack into the corner before sliding in herself. William hopped up next to her, and Luca and I fell into the booth facing them.

The tables looked nondescript, a whitewashed pine. But as soon as we were sitting, I could feel the slight distortion that came with ingrained spellwork: a noise-canceling spell, certainly, and perhaps a privacy spell as well. I was no magical expert, but I noticed William sniffing the air, testing the spells himself. He seemed satisfied, and I trusted his judgment.

"Alright, then," said Officer Thorn, leaning over the table with both elbows. "Let's finally get down to it."

I caught Luca's eye out of the corner of my own, and we exchanged a humorous look. *Oh, "finally," she says?* Across the table, William sneezed.

"Here's the deal," Thorn continued. Her voice was gravelly, as low as it ever got. Between this display of discretion and the spellwork around us, I felt certain that the happy families and travelers around us were none the wiser. "It came in over the wire this morning. Murder in the Maplehouse district in Brass."

"That's where the conference is," Luca interjected, his eyes worried once more.

I put my hand on his arm without a second thought. It was a comforting, but also a *wait-and-see* gesture. I kept my gaze on Thorn.

"There's a full station in Maplehouse, of course," Officer Thorn went on, as I knew she would. "Three recruits, six officers, and a chief. The chief's an old friend of mine; asked for me particularly when they saw how things were starting to go.

"I already told these ones," she added to Luca, indicating me and William with a shrug of one massive shoulder. "But I guess I might as well tell you—"

"How about you start at the beginning," I interrupted, "and tell us all everything, right now, as if we hadn't heard anything yet?" *Because we basically haven't,* I thought.

"I vote for that too," William panted.

With a lurch, the balloon above us was unmoored, and began to take flight. For a moment we lost Luca as he turned to the window to watch Pine fall away. I put my hand out, asking Thorn to wait, grinning at my country boyfriend's excitement. Once the balloon was well into the air, we resumed our huddle.

"Settle down and listen up," said Thorn. "This is everything I know. There's a big campaign going on in Brass right now. At

Yule, they're going to be voting on a new proposal—something about the rights and recognition of magical creations. Familiars, charmed children, the like. It's a hot topic all over the city, to hear my friend tell it.

"As things stand now, there's this term they use—'magical near-life forms'—don't give me that look, Red, you said I should go over everything, and this is part of it—that covers familiars, magically-created kids, puppets, those automata thingies Red's always going on about, and whatever else I've forgotten."

Luca was nodding along. "It's a big theoretical issue at the university, too," he said, when I caught his eye. "There's going to be several papers on it at the conference. I have a friend in Brass who says that for people on both sides it's a very personal issue. Which I completely understand," he added, with a look at William.

William seemed to be focused on Thorn, though.

"Right. So," Officer Thorn resumed, "the local Guild decided that they'd better bring in an outside opinion, what with this being a political matter and whatnot. You always have to remember, the primary goal is to make sure the victims—or, if they're gone, the witnesses—are being fairly heard. That's the guiding principle of the handbook."

By "you," naturally, I assumed Officer Thorn meant *police guild recruits*. Often in the throes of a new case, she forgot that William and Luca and I were *citizens*, and that not all citizens had memorized the police handbook the way she had.

"The crime has to do with a familiar, then?" Luca's voice was a little breathless as he leaned in.

Officer Thorn glanced seriously at each of us, her brown eyes dark. "Two victims: a gnome who went by the nickname

'Bricky,' and a familiar known as Sweep. Some kind of magicked sentient broom, I take it. Both found attacked with a kitchen knife in Bricky's home early this morning."

William had startled, and I was uneasy, too. "You said there was a witness?" I asked.

"Not to the actual crime," Thorn said, to my immense relief. For Luca's benefit, she went on, "A child who lives in the neighborhood, one rock child named Meteor, overheard signs of a struggle. Since the front door of the apartment was locked, Meteor ran to the local police station for help. Unfortunately, the station didn't take the kid seriously, and Meteor ended up running to an entirely different station before anyone responded to the call. By then, it was too late for Bricky and Sweep."

"They didn't take Meteor seriously because of them being a child?" Luca asked quietly. "Or because a rock child is a magical near-life form, so they thought it might be a magic prank or something?"

"The latter," Officer Thorn confirmed. "You see, then, why they're bringing me in."

"*Us* in," William corrected, his words barely more than a growl in his throat. I looked at him in surprise as he continued, "Has anyone else been threatened?"

"No threats or claims of responsibility as of yet," Officer Thorn reported. "Local staff will be finishing up initial interviews and processing the scene now, and they'll brief us when we land."

"Luca has a conference," I pointed out. "And while I do feel for Meteor, and Bricky and Sweep, I'm not sure what I'll be able to do for you, Thorn. I mean, a police station the size of Maplehouse's must have forensic scientists or alchemists on staff already."

"I don't want you because of your alchemy, Red," Officer Thorn said unexpectedly. "Isn't it obvious?"

I glanced at Luca, who looked concerned, and then at William, who ignored me. "Um, no?"

Thorn sighed heavily. "You're the one who got Magica to talk," she reminded me. Technically, that had been both Luca's and my own doing, but I didn't think to correct her. Magica had been at the center of a Cinderella-type mystery over the summer. Fairy tales do that often, in Beyond— repeat themselves, in slightly twisted or even murderous ways. Sometimes just recognizing the pattern of the tale wasn't enough; sometimes you had to take a good close look at its characters to really understand what was going on. I knew that personally. After all, my mothers had been very purposeful in giving me the nickname *Red*.

"This wouldn't be Cinderella, though," Luca said, still quiet. "If questions about *life* are involved, it's probably . . ."

"Pinocchio," William growled.

"And *you*, Red," said Officer Thorn, "are the perfect person to act as the bridge between living and near-life."

# 4

# Wish Upon A Star

For the first few hours of our flight, I brooded.

The trouble was that Officer Thorn was absolutely right. Alchemy has a reputation for crackpots and the endless search for Philosopher's Stones, but at its heart, it is the science of transformation. It is the science that brings all the others together in pursuit of *making things better.* The phases of the moon and the botanical particulars of a glowing moss? An alchemist combines those to make ever-popular light sticks. The geological makeup of shale and the physics of pressure and the slipperiness of time? Combine those, and you have an alchemical slime potion. As my old teacher used to say, *alchemy takes hidden strengths and brings them into the light.* So, theoretically, it wasn't a stretch for Officer Thorn to say I was in a good position to help her understand and mediate between all different kinds of witnesses and suspects.

*But I don't understand magic,* I thought rebelliously, watching on as Luca and William competed in completing a puzzle—Luca with relish, William begrudgingly, moving little wooden pieces with tendrils of blue magic. And I had had my own bad

21

experiences with "near-life forms" while living as a traveling alchemist . . .

It usually wasn't the creations' fault; it was often the creators themselves who were a bit *off*, if not to say, downright immoral. I mean, just take William as an example: he'd run away from the sorcerer who created him—a very unusual thing for a familiar to do—and seemed entirely happy to be rid of him. To be *free. Maybe that's why it bothers me*, I decided. *Because it's so hard to say when a creation should be free of its creator. Or even when, and how, to give the creation a choice.*

"Look, Red, it's a map of the desert isles," Luca said. He kept his voice down because Officer Thorn was snoring in her corner, but his hand found mine, capturing my attention. He gestured at the completed puzzle, which had been magicked so that it sparkled and moved, blue waves lapping along the edges of a golden brown archipelago.

"Did you choose that one on purpose?" I asked him, suspicious. The scene made me feel uneasy; it reminded me of how intuitive and magical my family, a group of Seers, was. I had always been the black sheep.

"No, Red, he just happened to get a picture of your homeland from the stack of dozens of puzzles," William said, sounding bored. "I'm going to go find a snack."

Frowning, I watched him hop out of the booth and trot off, tail in the air.

"Is it me," Luca said gently, "or is this more resistance than is normal?"

One glance at my boyfriend told me he knew far more than he'd let on. For as bright and distracted as he could be, there was a deeper side to Luca too, a darker side that had endured curses and abuse. His comment now was purposeful, a quote from before we'd started dating, a time when William and I had been fighting and Luca had been trapped on the sidelines. And to add to that, the puzzle he'd chosen . . . *He sees it now, too, then.* I sighed, releasing tension I hadn't realized I'd been holding all along my shoulders.

"I'm sorry," I told Luca. "I really don't know what's going on with him. He didn't seem to want to come at all, until Thorn showed up with her murder case. And I'm not even sure why that changed his mind."

"Are you really not sure?" Luca's free hand played along the edges of the puzzle, drifting over waves so blue it seemed like his skin ought to come away dyed.

His voice was still soft, but I bristled all the same. "Am I supposed to know something I don't?"

"I'm not saying that. But maybe you're overthinking things. You *are* the person who knows William best, don't you think?"

"I don't know. Maybe we should have asked Dusty," I grumped. Luca and I had been together long enough that I understood the point he was trying to make. He was asking for my intuitive read of the situation. But I still wasn't sure I trusted my intuition as much as Luca seemed to.

For his part, Luca grinned. "Or Rhys. But since they're back in Belville, you'll have to do."

I sighed. "Maybe that's the problem, Luca. When this trip was just you and me, or even you and me and a grouchy William, that's one thing. But now with all of Officer Thorn's politics about familiars and another *murder*—it feels like getting in over my head. It reminds me of some of the worst times when we were traveling."

"I know." Luca slid his arm around me, and chuckled when I looked at him askance for being so knowing. "That's been one of your bugbears ever since you first came to Belville, Red. 'No, don't let Trent do an animation spell on that flowerpot, it'll only cause trouble,' and 'whenever some power-hungry tinkerer tries to bring a puppet to life, it's always the nearby alchemist that gets the blame!' Sound familiar?"

"It sounds familiar because it's *true*," I said, elbowing him—gently. "Have I ever been wrong about that kind of thing?"

"Not yet. So why are you worried now? We haven't even landed in Brass."

"Don't you dare say 'it probably won't be as bad as you're thinking,' because you know that's not true," I warned him. But I couldn't help chuckling a little at myself too. "I guess it's fine, as long as you don't mind that Thorn and William and I might be busy."

"You were always going to be busy, gathering your supplies and doing your own sightseeing," Luca reminded me, smiling warmly. "I don't need you to hold my hand the whole time, Red. Just knowing that you're nearby, that you were willing to come along, is encouragement enough."

"Of course I was willing. I believe in you," I said, the words coming thickly. "And I know what you're going to say, that I should believe in myself too. I just wish sometimes that William wouldn't be so darn stubborn about telling me how he feels."

"Maybe the apple doesn't roll very far from the traveling-alchemy-apple cart." Luca's attempt at a clever twist on *fall far from the tree* made me snort with laughter. "I'd say you'd be better off making sure he knows you love him rather than just wishing."

"Yeah, yeah, yeah." Though outwardly I brushed off Luca's sage advice, I felt my cheeks flush. I knew he wasn't wrong.

Fortunately in that moment our conversation ended as William trotted up . . . carrying with him, of all things, a bright red candy apple on a stick.

"All the stores are selling Yule stuff already," he grumbled, scrambling back up into his seat. "I thought Samhain was just barely over. What've they got to rush into the next holiday for? . . . And what's so funny?"

"Nothing," I assured him, chortling. "I'm glad you found a suitable snack."

* * *

The rest of the ride passed peacefully. Officer Thorn woke up about half an hour before landing—just in time so see the city of Brass in all its glory.

I say that a bit sarcastically, because I'm not fond of cities. But as far as cities go, Brass *is* an impressive one, I must admit. It stands proudly along a river delta, hemmed in by harbors and inlets and lakes, slowly stretching outward via bridges and well-worn roads and a never-ending parade of boats. To the south and west, the city is bounded by hills—*gentle* hills, in comparison with the mountains around Belville. The Current River flows down from the east and gently settles into the northern sea; I've always thought the name was particularly silly, but the residents of Brass have come up with all kinds of myths about it. Some say the river got its name because the city has always been a center for magitech and communication wires; others say it's because everyone in Brass prizes being abreast of the latest developments in fashion, gossip, and industry above everything else. It seemed like ancient history to me, though. My days training as an apprentice alchemist in the city felt like a past life.

"The old stomping ground, eh, Red?" Officer Thorn asked, as she shifted herself up and joined the rest of us in staring out the window.

"I'm sure it's changed quite a bit," I said, looking over the tree-lined neighborhoods and gleaming glass towers for familiar landmarks. "But I'm impressed you remembered I trained here."

"Oh, I have a file on everyone in town. Especially the newcomers." Officer Thorn winked, as if to say, *It's alright, you may have only lived in Belville for a few years, but we'll keep you around.*

"That must be the university, there," Luca said, his finger hitting the thick windowpane as he pointed down. Given how spotless the windows lining the passenger hall were, I could only imagine how many cleaning potions the balloon's crew went through.

"Let me see," William insisted, leaning over Thorn, paws on the table. I leaned on Luca, rather more gently. He'd pointed out a brick-colored patch amid the wandering streets and alleys, its own island—literally an island, bounded by the river on one side and a series of canals on the other. The university had long made its home there, growing to fill every inch of the space with dormitories, study halls, and tidy walkways. We were high enough up that the grounds, which easily covered half a dozen blocks, seemed no bigger than the size of my palm.

"The district just to the south of the university is Maple-house," I said, for Officer Thorn's benefit. "It's full of old homes mostly, the kind that had maples lining the sidewalks in front. But many of them have been converted into apartments, hotels, and shops that support the scholars and students now."

"And it should be fairly quiet this time of year, since the university's on winter break. At least, that's what my friend told me," she added.

I raised an eyebrow. "Aside from the annual conference of scholars coming in from every corner of Beyond . . ."

". . . Scholars who are going to spend all day huddled up in their libraries discussing esoteric secrets," the officer pointed out. "Aside from the odd night out, how much could they really get up to?"

As one, we turned to Luca to see how he'd take this judgment of his fellow academics. "Well, I don't know about esoteric secrets," he said modestly. "Probably just a lot of catching up on gossip and whatever new fads there are in preserving old paper, from what I hear. But I *was* very excited about seeing the libraries at Brass. They have them organized by subject. There's one for the sciences, and one for sorcery, and one for witchcraft and charms—"

"Thanks, we'll get the tour later—" Thorn hastened to interrupt.

But I had already heard enough to rile me up. "Wait, why does magic get two libraries and all of the sciences only get one?"

"—well there's actually *three* for magic, and a new building they just finished to be part museum, part archive for developments in magitech research—"

"Now you've gone and done it," William muttered to Luca.

"They get a whole *museum*?" I asked.

"Could any of you stay focused on what's really important here?" Thorn demanded.

My poor boyfriend sputtered, and an overhead announcement saved him.

*"All passengers, prepare for landing. Please ensure you have all luggage brought on board and all members of your party present. Form an orderly line along the starboard side . . ."*

"Looks like this is it," Thorn declared, lifting her backpack in one hand.

"This is it," I agreed, smiling at Luca, then at William. "Ready to be back?"

William gave a canine whine. "Here's hoping this time the truth wins out."

# 5

# Splinters and Scrapes

From the way Officer Thorn swaggered about, her pack swinging behind her, I half expected a police guild messenger to be waiting for us as we stepped off the gangplank from the balloon. Instead, we joined the masses in streaming down along curling ramps, watched over by mosaics that told the entire history of the city of Brass. That is, the history would have been plain to see had anyone been looking. But everyone—aside from Luca, perhaps—was focused solely on getting through the station and to their next stop. Since Brass's balloon station was much larger than the one in Pine, finding the exit was a feat in itself.

When at last we were deposited outside the station's massive, ornate doors, we found ourselves in good company. The trickle of black-robed scholars in the crowd became a flood as we approached the magitech trolley bound for Maplehouse.

"I think we wore the wrong uniform," Officer Thorn remarked to me. We were squashed into a trolley car with dozens of scholars.

"Sure feels that way. At least William fits in." I caught Luca's

29

eye and squeezed his hand, grinning.

With a shrill whistle and the grind of iron wheels on rails, the last leg of our journey began. The trolley managed to be both quick and scenic. We whipped through the streets of downtown Brass, passing carriages and food carts, fancy buildings and sightseeing tourists. I hadn't ridden the trolley in ages, but I immediately recognized the smell, a mix of hot grease from the steam-powered engine up front and sweet burned sugar from the vendors selling roasted nuts on every street corner. The wintry wind whipping by the open windows reminded me that city life was far from idyllic, but still, it had that undeniable feeling in the air—a childish excitement: *Yule is almost here.* The window displays and brightly bundled-up pedestrians were full of it. And even though, as William had pointed out, it was early in the season yet, many apartment windows sported wreaths or evergreen boughs.

As the trolley trundled out toward Maplehouse, the city-paced excitement eased into something older, something more sedate. Here the streetlamps burned proudly, even in the afternoon, and horses pulling coaches wore bells and red ribbons in their manes. Though the buildings were no longer scraping the sky, ancient trees rose up along the roads, their bare branches creating tunnels and sporting cozy birdhouses or swinging lights. The houses themselves had been painted vivid colors, many with shop signs in the windows or laundry airing from the balconies. William put his front paws up on the window next to me, watching it all go by. I ruffled his ears.

When the trolley crossed a bridge and stopped at the university, the scholars poured out. Officer Thorn remained unmovable, though, so I paused. "Luca and I—and William—

have rooms here," I told her. "Where were you planning on staying?"

"With the Guild," she said simply. "It's the next stop."

"Why don't you let me take your things, and you go on to investigate?" Luca offered to me. "I can get the room set up and pick up my registration packet. I'm sure they'll keep me busy. We can meet back here at six for dinner?"

I glanced at Thorn, who was obviously champing at the bit to get to her investigation, and at William, who shrugged. But Luca looked determined, so I handed over my bag, smiling gratefully. "Thank you, Luca. We will absolutely be back here at six. There's a big statue as soon as you leave the trolley station—you can't miss it. We'll be waiting there. Right?"

I glanced pointedly at Officer Thorn, who agreed at once. "Right."

Luca had to hurry off the trolley with our bags, especially since I held him back for just a second to give him a kiss on the cheek. As our now early-empty trolley car pulled out of the station, I turned to give Thorn a skeptical look.

"You agreed to coming back here at six pretty easily," I observed. "What is it—do you think you'll have the case solved by then?"

"Oh, I doubt it," she said, unruffled. "But I have to come back here at some point. Otherwise it wouldn't be much use me being undercover."

"I'm sorry," I said, taken aback, "you're *undercover*?" Helping Officer Thorn with big cases was one thing, but doing it on the sly was another. Lying was not a strength of mine, and the prospect of lying to a bunch of police officers was enough to make my stomach flip. *And besides, if she's here in some kind of disguise, then she really* should *have worn a different uniform!*

"I told you," she retorted. "I'm here as a personal favor to the chief."

I put one hand on my hip, still clinging to the swaying handrail with the other. "You told me no such thing. I thought this was an *official* favor. You know, like Seaside?"

"Seaside nothing," Officer Thorn said cheerfully. "Actually, that's my cover. I'm telling the folks at the Guild that I'm here to give all those scholars a talk on solving high-profile cases."

"Oh, you are, are you," I muttered. I half expected her nose to start growing at any moment.

"But of course since I'm in town I'll stay at the station and be friendly and helpful," she added. "The only one in on it is Chief Bakis. So keep a low profile, eh, Red?"

"A low profile as *what*, exactly?" I asked, though I already knew the answer.

Officer Thorn beamed a very wide, toothy grin. "Why, as my assistants, of course."

* * *

The trolley dropped us off right across from the Maplehouse police station, a stately old wooden building with a long, tidy porch. Officer Thorn did no more than poke her head in the door, deposit her bag, and ask for Chief Bakis's whereabouts. In one minute flat, we were headed into the neighborhood.

"Two blocks over, one block up," Thorn muttered helpfully to herself.

Even in my prior days in Brass, I hadn't spent much time in Maplehouse, so I looked around us curiously. The streets off the main drag were narrow, and many of the crossroads were no more than alleys. The houses were the same old wooden style, perhaps two or three stories tall, but most had clearly been split into apartments. Residents ambled down the sidewalks and sat chatting on porches, even in the chilly weather. A school was tucked among the houses, and children raced by, disappearing down a narrow, vine-encrusted alley.

As we turned onto the block we were looking for, though, it became clear something was wrong. *Maybe I'm developing a feel for crime scenes,* I thought, pulling my cloak tighter around myself. The only outward sign of a police presence was one lone recruit sitting on the front step of a prim yellow house trimmed in white and red. But even so, it seemed like sadness and unease hung in the air.

Officer Thorn again went to work, quickly and efficiently, exchanging no more than a few words with the guard. Apparently, she'd been expected. The three of us were waved right in.

The front door of the yellow house opened onto a landing, and from there three more doors split off. *So, it seems unlikely that someone randomly stumbled in here and found our victim,* I thought, looking around carefully. The doors to our left and in front of us were shut tight. But the door to the right was open, and so was the nearby apartment window, looking out over the street. *No question as to how Meteor could have overheard a struggle, then.*

William and I trailed after Officer Thorn as she led the way. The apartment opened up with a small sitting room, and a door beyond which seemed to lead to a bedroom. As we entered, a dining room leading to the kitchen was to our left. Every single piece of furniture seemed to be wooden, and carefully re-upholstered; and of course, much of it was small—Bricky had been a gnome, after all. The whole place had that unnatural stillness, but muffled voices could be heard from the bedroom.

"I'll go and say hello," Officer Thorn told us. "You two take a chance to look around."

*So that you can blame us for being overly nosy later?* I wondered, but didn't protest. I *was* happy to postpone meeting the others. I doubted I'd be much use talking to Thorn's police friends.

I nodded my agreement, and Thorn made her way into the far room. When we were alone, I turned to William, thinking. "Any magical impressions?"

"Nothing other than basic anti-theft spells and gnomish protections," he answered, shaking out his heavy fur. Blue sparks flared and leapt off him as he worked his own peculiar brand of magic.

*Gnomish protections* made me think of our friend Dusty back home, who had once refused to tell Officer Thorn where he lived—even under threat of arrest. As I moved gingerly toward the kitchen, I wondered, "It *is* a little strange to be in a gnome's house, isn't it? I mean, I got the idea from Dusty that they're usually pretty private about where they live. I could see how they have to live *somewhere,* and especially in the city, they might not get their first choice. But I never would have expected to hear of a gnome murdered in their house."

"Maybe Bricky was unusual," William offered. "Or maybe whoever killed him was a close friend."

"Not a happy thought. But you might be right." I drew level with the kitchen, and paused. The victims had been removed earlier in the day, of course, but bright white chalk outlined where they'd been, and the kitchen was in disarray—a splintered, smashed disarray, the kind that spoke of struggle rather than clumsy searching; even the pantry door was left open, hanging awkwardly. Apparently, Bricky had been found lying flat on the floor, almost as if he'd run into an invisible wall and fallen straight back. Sweep, the magical broom, had an outline too—that of a midsize house broom, perhaps four feet long, cut into three pieces.

"I'm not about to sample anything—I imagine Officer Thorn's friends have got that covered," I murmured to William as he came up next to me. "But I can tell you one thing. Whoever did this was downright vicious."

"Or felt cornered," he agreed. "To stoop to killing a familiar, you'd have to be desperate."

"Is it that simple?" I asked, choking slightly on the words, my eyes pinned to the smashed flour jar on the low kitchen counter. "Could a knife really have done away with Sweep like that, do you think?"

"You know it's that simple, Red." William sat next to me, and once again he glowed blue. I took a deep breath. I did know. William could be wounded like anyone else, and if his physical form was killed he *could* be re-summoned—but only by someone who knew how to work powerful magic. As far as I and my abilities were concerned, if my friend William was attacked with a knife, he'd be dead.

"I don't know why you're acting like it's such a big deal," he rumbled. "Knives are fatal to basically *everyone.* Not just familiars."

"I know, I know. I guess it's because I've never heard of anyone killing a familiar before. I can't imagine why they would."

William gave me a look.

I swallowed, and teased him half-heartedly. "I mean, if you're trying to get me to admit that you've probably goaded some people into murderous thoughts with your attitude, then . . ."

"It could also have been that Sweep was protecting Bricky," William pointed out with a huff.

I glanced around at the scene again. A fight had definitely taken place, but the broom outline was *behind* the gnome outline. And I didn't see any back door. The attacker must have been standing right where William and I were.

"Could be," I agreed slowly. "Does that seem likely? I mean, I know protection magic is your specialty, obviously. But would it be different for a broom familiar?"

"If your thinking is that Sweep was probably created to handle magical clean up and general tidying, you're probably right," William said. He still sounded a bit gruff. "But that doesn't mean that somewhere along the line, Sweep didn't decide to do something else. Maybe it felt strongly about Bricky for some reason."

"Of course. I didn't mean to sound insensitive," I said.

William sighed. "I know. There's a lot of things about familiars that people don't understand. It isn't just you, Red."

I let my hand rest on top of his head, distracted from the scene. "Is that why you decided to come along?"

"I . . ." William hesitated, then sniffed. "I *do* think something's off here. I thought it all along. Look at the floorboards."

I did so, but I didn't see any footprints—just a few dust bunnies and cobwebs in the corners. "Why? What for?"

"Even if Sweep wasn't *just* cleaning, it probably did still feel an urge to clean," William explained. "Especially if it was in one place long enough."

"But this kitchen was obviously a bit dirty even before the fight," I reasoned, starting to see where this was headed.

William nodded. "No matter how Sweep might have felt about Bricky, I don't think it was actually *his* familiar."

"And in that case," I concluded, "the question becomes, why was Sweep involved at all?"

# 6

# Family Matters

"Red? William? Where did my assistants go?" Officer Thorn's voice came from behind us.

Though I made a face at William, unenthused about the conversation we were about to have, we both dutifully turned away from the kitchen and emerged into the sitting room. Our audience was smaller than I'd feared; where I had been dreading a roomful of recruits and officers, only Thorn and a tall, black-haired vampire in a deep blue uniform faced us.

"This is Chief Bakis," Officer Thorn said, without pause. "They were just running me through the details of the case. Bakis, this is Red and William. They've helped me out with big cases back in Belville."

"The quintessential backwoods post," Chief Bakis said with some humor as they nodded at me and then William in turn. "But not, I think, the quintessential backwoods companions. Do I remember correctly that you are an alchemist of some repute, Red?"

I raised my eyebrows, glancing at Thorn. I wouldn't have

suspected her of telling her police friends about me, much less remembering to mention that I was an *alchemist,* not a police trainee. "I'm afraid I can't claim any repute, Chief Bakis, but I do my best."

"Actually we do our best to avoid repute of any kind," William chipped in, sitting at my side.

The chief laughed at us both, a genteel sound. I'd noted their preference for the pronoun *they,* and now was preoccupied with their eyes, a striking golden brown peering out from an almost arch expression. The effect was more erudite than forceful. Chief Bakis stood even taller than Officer Thorn, but appeared reedy where she was broad; black hair cropped close, where hers was long; and pale-skinned to her green earthy tones. In short, aside from the uniform, there really wasn't much the two seemed to have in common.

"I've told Bakis all about you," Officer Thorn said, and she even managed to make it sound like a good thing. "And I told them you'd be taking a look at the crime scene. No need to act so guilty, Red."

"Indeed. I'd be very interested in hearing your opinions," Chief Bakis put in. "But first, allow me to offer some explanation. You may have heard that just before Yule, the city's annual elections are held, and this year one of the topics is a new law that codifies definitions and regulations for magical near-life forms. That includes familiars, of course, and a great many magical beings which, up to this point, have lived in the city just like anyone else. This has caused a great deal of distress. While on one hand, magical life forms and their champions fear that the law may lead to persecution, on the other, those who are skeptical of magic or who have run afoul of magical beings say the law is necessary for public safety; they cite a number of recent cases in which magical beings, in particular magically-created children, were at the center of large-scale disturbances. One memorable occurrence involved a whale crashing into one of the city's primary shipping docks.

"Naturally, the police guilds of Brass find themselves in a difficult position. It is a time when shadowy forces are at work in the public mind. With this said, please, any assistance you can provide is most welcome."

I glanced down at William and cleared my throat. "Well, we didn't want to step on the toes of your own investigation, Chief. And we certainly didn't touch or move anything. But we couldn't help wondering how Sweep and Bricky were connected?"

"You don't believe Sweep was Bricky's familiar?" the chief intuited, addressing William.

"Does this place look like the home of someone who keeps familiars?" William rumbled, not entirely politely.

I nudged him. "I think what William means is—"

"No, no, Red," Officer Thorn headed me off, stroking her chin. "It's a good point."

"And did anyone *look* in the pantry?" William went on.

I hesitated, knowing that I hadn't. I'd been preoccupied by the crime itself. My mind raced through the details of the Pinocchio story. *Is there a cat in the pantry, or a fish, or some other character from the story?* I wondered irrationally.

"There's a broom in there," William said, rolling his eyes at me as though he could hear my thoughts. "An actual, plain old *broom.* Gnome-sized, but still, big enough that a police recruit shouldn't have missed it."

"William," I protested, "can't you try to be a *little* nice? We're the new ones here, you know!"

"But again, he has a point," Officer Thorn put in.

"And it is precisely why I'm grateful you came," Chief Bakis said. "I had not been informed about the—ahem—broom. And the question about Sweep belonging to Bricky never occurred to us. I doubt if any of my officers inquired into the familiar's status or connections as of yet."

"But you *do* know something about Bricky?" I asked hopefully.

"Even better," Officer Thorn told me. "We're going to do a follow-up interview with his brother and sister-in-law right now."

***

With a sense of calm and poise, Chief Bakis led us into the entryway—and then, to my surprise, continued straight to the facing apartment. They rapped three times on the door, and as we stood waiting, I realized something I hadn't before. The doorknobs on all three apartment doors were set very low. And judging by my experience of the floor plan in Bricky's apartment, the center door probably led to a set of stairs going up to the second floor. *Gnomes on every level, then?*

I nudged William, and he nudged me back. We'd been friends so long I could understand his sentiment as clearly as if he'd used telepathy: *of course the family lives next door, Red, didn't you notice this before?*

Officer Thorn frowned at us as if to add, *good assistants don't cause trouble.*

Before I could defend myself from either of my friends, the door opened. A gray-haired gnomish woman, perhaps two feet tall, with weathered brown skin and a face largely obscured by a blue floral handkerchief held to her nose stood looking up at us.

"I'm very sorry to bother you," Chief Bakis said, sounding truly apologetic. "But I hope the officers earlier did explain that we'd be back for a follow-up interview?"

The gnome nodded, sighing. It wasn't a resigned or annoyed sound, but a very, very weary one; my heart went out to her. She stepped back to allow the four of us to troop in.

Where Bricky's home had been bare and utilitarian, this home was cluttered and cozy. It was clearly a gnomish home, too, with low furniture and hand-carved woodwork. The floor plan mirrored Bricky's, so we came straight into the living room, which hosted couches of various sizes, a low bookshelf, and a pile of hastily-tidied children's toys. The rug showed wear patterns from the door to the kitchen, as if many, many eager feet had run that path, looking forward to a meal or going out to play. A deep burgundy wallpaper gave the home an almost cave-like closeness, but the floral patterns and cheerfully jumbled furniture made that closeness comfortable rather than stifling. It was a home which couldn't help but feel inviting, even in upsetting circumstances.

"Please sit," the gnome told us—the first words she'd spoken. Her voice was low, and a bit rough, perhaps because it was clear from her face she'd been crying. "I'll go and get Shades and Meteor. They've just been lying down," she explained. She stepped toward the door that led to a bedroom, but didn't have to say anything before another gnome and a small, shadowy figure emerged.

*Oh,* I thought, as another piece fell into place. *Meteor must have been Bricky's nephew . . . No wonder he was on hand to hear the fight.*

"Let's start from the beginning," Chief Bakis suggested as the family silently took seats all in a row on one couch. Officer Thorn and I sat carefully on the couch under the front window, at right angles to them, while William sat near the door and the chief remained standing. "My name is Koda Bakis, and sitting beside you is Officer Thorn, from Belville, and her associates Cinnabar and William."

"Please call me Red," I added politely, as we each bowed slightly to the grieving family.

Chief Bakis nodded, and then went on smoothly, still addressing the gnomes. "Would you please introduce yourselves for my colleagues?"

"Everyone calls me Mix," our hostess said, lowering her handkerchief. "My husband is Shades. He is—was—Bricky's little brother. And our little boy is—"

"Meteor," the child supplied. "Are you going to catch the murderer?"

Though his mother shushed him gently, Meteor's gaze on Chief Bakis was intent. He sat securely under his father's arm, and yet his little feet kicked at the cushion beneath them as he swung his legs. I haven't met many gnomish children, but my understanding is that they grow very quickly, and are often as tall as their parents in their first few years; by contrast, Meteor was shorter than his parents—maybe a foot and a half, only the size of a human baby, really. But he was solid. His skin was a mottled gray, and a knit purple cap with multicolored pom-pom covered his head. Despite the chilly time of year, he wore only a short-sleeved blue shirt and the same rough brown overalls his parents had donned. There were no shoes on his feet.

"We plan to," Chief Bakis said, answering Meteor's question sincerely. "But murderers are sometimes very clever. We're going to need your help."

"I don't think this one was clever," Meteor said, looking to his parents for confirmation. "Because why would they be so loud?"

Meteor's father, Shades, simply held the boy close.

Mix sighed once more. "We'll tell you anything we can," she said simply, "but the truth is, Bricky kept a lot of things to himself. He was always very kind to us, and to Meteor, but we never knew—we never knew—"

"Why don't we start with the basics," Officer Thorn broke in kindly. "What do you do, and what did Bricky do? Were you in business together?"

"Shades and I have a painting business," Mix said, and for a moment her pride shone through her sadness. "Interiors, apartments mostly. We built it up from scratch."

I knew myself how hard it was to run a business, so I could appreciate Mix and Shades' determination. In fact, as I glanced around the room once more, I saw that what I had taken for wallpaper was in fact an intricately detailed paint job, and the trim—even near the ceiling, which was easily ten feet high— was pristine. I also happened to notice a pair of children's shoes tumbled over by the door. *So Meteor does have shoes,* I thought, interested, *but chooses not to wear them. Nothing too unusual about that. It seems the family is doing well, overall—or was doing well until this happened.*

"Bricky worked construction," Mix was saying. It seemed she did the talking for the family. "He's been at it thirty years now, since he was just a boy. Said nothing was more satisfying than seeing a building come together. For the past—I don't know—" she turned to her husband, who signed to her briefly. She concluded, "He'd been with Skeen Construction for nearly twenty years now. For the last five, he's been in charge of their stonework team."

"Happy in his work?" Chief Bakis asked.

All three family members nodded, and Meteor said, "He promised me he'd take me to see how it's done some day!"

*So, work seems fairly normal,* I thought, checking it off my mental list. In my experience with Officer Thorn, I'd found that most mysteries could be solved if you focused on outliers and discrepancies in the stories told.

"Whose idea was it to live here?" William asked.

Mix seemed to hear the layers in the question. She sat up, her hand on her husband's knee. "We were the ones to move into the area first. You might know, most gnomes in the city have their own set of apartment buildings, built into basements and underground, places only gnomes go. But we wanted—Shades and I wanted—well, it was better to be where our customers were, we thought. It would make it easier for the business, and—and for Meteor, too. So it was our idea. When we found this place, Bricky said we shouldn't go off and live all on our own, with no friendly face nearby. So he got the place across the hall."

"Would you say you're a close-knit family, then?" I asked, cautious because I didn't want to hurt their feelings, but curious as to Bricky's reasoning. *So it is odd for gnomes to live in this neighborhood,* I thought. *And that still supports the idea that the murderer was targeting Bricky specifically, and the fight wasn't due to random robbery or an accident.*

"Bricky was always very good to us," Mix repeated tearfully. "He wanted to look out for his younger brother. And he never had an unkind thing to say to Meteor or me. In fact, when Meteor came to us, he insisted on helping."

All of this detail just served to remind me of our friend Dusty back home, who was fiercely devoted to his sister's children and, from the beginning, had treated myself and William like family. But apparently it meant something different to William. He cleared his throat.

"Can you tell us about when and how Meteor came to you?" he asked Mix.

Officer Thorn and Chief Bakis both tilted their heads back at William, as if to say in unison, *is that really necessary?* And, naturally, William stared them both down. Apparently, it was.

"Meteor came to us eight months ago," Mix said, glancing at her child. I could see love in her dark eyes, but something else as well—trepidation, maybe? "I couldn't really tell you how. It was—a miracle."

"*I* am a miracle," Meteor piped up proudly. "Uncle Bricky told me so."

"I am very glad to hear that," a solemn Chief Bakis replied. "Now, Meteor, could you tell my friends what happened this morning, please?"

"Yes, I can do that." Meteor turned to face Officer Thorn and me, his feet swinging once again. "Ma went out to shop at the farmer's market before breakfast, *really* early. She has to go really far to get there. Dad and I stayed home. I was playing with my trains on the sidewalk when I heard noises from Uncle Bricky's apartment."

"What kind of noises?" Officer Thorn asked.

"Had you seen anyone go inside?" I added, since she'd already interrupted.

Meteor shook his head. "I thought Uncle Bricky already

went to work. He gets up really really early, too. I never saw anyone go in. I just heard crashes and bangs. It sounded like someone was breaking stuff. I knew Uncle Bricky wouldn't like that. But I couldn't get in the door. So I went to go get the police so they could get in."

William cleared his throat. "You didn't take your father with you?"

"Dad didn't hear it," Meteor said simply. "So he wouldn't be able to tell them like I could."

*Ah.* I had wondered why a child was the sole witness, but now things made more sense. Shades, Meteor's father, must have impaired hearing; that explained the signing earlier. Any police station, especially in a big city like Brass, would have people who could communicate via sign—but if Shades hadn't heard the commotion in the first place, then he might not have much to say about it, just as Meteor had pointed out. *Unfortunately, given the fact that the first station didn't take Meteor seriously, perhaps it* would *have been better to take Shades along,* I thought. But of course, Meteor was a child, and that level of detailed decision-making would have eluded many adults in such a stressful situation.

"You were in here at the time, I take it?" Officer Thorn asked Shades delicately. As she spoke the words, she signed along.

Shades nodded and pointed to the kitchen. Meteor added helpfully, "He makes breakfast for me every morning! I like pancakes. But only if they come in cool shapes."

"Our kitchen doesn't share a wall with Bricky's, though," Mix added. She was clearly savvy as to where the police officers' questions might be heading. "Shades pays much more attention to vibrations than any of us do, of course, and he can sense quite a bit. But there was too much house between him and Bricky."

Shades seemed to sense what she was saying, especially as she glanced sideways at him; he looked like he might start to cry all over again.

"Of course, I understand completely. And you did very well," Chief Bakis told Meteor. Now that the chief had realized that Shades probably couldn't hear us—information that must have gotten lost in the initial interviews—they were signing along as they spoke, just as Officer Thorn had. "Allow me to extend my deepest apologies, once again, that my station did not initially respond to your call."

Meteor's gaze on Chief Bakis was fixed. "They said someone put me up to it. Someone told me to say it as a prank."

"But they were wrong, weren't they?" Chief Bakis said gravely.

"Yes. No one told me to say it. At school they say you should only tell the truth," Meteor said. When he glanced back at his father, Shades pulled him into a side hug. Husband and wife looked meaningfully at each other, communicating without words.

"Meteor, your father's going to help you get a snack," Mix said aloud. "It's past time you had something to eat."

"Are you going to eat too?" Meteor asked, hopping up.

"I will in a minute. First," said Mix, and her eyes hardened, "I have some things to say to our guests."

# 7

# Tragedy and Dreams

Shades and Meteor made their way toward the back of the apartment, the kitchen. Meteor walked with the energy of a child, even a sad one; Shades held his shoulders stiff and high. I got the feeling that perhaps it was Mix who'd remained to talk to us because she was the one who would be more measured in her reproaches.

In the momentary silence that ensued, Chief Bakis spoke up, subtly regretting the sudden end to the interview. "We did not get a chance to inquire as to the child's name—I understand he is an exceptionally fast runner?"

I perked up my ears at this. I wasn't sure why a rock child would have such a skill, but it could be to do with momentum— or magic. I myself could run very swiftly, although that was something only the magic in my blood could explain.

"Yes, he is," Mix answered, more steely than before, and I refocused on her face. "I have no doubt he made it to the station in seconds flat. We have always told him to do that, you know. Not every gnome family would. But we wanted our child to grow up trusting the local police and not afraid

49

to ask for help."

"An extremely admirable goal, and one which I appreciate," Chief Bakis replied. "I assure you, the officer who responded to Meteor in that fashion was *not* following Guild policy. We will be addressing the matter, and we will keep you informed as to the results."

"Please do," said Mix, more a demand than a request—as was well within her rights, I thought. "And I hope your investigation since has been *much* more in line with your guild policy."

"That's why Chief Bakis asked us here," Officer Thorn said. From the look on Bakis' face, I could see that they hadn't fully intended to admit this to Mix; but I knew Officer Thorn well enough to know that such transparency was important to her. She might deceive her fellow officers about her reasons for visiting, but she was always forthright about her actual investigations. It seemed to go over well with Mix. The gnome turned to Thorn with considerably more interest as she went on, "We're from a small town, well out of Brass and everything that's going on here. Like outside observers, you might say. But our main goal isn't just to look on, it's to actively help you find justice."

"You're like special detectives?" Mix asked, glancing from Thorn to me to William. "All of you?"

"Some of us more than others," I said wryly. "Officer Thorn is with the police, but William and I are—"

"Special consultants," William declared.

Mix's face softened as she looked at him. "You're a familiar?"

William nodded.

"So you know," she decided, sadly.

"I know more than some do, at least," he agreed, shaking out his fluffy ears.

"William pointed out to us that Sweep was not Bricky's familiar," Chief Bakis said, looking down at him thoughtfully. "I do not believe my officers thought to ask."

"They didn't," Mix said, some of the pertness returning to her voice. But she deflated a bit once more as she explained to Thorn and me, "But we didn't even think to say anything. I hope you don't think we're so very angry or upset. We *were* frustrated, of course, when Meteor told us what happened, and I'm afraid I might have given the officers earlier *quite* a piece of my mind. But even for as fast as our Meteor is, the police might not have been in time to save Bricky, no matter what station they came from. We know that. And I know—I know how much disinformation there is in the world about familiars and magical children these days. So I don't mean to seem unreasonable. Only, it is so—it is very—"

She broke into tears, burying her face in that same handkerchief, and I leaned forward. "Of course it is," I agreed, my heart wrenching as I thought how I might feel if William had been disbelieved about something so important. "To be angry is completely reasonable. We won't try to argue you out of it."

"What Red said," Officer Thorn agreed. "Although, unfortunately, you may be right about the time of death."

"We'll know for certain when the exam is complete," Chief Bakis added. "However, my station is at fault regardless."

Mix wiped her eyes and looked up at the chief. "You've been very good about that—I must give you that. It is just—a difficult time."

"There's always going to be something difficult about someone disbelieving your child," William growled. "But what about Sweep? Can you tell us anything?"

"I knew *of* Sweep, from Bricky," Mix said slowly, gathering herself. For the first time, rather than look at any of us, her eyes strayed to the door—almost as though she was looking right into her brother-in-law's apartment. "When we moved here, six months ago, Bricky came too. We told you that already. He joined a local club—very quickly, I thought. A sort of excuse to go out some nights, he said. Just a social thing. He knew Sweep from there."

"What was the name of the club?" Officer Thorn asked, her notebook handy.

"The Lost Rabbit Supper Club," Mix said, after thinking about it for a moment. "I think that was what it was called. He—Bricky—he'd go there once a week at first, then more as time went on. It seemed a little silly, just an excuse to go out to eat with friends, really. I think Sweep was sort of their—messenger."

I glanced at William, wondering what he thought of this development. The club itself sounded innocuous, but Mix's attitude had been a little strange when we brought up Sweep.

"Wrong place, wrong time?" Officer Thorn speculated, glancing up at Chief Bakis.

"Possibly," the chief agreed, "but it's worth looking into."

"How did Bricky feel about Sweep?" William asked abruptly.

Mix hesitated. "Oh—not antagonistic, at all—"

Officer Thorn caught on, and leaned in. "You wouldn't have said they were friends?"

"I—I never had reason to think so—"

"Sweep had never come over before?" Chief Bakis asked, eyes sharp.

"No, not that I ever knew of—"

"Mix," I interrupted gently, because I'd seen what William

was getting at. "Could you tell us again how Bricky felt about Meteor?"

"That's the thing." Mix collapsed in on herself, looking no larger than a well-fed house cat. "Shades and I tried for years," she told us, with the air of a confession. This, I felt sure, was what had been bothering her all along. "We tried so hard to have children, but it wasn't to be. Many gnome families *do* have trouble conceiving, you know, only no one ever talks about it. Bricky was always very good about it. He knew how much it meant to us. When we got Meteor, it was like—everything changed. I think before Meteor, Bricky never much cared for *anything* magic. That was always what I thought. I don't think he ever would have been friends with Sweep. He wouldn't have trusted Sweep at all. He used to talk about how magical things can go haywire and can't be trusted. But he *did* love Meteor. He loved him very much, and he was always a very good uncle. I hate to think that had anything to do with his death!"

*　*　*

"Complicated case," Officer Thorn murmured several moments later, after we'd finished up and taken our leave. She, Chief Bakis, and I loitered on the street as we waited for William. "Nosy onlookers common in the city, Chief?"

"Always," Chief Bakis said, glancing only briefly at the shadowy figure across the street that Officer Thorn had indicated.

I looked up and down the block but saw no one else. Evening was falling early; we'd been talking to the family for a while. Even without any wind, the neighborhood street was chilly and all the neighbors were no doubt huddled inside.

"Common in small towns too," Officer Thorn grunted. She winked at me, but like Chief Bakis, I was distracted.

"Where do we go from here?" I asked. "In terms of the investigation, I mean. Thorn, we need to head back to the university soon to meet up with Luca. Or if you want to stay, that's fine, but I'm definitely going."

"I'm going," she said affably. "The chief's in charge for the next steps. Right?"

"Right." For as different as their styles might be, Chief Bakis smiled briefly, agreeing easily with Thorn's assessment. "It's high time I was back at the station. The examination of the body should be concluded by now, and I'll assign teams of officers to interview the rest of the neighbors, Skeen Construction, and the dinner club. I'm hoping we'll have word back from the rest of Bricky's family, as well. Besides—there are still disciplinary measures to attend to."

I had to admit, I was surprised. I hadn't expected Bakis to take the night off—far from it—but I hadn't fully realized how much went into coordinating a police investigation . . . especially one that had full support and multiple "teams." I was used to my friends and me simply responding to Officer Thorn's investigative whims.

"The dinner club should give us more information on Sweep," Officer Thorn agreed thoughtfully, tugging at one ear. "How about the physical evidence from the scene? Any leads to follow up there?"

"So far, our best leads have been traces of mud found in the home, which my officers will compare at Skeen sites, and the knife block left in the kitchen. The largest knife was missing," Chief Bakis said quietly. "A pair of the recruits are out looking for it, but—"

"A knife in a city this size might as well be a needle in a haystack," Officer Thorn supplied.

"Precisely. Effectively, at present, we do not have any murder weapon," Chief Bakis admitted. "That said, Red, if you would like to take a look at any of the things we *do* have, you are more than welcome."

"Oh—I do appreciate that," I said, hesitating. Even though I still didn't want to step on anyone's toes, as I'd told the chief earlier, it was strange how much I already missed being in my lab. Maybe the challenge of investigation was what made me notice it so acutely. *I did bring my travel kit,* I thought. *More eyes, as long as they are careful eyes, can always be a help . . .*

"Red's spoken for tomorrow morning," William announced, trotting past the guard and down the front steps to join us. "She's coming with me to check something out."

"Naturally," Chief Bakis agreed politely. "Any of you are welcome to stop into the station any time you choose. In addition, Officer Thorn is able to contact me directly."

After the chief had bowed and said goodnight, Thorn added, "Officer Thorn is also feeling out of the loop. What are we doing tomorrow morning?"

William looked up and down the street, nose twitching. "We can talk about that later. I'm surprised Red isn't dragging us to the trolley station already."

"We have plenty of time. I can be reasonable," I protested.

William huffed. "Are you sure? I don't think you've been out of sight of Luca this long for months."

"I have so too!"

"Can't *either* of you be professional?" Officer Thorn complained good-naturedly. When we both gave her a *well isn't that the pot calling the kettle black* look, she tossed her hair over one shoulder and chuckled. "We might as well get a move on, anyway. Some fresh air will be good for our heads."

As we began moving slowly down the street, she added, "Who wants to bet me that Luca's already lost in a library, and doesn't even realize how much time has gone by?"

8

# Money to be Made

We stepped on to the university station platform with five minutes to spare, and walked over to our meeting spot in thoughtful silence. Neither Officer Thorn nor I had been able to convince William to talk on the trolley, so we'd given up. And I must admit that as soon as we were on the university grounds, I *was* a bit distracted. I couldn't wait to hear how Luca's first foray into conference-world had been.

The university station opened up into a wide stone plaza dominated by the statue I'd told Luca to find us beneath. Tall brick buildings and ivy-covered walls surrounding us made the shadows deeper and colder than they'd been in Maplehouse. Nonetheless, the atmosphere was bright and buzzing. We weren't the only ones to have thought of meeting outside the station. Clumps of scholars littered the plaza, some sporting seasonal scarves and others hauling armloads of books. Voices were light as everyone seemed to be catching up with conference friends and discussing where to have dinner.

Overseeing it all, the statue itself was a larger-than-life

57

lady cast in bronze. She wore cascading scholar's robes and carried an armful of scrolls; I was surprised to learn from reading the plaque that she had been lovingly nicknamed "the Puppetmaster," because of the way ribbons trailed from her scrolls. Her expression was distant, but benevolent. I'd known of her vaguely as a city landmark, but now I wondered exactly what—or who—she was meant to represent.

I didn't immediately see Luca among the loiterers, but we didn't have long to wait. We'd barely settled into position at the statue's feet before I heard a familiar call.

"Red! How long have you been here? Did I make you wait?" Luca came around the corner and wrapped me up in a brief but warm hug, which was very welcome because the stone I'd been leaning on was bitterly cold. In spite of our difficult day, I smiled.

"We only just got here," I assured him. "How was registration?"

"Fantastic. Remember Rachel from Seaside? She got in today too. She already had plans for dinner, otherwise I would've invited her to join us!"

"It's a good thing you didn't," Officer Thorn said sternly, though her gaze was more on William than Luca. "We have matters to discuss."

"Oh! The case? Did something happen? I guess it must have, of course, how was the—"

"Can we *not* talk out in the open in a crowd?" William huffed.

"Fine. Where can we go to eat that'll be discreet enough for you?" I asked him. Judging by the crowd around us, we wouldn't be the only people looking for a place to eat in Maplehouse.

His tail wagged. "I know a place. Follow me."

* * *

Let me just say, that is the *last* time I'm letting William choose where we eat.

It was an adventure getting there—that wasn't the bad part. Rather than leading us back to the trolley, William took us out over the bridge away from the university grounds. On the opposite bank, the houses of Maplehouse were cozily lit and the streetlamps flickered against the dark. Holiday bells echoed down the streets, as many people had opted to travel in festive coaches or even sleighs. Before I could comment on this to Luca—*they don't even have snow, and yet they've got sleighs?*—William ducked down an alley. He proceeded to duck down four *more* alleys, turning this way and that, until I was fairly certain we'd come full circle and could have simply stuck to the main road. But once more before I could say anything, William dove through an old wooden door.

*Not* the door to the sprawling, family-friendly tavern that took up two lots, mind you. Oh no; William dove into the seedy bar set practically below street level, basically in someone's basement. I'm pretty sure there was laundry hanging from the rafters.

But if there was laundry, there were at least tables and booths, as well. Officer Thorn, who seemed to be enjoying this little charade, stepped up and claimed a corner booth with an efficient nod to the bartender. Luca stayed close to me as we crossed the room. Several people were hunched along the bar, and groups chatted at tables; they might have been perfectly nice, but the dim lighting and rough, unfinished stone walls gave the place a dingy feel. The only thing missing was a bar fight, and I knew from experience that neither William nor

Thorn would hesitate to start one if they thought they were in the right.

"Please tell me the crunching beneath our feet is just peanut shells," I muttered to Luca as we waited for Thorn and William to slide into the booth.

"How about I promise not to look if you won't." Luca's voice was light, but I could see from his sharp gaze that he was a little worried. Admittedly, I was too—but I was also suspicious and annoyed. It was starting to feel like William had been toying with me all day long. And it had been a *very* long day.

The bar did not seem to have a name, nor menus, so after a few cautious questions we gave our order to a rather bored-looking waiter who disappeared into the kitchen. Apparently, he doubled as the chef.

As soon as he was gone and we were assured of privacy, I glared across the table at William. "Would you mind telling us what this is all about?"

"Mix told me the name of a special school Meteor goes to," he replied, looking quite pleased with himself.

I, however, was exasperated. "And why is that top-secret news? All of his neighbors probably see him walk off to school every morning. We could have asked anyone 'hey, where would a rock child go to school in this neighborhood?' and I bet they could tell us."

"Be that as it may, what we don't want is for anyone to know where *we* are going," William shot back.

I set my elbows on the table, ignoring any thoughts of stains or dirt, leaning in. "Why is that? Exactly how undercover *are* we?"

I had meant the question as a pointed but mostly teasing remark, but William stopped panting, turning to look at

Officer Thorn. And Officer Thorn looked serious.

"She didn't notice," she said to William.

"Of course not. Her head's in the clouds," he growled.

"Be *that* as it may, I am still right here!" I protested. Luca set his hand on my arm, no doubt hearing the frustration in my voice.

Officer Thorn took over. "We were followed," she said, not to me but to Luca. "Someone was watching the scene of the crime, and they watched us catch the trolley to come back to the university."

"Do you know why someone would be watching *you*, specifically?" Luca asked, tightening his hand on my arm. I seethed quietly. I *had* noticed someone watching the house, but I hadn't thought anyone would bother with our movements after that. We were strangers in town, after all.

Apparently, Officer Thorn was thinking along similar lines. "No. Bakis has only given people the official line—that I'm here to give a talk at the conference. And they didn't mention anyone following any of the rest of the officers."

"So you *are* undercover?" Luca clarified, trying to keep up.

As Officer Thorn filled him in on our afternoon, I let my attention wander to William. He was looking out into the bar, ignoring me. To be honest, that hurt more than anything else.

*What is going on? Why come if he was going to be like this about it?* I bit my lip. *Does he really think I couldn't have handled helping Officer Thorn on this case—that I'd just miss things and get in danger—because of Luca?*

William thinking he kept better watch than me was nothing new. It was probably true, too. But I wasn't some naive country mouse, and William should have known me better than to think so.

*Although—I really didn't notice anyone on the way to the trolley . . .*

Across the table William gave a low *woof,* interrupting my thoughts. Once he was certain we were all paying attention to him, he said very quietly, "The pair at the bar is from the same house as Bricky."

"How do you know?" Luca asked, swinging around to look.

"The one on the left is about to lose his keys," William growled, "and on the key fob is the house address."

I looked too, though I tried to be a *little* more discreet than my friends. The pair William was talking about weren't gnomes, but they were about the same size as Mix and Shades; from their shabby clothing, thin limbs, and scraggly hair, I guessed they were house elves. House elves are fairly common in Brass; many of them like the old wooden mansions. Where gnomes often tinkered or lived underground, house elves preferred to live in apartments and usually took jobs in house cleaning or child-minding. Most could do small bits of magic, like levitating light objects. They were also, however, known for being a bit mischievous. And one of them was indeed in danger of losing his keys out of his back pocket. He was leaning forward so far on his tall stool that the keychain was apparent, even in the dim bar light. How William had read the house number on it, though, I had no idea. All I could see was that the fob was the same color as the house had been, a creamy yellow.

"So—do we think they're involved? I wonder if they've heard about it," Luca added, curious.

"We can't hear anything from here either way," Officer Thorn said. "I'll go up to them."

"No—wait." Luca sounded decisive enough that she did just

that. "You're in your uniform, and apparently you all have been seen snooping already. Let me go."

"Are you sure?" I asked, hesitating to let him out of the booth.

"Sure. I'll just say I want to change my drink order. Think a place like this has hot chocolate?" Luca grinned at me, but his eyes were serious. I let him go.

We sat for a tense moment, just watching him, before Officer Thorn said something about acting more natural. She and William fell to talking; I tried to keep up, really, but found it nearly impossible between my own confused feelings and my anxiety about Luca at the bar.

In a few moments, though, he was back. Trying not to make my relief too obvious, I slid further into the booth so that he could take my seat.

"So?" Officer Thorn demanded.

I almost told her that wasn't very "natural"—but then, it kind of was.

"Bricky was the name of the victim?" Luca asked, to clarify. When we nodded, he went on, "They *were* talking about him, then. Or actually, his apartment. They didn't even stop when I walked up next to them. I guess they thought I was just another scholar who got a little turned around."

"But what were they *saying*?" William insisted. "Anything good?"

"What exactly would count as 'good' in this situation?" I wondered.

"Both of you be quiet," Thorn said. "Luca, you talk."

"I wouldn't call it good exactly," he hedged, keeping his voice low. "Like I said, they seemed to be talking about his apartment, his 'place.' Apparently they think that since it's empty, now that he's gone, it'll be much easier to get someone else to leave—'the family'?"

"Relatives who live in the adjacent ground floor apartment. We met them. Go on," Officer Thorn urged.

"One person kept talking about 'underneath,' so I think he lives on the second floor, if that makes sense. The other person seemed to be an interested party, waiting for the property to come available. But there was some kind of secrecy about it all," Luca said. "I specifically heard him mention something about a 'puppet buyer.'"

"What in Beyond is a puppet buyer?" I asked, bewildered. "Don't tell me it's someone who actually buys puppets?"

"Of course not, Red," William snorted.

I pursed my lips at him. "Well, then?"

"It's not really a thing." Fortunately, Officer Thorn had decided to intervene. "Not an *official* thing, that is. It's a term sometimes used in the underground as slang for a proxy. Someone who goes in and buys something or sets up a deal, acting on behalf of someone else who doesn't want to show their face."

"That makes sense to me," Luca said, nodding along, "it fits the tone of what I heard. But do we have any idea *why* such a thing would be necessary?"

"Someone—maybe the other person at the bar—wants Bricky's old place?" I guessed, slowly. "But they don't want the landlord to know?"

William sneezed. "Seemed like a pretty boring old apartment to me."

"Do we know who the landlord is?" Luca asked.

"They do at the station, I'm sure," Officer Thorn said thoughtfully. "If there was talk about Meteor's family, too, then maybe it's not so much about the apartment as it is the whole house."

"This is how this whole case has been so far," I told Luca. "Each tiny string seems to lead to something *huge*."

"Come on now, Red," Officer Thorn said, grinning. "You're *knot* worried already, are you?"

Fortunately, our food arrived before I had to voice my opinion of her pun.

# 9

# Friends Close

One strained meal and very cold walk later, Luca and I were still talking over the case. Officer Thorn had gone back to the police station, ruminating about landlords and houses, while William had *insisted* on staying out to stargaze, no matter how much I protested that the city was dangerous right now. Especially since we were being followed, on top of everything else. But William, being William, was adamant that he could handle it. And since starlight was important for helping him "recharge" his magic, or regain energy somehow, I certainly couldn't *forbid* him from going outside.

Besides, it's not like I'm his parent or anything, laying down rules and curfews . . .

I sat hugging my knees on a dorm room bed, moping over this and everything else, while Luca thought his way through the mystery. Aloud.

"It's too bad those two left the bar before we could overhear any more," he mused, as he transferred scholarly robe after scholarly robe from his pack into the dresser that came with the room. "Although they might not know anything more, when you think about it, they could just be like cogs in the engine, right? That's the trouble with cases like this, I bet. Figuring out *who* would know what you need to know in order to solve the murder. It sounds like the family told you everything they know. I wonder if the people at Meteor's school will know any more? I suppose it's worth a try, especially since we don't have any ideas about motive yet. And you did say it seemed like Bricky was very supportive and involved in Meteor's life. Really, it could have been *anyone* that had contact with either Bricky or Sweep at this point. Except, of course, the family. It doesn't seem like they'd set up their one child to be the witness and make him deal with police skepticism at his age, not when they could have just lured Bricky somewhere else to kill him just as easily. I mean, it's not like he'd turn down an invitation from his family if they wanted to go somewhere, right?"

Belatedly, I realized that Luca was looking at me, and that this rhetorical question hadn't been so rhetorical after all.

"Oh, Red." Luca crossed the tiny room and sat beside me on the bed, wrapping his arm around my hunched shoulders. "Something about this has had you feeling 'off' all day—even before we left town. Is it William? Like what we were talking about on the ride here?"

I leaned into him. "I'm sorry, Luca. I really wanted this trip to be fun for you, and for it just to be about you going to your conference and making friends."

Of course, I hadn't answered his question, but I still meant what I said. Fortunately, Luca knew enough to be patient with me: I'm not the best when it comes to talking about emotional things. He chuckled gently, pulling me closer. "Murder is definitely not within your control, Red, don't worry. And besides, I can still have fun and make friends and sit through all kinds of boring lectures to my heart's content. Unless you need me to help with the investigation, of course. *You* are what I'm really worried about here. So . . . do you?"

"Need you to skip out on the conference and help, you mean?" I sighed. "No, no. At least, not yet. It's just—everything we talked about on the way here, it only got *weirder* while we were investigating this afternoon. For a moment there it was like William didn't even feel like I knew him at all. And—I mean, how well *do* I know him, really?"

"Stop right there," Luca interrupted. "You and William are peas in a pod. Everyone can see that."

"Well, that's how I've always felt, even if we don't necessarily always get along. But I don't really know anything about all this familiar business. Like how it actually *works*. All this stuff about Sweep, and even about Meteor being a magical child—I feel like it's going right over my head. Like I'm trying to run to catch up, but all I'm doing is treading water. Is this making any sense?"

"Your metaphors are definitely mixed up, but you make perfect sense," Luca assured me, pressing a kiss into my hair. "But I'm still not sure you're admitting what's really bothering you. I mean, I've never known you to be mopey just because you don't know something. Usually you love learning."

"You're an absolute nightmare, you know that?" I teased him, pulling my head up to meet his eyes. "Who gave you permission to be so enlightened?"

"Oh, just a magical curse, tortured past, and a couple extra centuries under my belt. Typical fairy tale backstory," Luca said with a completely straight face. It was true—when I'd first met him, Luca was under the thumb of a manipulative criminal called Owl, and a curse had left him to live with qualities of a monster, a sort of dark, shadowy anti-unicorn. Normally, he was able to hide all the marks from the curse—with the help of a little magic. And now that Owl was gone, Luca didn't talk about him often, though I knew he was still working through things in his own way.

After a mere second, Luca's serious facade broke, and he laughed. "I'm not enlightened. It's just that we have different strengths. Pretty sure if I *was* enlightened, I wouldn't have been so relieved when you agreed to come along on this trip in the first place," he added, when I refused to look convinced.

That did make me smile, which I knew was his intention. "Please. You would have been fine."

"On the contrary. I would have been stuck at the meet-and-greet drinks event in the library, which is probably still going on at this very moment, because I couldn't think of an excuse to leave."

"You love libraries," I reminded him.

"Within limits."

"And you're *supposed* to be here to meet people."

"The drinks were non-alcoholic."

"Any hot chocolate?"

"Nope. Stains the books."

This was the last straw. I elbowed him, ducking my head to hide my laughter. I knew exactly what he was doing. And as much as I wanted to hate it, I actually appreciated it deeply. After the momentary release from the tension that had been following me around all day, I was able to clear my throat and admit quietly, "It's not the case. And it's not all the esoteric magic. I'm afraid of hurting William. Or losing him."

"Of course you are," Luca agreed companionably, putting his arm around me once more. "But does it really seem likely?"

"I don't know. With Sweep being one of the victims, and with the whole political situation in Brass regarding familiars—I just don't want to say the wrong thing. But it's *William*. Who knows what the wrong thing might be, with him?

"And," I added, when Luca was quiet, "shouldn't I know all this already? If I really was a good friend to William, shouldn't I have figured out everything there is to know about familiars?"

"Do you hear yourself speaking right now, Red?" Luca asked, his voice soft.

"I know. I know I'm being unreasonable. Maybe I shouldn't know *everything* about familiar magic, but still—I shouldn't be making mistakes, at least—"

"It's always seemed to me," Luca said, "that one of the reasons you two work so well is that you respect each others' strengths. Ever since you came to Belville, I've heard you say that William covers the magic . . ."

". . . And I cover the science," I finished, as Luca kept looking at me, his green eyes far too understanding. "Yeah. I know. But—"

"No 'buts,'" Luca said, squeezing my shoulder. "I was just saying that you and I have different strengths, too. So what would you do if it was me in William's position?"

"Probably exactly what I'm doing right now," I said sourly. It wasn't *necessarily* true, but I was keenly aware of my lack of emotional intelligence, and it was starting to get me down.

Luca took it in the best way possible, though, grinning and shaking his head. "I would *hope* that you would just talk to me about it. I mean, think about it. Who knows the answers to all the questions you're asking me right now? William."

"True. But that's part of it too. I feel like I keep *trying* to start that conversation with him, but he's being really strange about it. All day, he's been impulsive and secretive and bounding off to lead us into sketchy bars and insisting on walking through a strange city full of murderers at night instead of just *talking* about something for once."

Luca's eyes sparkled. "You're starting to sound like his mother."

"Ugh, I know, I was just thinking that earlier." I covered my face in embarrassment.

"And here I thought that of the two of you, *he* was the one who considered himself the guardian," Luca added.

"He does! So what's he doing off on his own?"

Luca shifted on the bed, pulling me—covered face and all—into a hug. "Maybe he's just as worried about you as you are about him."

For a moment I savored the gesture and thought this over. Eventually, my voice muffled by Luca's sleeves, I asked, "But why worry about *me?* No one in this city knows us. That's what bothered me when they were talking about someone following us earlier."

"I honestly don't know, Red. But do you really think it's true that *no one* in Brass knows either of you? I mean, this *is* where you did your training, right—and isn't it where you first met William?"

"I hadn't thought of that. It was so long ago." I sat up abruptly. "Do you really think something from the past might be involved?"

"You would know better than me," Luca reminded me.

*Of course. Poor Luca, being pulled into all of this,* I thought briefly, before mentally flipping through all the people I had known in Brass. Most were associated with the alchemical institute I'd been to. Many of my fellow students had moved on and established themselves elsewhere in Beyond, but I knew for certain that some had remained. And of course, my old teacher, Paracelsus, would probably be there forever.

When I mentioned this to Luca, he tilted his head and asked, "Weren't you planning on going there anyway, to get some hard-to-find supplies?"

"I was," I said slowly. "And I guess this just gave me one more reason to check it out."

## 10

# Children at Play

The next morning Luca skipped off to his conference breakfast at an ungodly early hour—and not long after that, William and I were on the road, too. We picked up Officer Thorn from the police station on our way to Meteor's school.

"No luck as of yet on the landlord," she informed us, in lieu of a *good morning.* "Seems they're out of town for the holiday. What a time to be gone, eh? Anyone want an almond croissant?"

I was still brushing crumbs off my crimson cloak when, rather abruptly, we were at the school gates. It turned out that Meteor's school was in fact two residential lots put together. On one side, an old house had apparently been remodeled to fit classrooms; its double-paned windows were plastered with hand-cut paper snowflakes, and its porch was fenced all the way around. In the empty lot next door, a playground had been erected, slides and swings visible over another fence. A sign hanging from the peaked roof of the house read *The Blue Fairy's School for Magical Children.*

"I'm guessing that's 'magical' as in magically-created, not magically adept," I murmured to William as we looked over the wooden siding. It looked like one wayward flame spell might spell the end for the old house.

"I'm sure they have all kinds of protections on it," William sniffed.

"Either way, they committed, you must admit," Officer Thorn observed beside us. She was right: the entire three-story building was painted in various shades of blue. Even the fence rails were a vivid cobalt. "Let me go on ahead and handle introductions."

As we stood on the sidewalk, waiting, I could have sworn I saw a shadowy figure lingering on the nearby street corner. But before I could decide whether to point it out to William, Officer Thorn had returned—and not alone.

With her, there was a very solemn-looking official. He stood just as tall as Thorn, his shoulders just as wide, and his uniform—a black peacoat and collared shirt underneath—was just as severe. He seemed to be bald under his woolen hat, and his bare chin might as well have been cut out of marble. Like veins in stone, small scars criss-crossed his pale skin. The moment he saw me, he frowned, as though he could just *tell* I'd be a problem in class.

For the record, I never *was* a troublemaker in school. Nevertheless, I squirmed uncomfortably.

"This is the headmaster, Adam," Officer Thorn told us. "He's offered to give us a private tour."

"Anything to help Meteor," Adam said, his pale blue eyes skating over mine as if giving tours was approaching the limit of *anything*. He did not offer to shake hands.

William, however, was unaffected. He was up and at the

front of our little group at once. In fact, as we paced the hallways, peering into classrooms full of young kids of all shapes and sizes, it was William who asked most of the questions. What had seemed like enthusiasm to be *doing* something on his part soon became more serious, almost interrogative. To Adam's credit, I could tell from his answers that he cared very much about the children there. Enough to do *anything* . . .

"The children here age differently than others do," Adam was saying as we climbed the stairs to see the upper-level classrooms. "Many of them know things differently, too. Because they come to us in all sorts of ways, they each bring their own unique understanding and skills. Honoring that and protecting them is one of our most important duties. You can be assured we take it *very* seriously . . ."

We took turns peering in classroom windows from the hallway. As Officer Thorn asked Adam about registration and family checks, I looked at the art on the walls, musing over what Adam had said.

The tour ended as abruptly as it had begun, as we arrived at Adam's office at the end of the hall. The space was crammed with files and books on education, leaving little room for living visitors. "The attic is being converted into an indoor gymnasium," he told us, almost reluctantly. "You've seen everything. I suggest talking to some of the parents. You'll find them setting up for lunch."

"The parents are very involved, then?" Officer Thorn jumped in. "Did you often see Bricky?"

A flicker passed across Adam's broad face, but it was gone too soon for me to see what it was. "We did often see Bricky, whenever Mix and Shades were busy painting. Meteor loved him very much."

"How did everyone else feel about him?" Thorn asked.

Adam shrugged. "I don't think anyone else knew him well enough to have an opinion. He came to help with lunch or study periods, but never stayed for any of the parent mixers. I gather he had his own social circle to focus on. He made it sound very . . . exclusive."

William and I exchanged a look. *The supper club, maybe? "Exclusive?"*

"If that's everything?" Adam asked, interrupting my thoughts.

Officer Thorn and William thanked him, practically in unison, and turned to go back to the cafeteria. But a thought had occurred to me.

"Wait, there is one more thing," I said, hanging back as Thorn and William left the office. "I just thought of one last question, if that's alright."

"And why wouldn't it be?" Adam asked. But as I noticed before, his tone wasn't light—in fact, it seemed downright menacing. And the way he loomed over me in the suddenly too-small office did *not* feel good.

"Um," I said, reminding myself to *stand up straight* and *don't leap to conclusions.* "Well, I was just curious if you have any dealings with any of the, ah, further-education institutions in Brass. Like, do you ever send students to the university, for example, or do any outreach with them? Or—the alchemists' institute?"

"And why," asked Adam, ponderously, "would we send any of our children to the alchemists?"

There was no "leaping to conclusions" about it: he was *definitely* looming now. My feet itched to escape out the door and down the hall with the others. But I was desperate to figure out how to tie all the loose threads together, somehow. "If they showed any interest in alchemy as a career, perhaps?" I suggested, keeping the quaver out of my voice. "Or maybe if you wanted some support for your science program?"

Adam stared at me for what felt like a *very* long moment. Then he reached out one long, bulky arm and snapped the door shut at my back.

*Crossing the line,* my internal mother warned me. The itching in my feet was a full-on siren playing out behind my thoughts now. "There's no need for this to be a private conversation," I began. "I'm going to leave—"

"You're an alchemist."

The way Adam said it made me pause with my hand on the door. In my old days, my traveling days, the distrust and judgment woven into his voice would have made me run away all the faster. But I suppose living in Belville, surrounded by friends, had nurtured my pride—even to the point of foolhardiness. I turned back to face him, angry now. "Why does it matter if I am?"

"You are," he said doggedly. "The goggles. The vials on your belt. I saw them at once."

I bit the inside of my cheek, seething at this unwarranted derision. He was right, of course—I don't go anywhere without my goggles plastered to my forehead, and Officer Thorn herself had *asked* me to bring some tools along "just in case." But I still didn't see that it was any of his business, or that it merited such attempts at intimidation. *Is this why he's been rude to me, this entire time?*

"I'm an alchemist," I agreed, my voice clipped. "And you're being a bully. If you didn't want to answer my question, you could have just said so. I don't know what your problem is with the alchemists in Brass, but I'm not one of them, not any more, so it's nothing to do with me."

Adam's face went slack. "You *don't know what my problem with them is?*"

"I don't," I confirmed. "But your attitude is causing a problem with *me*. I'm going to join my friends—"

But once again, I didn't get a chance. This time I had the door just barely open when Adam's words stopped me.

"They made me."

* * *

That moment with my hand on the doorknob, the door cracked open and the safety of the hallway beyond, seemed to last an hour as I remembered. The voice of Paracelsus echoed in my mind:

*Each being is a microcosm, or a little world, an extract from all the stars and planets of the whole firmament, from the earth and the elements . . . alchemy's greatest, most unachievable aim is to understand life itself . . .*

All my anger was forgotten when I came back into the present moment. I didn't even disbelieve him. I was simply in shock. "What did you say?"

I heard Adam sigh, and his footsteps shook the room as he walked back to his desk. "Could you shut the door? I'll stay over here. Promise."

There was no question in my mind now that I would stay to hear him out, but I was still moving slowly, my mind turning over all the new—and awful—possibilities. Carefully, I shut the door and turned to face him, crossing my arms over my chest.

It was so obvious now. The scars on his face and hands—things that, if magic had created him, magic might have been able to cover up. None of the children were scarred this way. *Thank goodness, none of the children . . .*

Adam must have been able to see my dismay and surprise very clearly on my face, because he sighed again, and his anger seemed to subside. "I guess you'll say you didn't know."

"I think you can tell I didn't know," I agreed. "And I can tell from your reaction to my lab equipment that you're not a fan of the guild, so I'm guessing it didn't go well."

"I'm walking and talking," Adam said bitterly, lifting his hands and moving his wrists as if to prove the point. "The experiment worked."

"I didn't mean the experiment," I told him.

Adam blinked. For a moment he tugged at his ear, looking vaguely reminiscent of Officer Thorn on those rare occasions when she was at a loss for words. Then he refocused on me. "To answer your question, then. No. We don't have anything to do with them. *I* won't have anything to do with them. And if the university knows we exist, they won't admit to it. Too political, I guess."

"Political, my foot," I blurted without thinking. My hand flew to my mouth immediately—*I just keep saying the wrong things in this case!*—but, luckily, Adam seemed amused. He didn't smile, exactly, but his face relaxed into a sardonic weariness that was welcome after all the animosity. I cleared my throat. "Sorry. And I'm sorry if I said anything insensitive earlier, too. As you've probably noticed, this entire situation with magical and—ahem—alchemical people is far beyond us out in Belville."

"In a way, it's nice to know that there are places where it *isn't* a source of constant conversation and anxiety," Adam conceded. "I'll accept your apology. But you'll have to forgive me if I don't seem friendly."

"I certainly wouldn't expect you to," I said, and hesitated. "I'm sure there's really nothing I can say in this situation. But . . . I have to admit, I never would have thought that Paracelsus would allow anyone to . . ."

"Never?" Adam repeated, pointedly.

I tensed—and then sighed. "You have me there, I will admit. He was always interested in extending life—that was the golden standard for alchemists of his generation, from what I gathered. It never did interest me as such. But still, to go from extending life to *creating* it . . . I can't see how anyone could have justified that leap."

"Then it's good you're in Belville," Adam decided. "You haven't had any communication with them at all?"

"No. For years I was traveling, and—" I waved my hand, realizing that the details weren't pertinent here. "Anyway, to be totally honest, it's on my list to visit them. This afternoon, in fact. I was—well, as I'm sure you can understand, now—I'm a little suspicious they might be involved in all this, somehow."

"In the murder?" Adam's gloom lifted momentarily into surprise, and then resettled. "I won't say I wouldn't be glad if you could prove that they were. But I doubt you can."

"Why?" I asked, cautiously.

"Even if they were responsible, they wouldn't have done it themselves. They would have hired someone. Someone they've probably already disposed of."

I did my best not to dwell on that last bit of speculation—or to think about the massive amounts of poison any alchemist has access to at any point. Instead, since Adam now seemed much more willing to talk, I pressed for details. "You never knew Bricky or Sweep to deal with them, though?"

"I didn't know Sweep. If Bricky had, he wouldn't have told me. No one brings them up in my presence. I haven't even spoken to an alchemist in two years," he added, eyebrow lifting as he looked at me.

On one hand, I could completely understand where he was coming from. On the other, it was a little hard to blame *all* alchemists in the city for what must have been the work of one or two extremely elite practitioners. I let that point slide, and instead thought about what else he'd said. "Would you like me to conceal any details about you or the school when I question them?"

Again, Adam seemed surprised. *So, he didn't think I was a spy?* I guessed, hiding an inward bit of amusement.

In the end, he shrugged. "The school is a private institution, and we have protection, like I was telling your friends before. I'm not worried. They've probably moved on to their next experiment by now."

"How many times have they done something like this?" I asked, alarmed.

"As far as I know, I'm the only one." Adam held eye contact. "I made sure it ended badly enough that they'd never try again."

*Well* there's *a story it's probably best not to inquire about,* I thought, a shiver racing down my spine. But given how he clearly felt about alchemists, it brought up another question. "What about the kids here—the magic that's made them?"

"If you're asking if I hate sorcerers too, I can't answer," Adam said, rather savagely. "But as for the children . . . it's different. They *have* families, they have people to take care of them. They always will. That's why I made this school. And they'll grow, and live, and lead happy lives . . . turns out," he added, with excusable snideness, "magic is stronger than alchemy."

"In this way, it seems so," I agreed diplomatically. I had to wonder, though. Adam's bitterness seemed to stem partly from the fact that he'd apparently been created as a full adult, with no support or home in place. While I could understand that, it seemed to me that either way, there were massive amounts of power at play.

Apparently, my thoughts were once again plain on my face. Adam ended the conversation with a heavy hand on his desk. "Go and talk to the parent helpers," he told me. "You'll understand."

"Alright. I can see there's a lot here," I agreed, turning to go. One last time, I paused before stepping out of the office. "Adam? Thank you for letting me in on all this. And—for what it's worth, what they did *was* wrong. But it's impossible to see this school and not see that you're doing something right now."

"You're not welcome, alchemist." But Adam looked up and, for the first time, seemed to just barely smile. "You'll see."

# 11

# Home and Heart

It wasn't hard to retrace my steps to find the cafeteria; even if the school *had* been bigger, or if I had gotten lost, I could have easily followed the sounds of Officer Thorn's voice. I turned the corner into a galley kitchen and found her enthusiastically helping a willowy elf in a hair net scoop salad into bowls.

"So you rotate volunteer responsibilities weekly?" Thorn was saying, cheerfully flinging an overflowing serving of leafy greens onto the counter.

"Yes, we have a sign-up system. We try to keep it regular, for ourselves as well as the children, but many of us do have careers to juggle, too," the elf answered in a long-suffering voice as she snatched a few stray clumps of lettuce from the bowl and surreptitiously added them to another, scanter portion. Her hair was streaked, silver and gold, and the smile lines around her mouth were deeply worn. Bright necklaces, loaded with beads in a way that suggested a child had made them, clinked and swung over her paisley dress as she moved.

"I must say, I admire the spirit," Officer Thorn declared,

banging another heaping serving onto the counter. She looked up and saw me standing in the doorway. "Oh, there you are, Red. Bit tight in here, as you can see."

"I can." *Particularly when you're throwing things every which way,* I thought, amused, though I wisely kept that part to myself.

"Carla here's been explaining the whole set up," Thorn continued, deftly wielding tongs to overfill yet another bowl. "Thirty-two mouths to feed."

I looked politely at Carla, impressed but uncertain how these lunchtime stats were advancing the investigation. She pressed the back of one gloved hand to her forehead, and smiled back at me. *At least she has a sense of humor about her 'help' today,* I decided.

"That's twenty-four students, as I'm sure Adam explained, and then the eight teachers and helpers," Carla told me. "We parents usually eat whatever's left over. Volunteer rights, you know."

"Certainly," I agreed, smiling in earnest now. "When we were looking at the classrooms and the playground, it seemed like ample space, but seeing this kitchen I can imagine it gets hectic sometimes."

"Yes, Red, hectic enough that no one keeps tabs on the helpers. I already asked," Officer Thorn interrupted, addressing her sixteenth salad bowl, which spun and sputtered as she set it down.

"I really don't know very much about Bricky," Carla agreed, shrugging her thin shoulders at me in a *I'd be more help if I could* sort of gesture. "Or even about Meteor and his parents. He's relatively new here, you understand."

"That's true, I think they mentioned having only just moved

here a few months ago," I mused.

"Well, and you know how gnomes are," Carla said as she reached for a truly enormous bottle of salad dressing and began to shake it expertly.

From the safety of the doorway, I gave her a tilted look, my gaze sliding from her to Thorn behind her. "Do we?"

Carla looked up from her dressing, having caught the hesitant note in my voice. "I only meant that they don't usually go in for play dates and that kind of thing. Oh, they're nice enough around the school, but honestly . . . Well, to be honest, it's a surprise to me to think that Bricky had someone over who *wasn't* a gnome."

"It is?" I asked, crossing my arms.

"Don't be mad at the Officer, now," said Carla. "Everyone's heard the stories about the familiar who was found at the scene, too. But that's just what's so strange about it. I really wouldn't have thought Bricky would be the type. Oh, he always seemed nice enough with the children here. But a little *helpless*, too. Like he really had no idea what to do about magic."

*Huh.* I got the feeling that Carla's ideas about gnomes might be a tiny bit outdated, but her insight about Bricky was interesting because it echoed what Mix had said, too.

"But I've been around a long time," Carla added. Elves had notoriously long lifespans, and judging by the tone in her voice, I inferred that she meant centuries rather than decades. She went on pleasantly, "Sometimes I just get these little notions about the people, that's all. And my boy and I have been with the school since it began. Sometimes it's difficult to remember that not everyone sees things the way we do."

"Speaking of 'everyone,'" Officer Thorn chipped in, "Red, why don't you go track down William? You're not helping anyone standing in that door."

I rolled my eyes at that, I must admit, but still managed to grin at Carla before heading a few steps down the hall to find the diners.

The cafeteria was really the old back porch, screened in and spanning the length of the building. In this weather, windows glimmered firmly in place, and every bench sported a cushion—cushions which seemed to be radiating heat. Two neat rows of tables sported place mats, napkins, silverware, and plates. At one end of the room, William sat upright atop a robin-egg blue cushion, talking to a man with a short dark ponytail wearing a thickly knit brown sweater.

"Like Effie was saying earlier, there was just something *off*," the man was saying in a seafaring lilt as I walked up. He couldn't see me, and I gave his seat a careful berth, because at the last minute I saw he had a polished wooden cane leaning against the corner of the table. If I tripped over that and made a scene, William would never let me hear the end of it.

"But you can't say what." William's question wasn't really a question, and he followed it up immediately by tipping his nose at me. "Hey, Red. Turns out everyone thinks Bricky had iffy friends."

"I wouldn't say *that* exactly," the man hastened to explain, nodding briefly at me as I sat beside William. "I never met them. It was just the way he spoke. About his friends, sure, but also just about his *life*. There was something . . ."

"A divide of some kind?" I suggested. That would fit in with Carla's assessment.

"Exactly." The man nodded again, this time gratefully, and as he lifted a leathery brown hand at me in greeting, I saw seafoam-colored scales flash at his wrist. "Giovanni."

"Hi, Giovanni," I returned politely. The scales, along with matching seafoam-colored eyes and thin ears that disappeared into his hair, suggested Giovanni was merfolk, which wasn't uncommon in Brass because of all the shipping trade. It made me think of our friends at Seaside, which made me smile. "I'm Red, as you heard. I'm with William, and together we're—"

"I told him all that," William interrupted impatiently. "What, do you think I just cornered him and started giving him the third degree?"

"William was a very good helper," Giovanni assured me.

"Is that so? Maybe I should expect more help in the kitchen at home," I remarked, eyeing my companion. I hid a chuckle behind my hand. The sentiment was well-meant, I was sure, but I doubted William appreciated being spoken of like one of the students at the school.

"In your dreams. So," William said, resolutely addressing Giovanni, "If that's all you know about Bricky, can you tell us anything about the rest of the family? Or about Meteor?"

This was blunt, even for William, and I blanched as Giovanni looked uncertain. I couldn't imagine two strangers asking about a student in connection with a murder case was reassuring. But after a moment, he said thoughtfully, "The twins like him.

"That's my kids," Giovanni added to me with a smile. "Twin snow children, literal *snow* children. One white as snow, one black as ice!"

"Sounds—dramatic," I said, aiming for neutral and missing somewhat. Next to me, William snorted.

But for his part, Giovanni chuckled. "So was finding them. On an iceflow, they were. Drifted right into my boat. Seemed to come out of nowhere, as these kids so often do, and—

anyway," he said, his ruddy cheeks flushing bashfully, "you didn't ask about me."

"If you don't mind, though," I said, seeing my chance, "*could I ask you how most children come to be at this school? Just in general? This is all pretty new to me.*"

"Some find their families on their own," Giovanni said eagerly. "Like mine. They just know where they're needed, bless them. But many of them come because their parents were wishing for them."

"You mean, an actual wish is what makes them? They come from the magic *in* a wish?" I asked, feeling silly. William stirred next to me, like maybe he was impatient, but Giovanni seemed happy to talk about the kids he loved so much.

"I wouldn't say that exactly," he said, leaning in. "I guess that can happen sometimes, but it's rare. Thing is, you need someone to *supply* the magic to make a wish come true, don't you? So most of the parents here, after they'd spent long enough wishing, they sought someone out who could help make their wish come true. Someone in the city's been good about helping families out, you know how it is—one family goes, and it's the best gift they could imagine, so they tell another family, then another. Word gets out. I never paid much attention myself."

Giovanni's voice dropped on that last sentence, and he glanced around us. William was stiff as a board next to me, but from what I could tell, we were alone and perfectly safe. Just in case, though, I lowered my voice too as I said, "Correct me if I'm wrong, but that's got to be some really powerful magic, right? To make a whole new being?"

"I might not say 'whole' exactly," Giovanni said, and instantly stopped, as though he regretted it.

I blinked, surprised. "What about them isn't whole?"

"Nothing about the kids exactly. The kids are perfect, all of them. Only—" for the first time, Giovanni seemed hesitant. His voice was lower than ever and more rushed as he went on, "My twins, see, they're just fine on their own. As far's we can tell, of course, since we don't really know where they came from. But some of the kids here—a lot of them—well, they came with *conditions.*"

William stuck his cold nose into my arm, hard, but I couldn't stop the word from falling out of my mouth. "'Conditions'?"

"Things they gotta do, some of them, to be *real* kids," Giovanni said finally, sitting back.

I *knew* the story of Pinocchio, of course. I knew perfectly well that the fabled Pinocchio had faced several moral tests before he was considered a 'real' boy. But seeing the fairy tale play out in person was baffling. "What about Meteor isn't *real*? Are you saying he'd—he'd transform or something, if he met certain conditions?"

"I'm not sure anyone rightly knows," Giovanni said, his heavy brows drawn. "He's one of the new ones, see, and—"

"Red," William growled at last, interrupting Giovanni's discomfort. Echoing voices could be heard in the hallway, and in the next minute, children poured into the cafeteria.

"I've got to go help distribute the food," Giovanni said, springing to his feet and grabbing his cane in one graceful motion. "Nice talking to you."

He might as well have been swallowed up by a whale, so complete was the clamor of children around him. The interview was definitely over.

William hopped up without a word. I followed his fluffy black tail through the crowd, until we'd reached the relative quiet of the empty hallway. There, we found Officer Thorn removing her food service gloves with the air of a job energetically done.

"Don't tell me you didn't learn anything," she said, seeing the stricken look on my face.

I half expected William to pipe up and say something about my pushing Giovanni too far, but he remained uncharacteristically silent. Eventually I admitted, "I—I got a little sidetracked. One of the dads was telling us about some of the kids, like Meteor, and how they're—"

"Conditional," Officer Thorn supplied, matter-of-factly. "That was the word Carla used."

"Of course Carla has a word for it," I mumbled, unsure what to think.

Officer Thorn cocked her head at me, her pointy ears making the look almost comical. "You *knew* it was Pinocchio, Red."

"I know. I know! That's what I was thinking, too. I don't know why I pushed him so hard on it. It just, to hear it all said out loud like that, it just starts to—not make any sense," I said, at a loss for a proper explanation.

With a rumble, William spoke up. "So there's a word for it. Does that mean it's *always* been common? Or is it more and more of the kids lately?"

"Giovanni seemed to think it was a lot of them," I said slowly. "At least, here at this school. But he did say 'one of the new ones'..."

"Carla spoke like it was a new phenomenon," Officer Thorn said, scratching her chin. "I didn't get too caught up in it. Don't forget, Meteor is a key witness, but this case is still ultimately about Bricky and Sweep."

*Is it?* I glanced down at William. He'd been the one to ask about Meteor in the first place.

"Although," Officer Thorn continued, her voice bouncing around the deserted hall, "that's not saying there's nothing in it. Could be worth looking into on its own. I'll bring it up to Bakis; they'll have the resources to follow up with the parents, see who'll talk about where their kids came from. Seems to me most of 'em are pretty tight-lipped about it."

"You can't blame them for wanting to protect their kids," I pointed out.

"That's not what she's saying, Red," William grumbled. "What she's saying is, it's *strange* how *secretive* some of the parents are."

"Is that what she's saying?" Officer Thorn repeated, looking down at William speculatively. "Well, now you mention it, I won't disagree. With me. But I still say it's a job for the Maplehouse force. The rest of us need to focus," she said, giving me a squinty-eyed look.

I resisted the urge to stick my tongue out at her. "Actually, I did have an errand in mind for this afternoon. I want to go check on some things at the alchemists' institute."

"Check on things involving the murder?" Officer Thorn pressed. When I nodded, she looked satisfied. "Good, then. We'll meet you downtown later. At the Guild this morning, I managed to reach out to the president of the Lost Rabbit Supper Club. We're all invited to their Yule dinner tonight."

*And when was she going to share this information?* I shook my head, sighing. "Well, okay, I should be able to make that work. But we should make sure Luca knows where we are."

"Luca's invited too. I already sent him a note. The more eyes at this meeting, the better," Officer Thorn said, before going on to give me the address of an old hotel downtown. Seeing that I had no further objections, she went on, "Me, I'm going to canvas the neighborhood and see what we can learn about that property lead. Landlord might be out of town, but I bet the neighbors still talk, and I'd like to hear what they have to say for myself. You up for it?" She added, looking down at William.

William nodded, tail in the air. "Let's see if we're followed again. I bet you *that* person knows more answers than the neighbors or parents do."

# 12

# Elixirs of Life

I left Officer Thorn and William on their way to the police station in Maplehouse. They were chattering all the way down the sidewalk. Though I felt a pang at leaving William when we still hadn't had a chance to talk privately, I was secretly glad to have some peace and quiet before facing my old training grounds—and whatever experiments might be going on there.

I caught the trolley back into the center of town, nursing my thoughts amid the sway and clatter and movement of the old car. Excited voices of young shoppers and folks getting ready for the holidays filtered in through the noise, making me smile in spite of myself. For all its bitter wind and politics, the city *was* a magical place at Yule time.

Like most of the other passengers, I hopped down onto the cobblestone streets in the city center, and spent only a moment looking around at the decorated evergreens and beribboned storefronts before flagging down a carriage. The alchemists' institute was on the city outskirts, near the harbor, and no trolley line went directly there. It didn't even really have a proper name—that is, it *did* have a very long and extremely proper name, but no one ever bothered to remember it: everyone just called it "the alchemists' institute." However, there was always a stream of carts and carriages going back and forth, picking up orders and delivering goods. Feeling a bit like a barrel of cinnabar or a crate of crystals myself, I perched on the backseat of a large, open-topped carriage drawn by a pair of donkeys festooned with red felt and bells. Pulling a thick woven blanket up to my shoulders, I let myself be rattled and bounced down the roads leading out of downtown.

Carriage rides in the city were nowhere near as meditative as trolley rides could be. Between keeping myself covered, keeping one watchful eye on the uncontrolled traffic, another keen eye on the buildings—and how they'd changed since I left, I didn't have space left in my brain to wonder over exactly what to say when I got to the institute.

As a result, I ended up standing speechless for a few moments on its front steps.

To be fair, this is exactly what the weary traveler was *meant* to do. I don't know who actually designed and built the alchemists' institute, but they'd encapsulated the grand glory days of alchemy right down to the foundations. The building itself took up an entire block. Polished white marble steps ran all along the front, leading up to a set of carved pillars that were holding up so much symbolism I'd always been surprised they didn't crumble under the weight. Twelve pillars at even intervals: as an apprentice, I'd been told alternately that each one represented a heavenly body—or a combination of elements—or an ancient god—or a symbol of the zodiac. Some of those legends made more sense than others. I'd never heard any definitive explanation, but then again, that was alchemy for you: grand meanings all wrapped up in an impressive and orderly package, so esoteric that you'd have to figure out what they actually *were* for yourself.

Behind the pillars, the actual building wasn't any less grand. Pyramid-shaped copper roof lines and shining walls hid the warren of labs and stockrooms within. This wasn't simply a school, not in the way Luca's university was, and it wasn't strictly a guild, like Officer Thorn's police system; it was an embodiment of its science.

For a moment I was young Cinnabar again, fresh off the boat from her family home, awed and excited. And at the same time I was Cinnabar the graduate, leaving these halls behind with a twinge of fear and determination. To be here now, suspicious and a stranger, was almost too surreal.

*All the more reason to begin the investigation,* I told myself, giving my shoulders a little shake. *It won't be strange for long once I dive in. Whether that's a good thing or a bad one, only time will tell . . .*

I fixed my intentions in the forefront of my mind as I climbed the wide steps. *One: Place my orders and re-establish a relationship here. Two: See if anyone knows anything about Bricky, Sweep, or Meteor. Three: Find out what in Beyond was going on when someone here decided to make Adam . . .*

Number Three was going to be a tough one, for sure. But as Luca had pointed out the night before, visiting the institute for Reason Number One had always been part of my plan. I squared my shoulders and stepped through the massive revolving door that led to the main hall.

(Revolving due to a mechanical process—one of the masters' attempts at perpetual motion—and not at all due to magic, of course. Although the rumor when I was an apprentice had always been that a magical spell was what kept the "perpetually in motion" gears turning . . .)

Just like the outside, the inside of the institute remained totally unchanged. The main hall stretched back into the building, but it was neither as long nor as wide as the building itself; lab rooms and study halls lined all three edges of the hall, their entrances hidden in the shadow of yet more pillars. Desks lined the interior side of those pillars: a desk for placing orders, a desk for picking them up, a desk for apprentice affairs, a desk for mail, and so on. The effect was a little grueling, as the visitor—me, in this case—had to walk through the two lines of desks in order to reach the main desk, set at the back of the hall, just in front of a massive mural depicting the mysteries of science. The entire room was lit by special skylights, but in the cloudy winter weather, this led to more gloom than anything else. Many of the desks sported candelabras or curious alchemical lamps to ward off the gloom, and some had already been decorated for Yule.

It was meant to be impressive as well as functional. But the further I walked into the hall, the more my body seemed to realize that *oh yeah, I've been here before. I used to live here.* By the time I neared the main desk, I was far from a wide-eyed and worried tourist. I approached the alchemist on duty with my shoulders back and confidence in my step.

"My name's Cinnabar Sunset," I told the alchemist, who looked to be the apprentice who'd drawn the short straw. I remembered those days well. "You can call me Red. I graduated from the apprentice program here, oh, probably eight years ago now. There are a couple of business matters I'd like to attend to, but I also wouldn't mind catching up on what's happened with the institute while I've been away."

It sounded pretty good, as far as explanations go, I thought. Entirely neutral so far—no *by the way did you send someone to stalk me and my friends* or *and while we're at it, care to explain who decided to meddle with life itself, and why?* But even so, the alchemist behind the desk jerked upright and stared at me as I finished speaking.

Her skin was a little darker than mine, perhaps as dark as the polished oak table between us, and her long, braided hair was deeply maroon. Her dark eyes were wide set and rimmed with a sparkly gold kohl, exaggerating her expression. Suddenly, she was brushing at her stained apprentice's apron and tugging at her gray flannel sleeves as though something about my winter cloak had reminded her that she was under-dressed.

"You're Cinnabar? Like, *the* Cinnabar?" she asked, her voice deep.

I ran a hand through my ponytail, a little surprised. "Um, I suppose so? Like I said, most people call me Red. But not so much around the institute, back when I was an apprentice. Paracelsus did always say—"

"—nicknames obscure the true nature of the object," she chorused with me. Apparently, my old teacher had held true to his pet phrases.

"Yep." I grinned at her, caught up in the moment. It had been so long since I'd had anyone to talk to about the institute that I'd even forgotten how much I missed it. "Although, personally, I never really agreed with him. Sometimes the common name tells you *plenty* about a plant or mineral."

"Oh my gods and goddesses," the apprentice said. "You are *so* cool. You're exactly how I thought you'd be."

I blushed. "Well, that's—nice of you. But what's your name? And why do you know mine?"

"My name's Nessalee. Gods and goddesses, I am *so* glad I was on desk today," she added, mostly to herself. "I can't believe it. I got your notes. First year. There's a legend about them and everything. They're lucky. Do you know how many people you've helped get past Phase One?"

"No. I had no idea," I admitted, leaning one hand on my hip as I chuckled along with her enthusiasm. Apprentice alchemists in their first few years used reference books and notes provided by the institute—essentially, recycled; you had to give them back when you moved on to a new phase, so that they could be shared with someone after you. Paracelsus had this whole speech about the point of an institution being the nurturing of future generations, but to be honest, I'd hated the policy. I would have preferred to keep all my books and notes—to then lug them around with me everywhere, I suppose? I hadn't thought through it at the time. But now, I was glad to hear that I'd somehow helped others.

"You're a lifesaver," Nessalee stated, as though it was proven fact. "We've always wondered what happened, like, why you didn't stay?"

"Well, everyone's recommended to go through a traveling period," I reminded her, even more embarrassed.

"Yeah but like, why did you never come back? Oh my goddesses! Is that what you're doing now? Are you going to come back and be a master?"

*Oh dear.* Immersing myself in complicated experiments and achieving high-ranking titles like *master* had really never been my cup of tea—I'd always thought it was a little vain, to be honest. But I couldn't just *say* that to a starry-eyed apprentice. "Ah, no, I'm not here to stay. I'm very happy with my shop, actually. My interests have always been a little more . . ."

"Practical?" Nessalee supplied, without hesitation. "We know. We could tell it from your notes. They're actually *helpful*."

"Yes, that's how I'd put it. And thank you." I was starting to wonder about this *we*—from what Nessalee was saying, I was picturing a horde of young apprentices gathered round my notes at bedtime, reading them out by lightstick. It was unnerving. I decided to change directions. "So, would you mind telling me a bit about what the institute is like these days? I mean, I do have some orders to put in, too, but we can get to those later."

"We totally can," Nessalee enthused. "There's, like, no one these days, since it's winter vacation and all. There's no rush. I can tell you *everything*. What do you want to know?"

"Oh, mostly I just am curious," I said, trying to stay casual. We were far enough away from the rest of the desks that no one could hear us—except when Nessalee got excited and raised her voice, of course. Her enthusiasm was actually a bit relaxing, after all my recent stress. "I really haven't kept up with anything here since I left. I promised everyone I'd write, but . . ."

"Oh my gods. The masters here barely even respond to *our* written requests. You should see the *piles* of unanswered mail that comes in each day," Nessalee confirmed.

I grinned. "So, that hasn't changed, then. And Paracelsus is still running things, I'm sure?"

"Like he'd let anyone else take charge!" Nessalee and I laughed together. For all his quirks, the headmaster was well-respected. His words were remembered for decades; I myself was proof of that. I'd always had a soft spot for him—until Adam's revelation, of course, but we'd get to that in time. "You should totally see him if you get a chance. He comes through here all the time, just checking up on things. You know how it is. But he definitely would want to see you. He still remembers you, you know. Once he saw whose notes I had and he just nodded and was like, 'you can't go too wrong if you follow her advice.'"

"Whoa," I said, catching myself from adopting Nessalee's pet phrase—*oh my gods and goddesses!* I never would have thought such a celebrated figure would remember me. "That's pretty incredible. I still can't believe anyone here remembers me, let alone people I never even met."

"That's what alchemy's like," Nessalee said proudly. "Right? That's why I'm in it. My uncle was really excited for me to come to the institute. He was here himself, but that was before your time. He has all these stories. I used to hear them all the time."

"You probably know all my stories, if you were reading my notes that closely," I chuckled. "Are there any new stories going around?"

Nessalee leaned in. The alchemy institute was home to a handful of masters, a few dozen researching alchemists, and an extra few dozen apprentices at any given time, and I swear, each and every one of them loved gossip. Even those who'd been close-lipped as children became nosy storytellers the moment they climbed the marble steps and claimed a bunk in the students' quarters. *It adds a human element to such scientific study,* I realized now, as I watched Nessalee's eyes dance.

"There's been some wild ones," she informed me. "There was the whole scandal with Albertus leaving—that was a few years back, right when I started. I never did get the whole story."

"I think we could have seen that coming, though," I mused, thinking back.

"That's what everyone says. Anyway, way bigger things have happened since then. They closed down the potions wing to do a deep clean, and found a body under the floor! Can you believe it? But the police said it was from a really long time ago, and no one here was responsible. Something to do with the construction. So that wasn't even the worst thing. The *worst* thing . . ."

"Yes?" I asked, leaning in.

Nessalee glanced into the corners around us before whispering, "Did you hear they kicked out Vincenzo because he tried to *bring someone back to life?*"

*Eureka. This has to be it.* But even though I'd met Adam, the story was still so egregious that my repulsed reaction was totally unfeigned. "Isn't that totally against the principle of *making things better?* After all, life isn't something that can be controlled. The alchemist would have no way of knowing that they're actually doing something *good* instead of ultimately harmful."

"Oh my gods. That's exactly what Paracelsus said. He was so mad!" Nessalee giggled behind her hand; apparently, a few years had eased the shock and pain of the incident.

Internally I breathed a massive sigh of relief that my old teacher hadn't been responsible. He still hadn't managed to *prevent* the experiment, of course, but—

"He said it was a shame to the institute, especially because they used shared resources to do it and somehow nobody ever knew," Nessalee continued, answering my thought. "But of course, how could we? Vincenzo was always so secretive. We all thought he was still stuck on turning stuff into gold."

"I guess he thought of another way of making money," I mused, my stomach turning as I thought of all the kids back at Meteor's school. *There's definitely money to be made if you could fashion life, or even bring someone back to life . . .*

"Yeah but like, is that not just the *worst?*" Nessalee asked, sharing my disgust. She shook her head, her braids swinging. "And in the end it cost him. Like, massively. I never saw the room myself, but apparently his experiment totally went wrong and the entire laboratory was destroyed. Paracelsus turned him over to the police for unethical practice. The trial was *such* a scene, I heard, but they wouldn't let us apprentices go. But we all heard that as part of his punishment, he has to pay the institute back every single coin, even for the resources he used."

It wouldn't help Adam, of course, but from what I recalled of Vincenzo, it would certainly hit him where it hurt. And knowing police procedures as I did, I felt confident that they'd made him sign some kind of oath—probably to swear off alchemy entirely.

"And what *did* happen from the experiment?" I asked, thinking things over.

"No one knows," Nessalee said solemnly. "Right after the lab was destroyed, Vincenzo was in total shock and couldn't even tell us what happened. Paracelsus said his greed cost him his sense. And now he can never benefit from either."

"True," I agreed slowly. I could already see how this story had become a sort of fireside tale, a ghostly legend for the apprentices—a warning of what could happen if they didn't stick to their principles. And honestly, that seemed fitting. Adam didn't want anything to do with them, clearly, so I wasn't about to change the story.

"Anyway," said Nessalee, "that's pretty much everything that's happened.  But we've all been dying to know what happened to *you*."

"Oh—you have?" I asked, surprised out of my reverie.

"Yes, indeed," said a cracked and ancient voice from the corner of the hall. "What has become of you, Cinnabar?"

# 13

# Old and New

"Paracelsus," I said, my surprise doubling and growing into delight.

From a doorway at the back of the hall, my old headmaster made his way to us at the desk. He looked exactly as he had when I was an apprentice: tall and straight as a young man, but with the long white hair and deep wrinkles of someone who's lived a *very* long life. He'd never been one for scholarly robes or fancy adornments; instead, he was dressed a lot like me and Nessalee—simple trousers and a long-sleeved white shirt under a thick protective apron. His was clean, though. He'd told us all when I was an apprentice that part of mastery is knowing when you're going so fast that you're going to spill something, and slowing down accordingly.

Despite his age and skill, his blue eyes beamed with a familiar warmth. He shook my hand like we were old comrades, not student and teacher.

"And here I was starting to think I might never see you in this hall again," he said, with good humor. Turning to Nessalee, he added, "I see you've already deduced who our esteemed guest is?"

I protested. "I'm really not—"

"Oh, I totally knew it," said Nessalee. "Even before she said anything."

I wasn't so sure *that* was the case, but I bit my tongue, smiling.

Paracelsus continued, "And I'm sure you informed her that we have openings available, should she wish to continue her studies?"

Nessalee wasn't even remotely abashed at being caught gossiping. "I tried, but she said she's happy at her shop!"

"Of course you are," Paracelsus said, turning back to me with a knowing grin. "Red's Alchemy and Potions, is it not?"

"How did you know?" I sputtered.

"Oh, we're not so out-of-touch here as you might think," Paracelsus said, with a wink that made him look vaguely like a Yuletide character out of childrens' tales. "In fact, your timing is most serendipitous. I was just on my way to complete a final check on the new potions wing, and the advice of a practicing expert is exactly what I need. Why don't you come along, Cinnabar, and you can fill me in on all your adventures along the way?"

Hearing a pinnacle of the alchemical community refer to me as a *practicing expert* had rendered me momentarily speechless. In the silence, Nessalee piped up. "But she still has to place some orders for things, she said!"

"There will be time," said Paracelsus.

"But I could do it now," Nessalee offered.

I was beginning to feel like a rope in a game of tug-of-war. I shook my head to clear it, and laughed. "I'd be honored to see the new potions wing. And Nessalee, don't worry, I'll be back. Even if it ends up being too late today, I'm actually in town several days more."

This seemed to at least halfway appease the apprentice, and she let us go without further protest. As I followed Paracelsus across the hall, I couldn't help but reflect that in a way, I *was* caught between him and Nessalee, on my own path between bright-eyed apprentice and methodical master. A calm, happy feeling in my gut assured me that this was exactly where I was meant to be.

* * *

Paracelsus led me down a familiar hallway, all the while asking questions about my travels and the state of alchemy in Belville. It took a few minutes, but by the time we'd reached the new potions wing, I'd gotten over some of my star-struck tongue-tied reserve. *Which was probably his plan all along,* I thought, smiling to myself as I stepped through the door he held open.

The potions wing, despite its unfortunate beginnings—Nessalee's story of a body in the floor still rang in my ears—was an alchemist's dream. It was a long narrow room, with exterior windows lining one side, letting in plenty of light across an unbroken workbench that spanned the length of the wall. Shelves lined the inner wall, freshly filled with glass bottles and ingredients, and a variety of hearths set into the floor at even intervals stood ready for heating and brewing.

"I tried to design it so that the traffic flows this way," Paracelsus said, gesturing the short distance between the benches and the shelves, "rather than the other way. But you know how apprentices are."

"Sure. They'll still find ways to get under one another's feet," I agreed, chuckling. I could already envision this room full of students, all shouting and running back and forth, despite Paracelsus' repeated reminders that *serious study leads to lighthearted results.* I glanced around the bare wooden walls. "Plenty of room for you to etch in your most popular sayings," I added, teasing. When I'd been an apprentice, the walls had been covered with reminders—most literally burned into the wood.

"Just a little hobby of mine. Something to pass the time when the students need supervision," Paracelsus said, with a mild smile. "You approve, then?"

I hesitated. "I think it's a great space. But you don't need my approval."

"And nor do you need mine. Come, sit for a moment. You must have traveled a long way to get here," Paracelsus said, gesturing me over to the workbench, where clean stools were waiting. After standing at Nessalee's desk for so long in my sturdy winter boots, I sat gratefully.

"Well, I didn't come to Brass just for the institute," I admitted as we relaxed. "My boyfriend is attending a conference, and—well—"

"And," said Paracelsus, intentionally, "you are assisting the police in some matter."

For just a moment, a little shock scared off some of my warm and fuzzy feelings. *What if the institute really is behind our stalker?* But I couldn't lie. "I am. It's a little complicated. Basically, ever since I settled in Belville . . ."

"Do not feel you need to explain yourself," Paracelsus said kindly, when my voice trailed off. "Alchemists make excellent police advisors. Your friend the officer of Belville has exceptional taste."

"Well, thank you, I suppose," I said, chuckling a little. "I have to admit, it's not something I ever saw myself doing. But my friend, Officer Thorn, she can be very insistent."

"The good ones usually are. We had a few here from Maplehouse the other day, wishing to check into your background," Paracelsus said casually.

I blanched. "Oh dear. I'm sorry if they inconvenienced you. I had no idea—"

"And nor should you," Paracelsus assured me, putting up one calloused hand. "I myself had only the best things to say. And I was given no clue as to their intentions, of course. I merely wanted to check that you are alright."

"Oh." I hesitated. Theoretically, this could answer my Reason For Visiting Number Two: see how much the institute knows. According to Paracelsus, they knew nothing. And it *did* make sense that Chief Bakis might want to check up on me before bringing me into his investigation. But could I really leave it all at that? "I'm fine," I answered eventually. "It's nothing to do with me, strictly speaking. I'm a sort of consultant. Not that I know much in this particular case," I couldn't help adding.

"The mark of a true alchemist is their skill at learning," Paracelsus said neutrally, his gaze fixed on the window.

I leaned against the workbench and sighed. "That's exactly what my boyfriend was just reminding me. But there's a lot to learn in this case, and not many people I can ask."

Paracelsus's gaze returned to me, and it was very calm and considered—not at all the look of someone who was secretly having someone else followed. In fact, he said, "I will refrain from prying. But I can certainly sympathize. Tensions are high in the city at the moment. It is a difficult time to find trusted sources to learn from."

I saw the chance, and took it. "Nessalee was telling me about the recent—experiment."

"The infamous experiment." Paracelsus nodded thoughtfully. "Of course, it was not the first time that someone under the institute's eye has attempted such a thing. But I must admit it is the furthest anyone has ever gotten before I realized what was going on under my very nose. I am growing old, Cinnabar."

"You've always been old," I said automatically, making us both laugh. More seriously, I added, "Nessalee said it was Vincenzo. I can see how you wouldn't have suspected him. There were so many false warnings with him it was almost a joke."

"Until it wasn't. Still, I appreciate your insight," Paracelsus said, and he seemed quite genuine. "If I may say so, understanding has always been one of your strengths, Cinnabar."

"In certain situations, maybe," I said, thinking of William. But then, with Adam in mind, I added, "It was a shock to hear about it. I don't see how someone could have that *lack* of understanding, to be honest. How could he do an experiment to create something, some*one*, and not see that it was problematic?"

"For the same reason you chose to make your home elsewhere, Cinnabar. The institute's foremost focus is science. And some of us take that so far that it becomes a focus on *power*," Paracelsus said sadly.

I skimmed over his comment about me choosing to stay at my shop—he'd hit on something else that bothered me. "But it isn't just science. Magic-users, sorcerers, are doing this kind of thing all the time. Animation spells are one thing, but then—then—"

"Life is a great gift." Paracelsus seemed to see where I'd been headed. "Not every field is fit to provide every gift."

"So you think it's okay when the sorcerers do it?" I asked, feeling like a young and confused apprentice again.

Paracelsus's answer was ponderous. "I think it is always dangerous. It is not an undertaking to be approached lightly. And yet . . . for those who *do* have an understanding beyond science, perhaps it is not so very different from the natural course of life."

"You're saying if it's done for the right reasons, it's fine," I summarized. My confusion was threatening to turn into a full-on sulk. "But how do you know what the right reasons are, and who has them?"

"I'm saying that every action is context-dependent," Paracelsus said, tilting his head. "But you already know that."

I knew exactly what he was getting at. "An experiment is only as good as the lab it's conducted in," I said, parroting a teaching from one of the other masters.

"See? You are more than capable." Paracelsus chuckled. "Your memory, *and* your actions, Cinnabar, do this institute proud."

"Thank you," I said honestly. "Sometimes I'm not sure what I'm doing, but I do try my best."

My teacher smiled. "I don't believe I've ever seen you do anything else."

"Paracelsus," I asked on impulse. "How do *you* feel about all this? Not the experiment, exactly—but all the politics right now about animation, and created life forms. Has it affected the institute?"

"Not as of yet," came the characteristically considered response. "As you may recall, we do our very best to stay out of politics. And in this case, of course, we wouldn't want to cause *additional* harm."

The way he said it told me instantly that he knew where Adam was, and what he was doing. I met his gaze quietly.

"One thing every student must learn for themselves," Paracelsus added quietly, "is that there is a crucial difference between *experiment* and *life*. It is not something I can teach. It must be discovered. Perhaps, indeed, we are all a part of someone else's grand experiment . . . but it avails us not. The truth of the matter is, there is no controlling life."

"I said something similar to Nessalee earlier," I admitted. "She laughed at me, because she said you'd said it too."

"She is already on the right track," Paracelsus observed with a smile. "If only I could lift up each and every one, and set them on the right track as well."

"Like you said, they have to make their choice," I said, although I could certainly feel the weight of his responsibility.

"Indeed. I must say, Red," Paracelsus concluded with a smile, "that your reminders are most helpful. What would you say to keeping up a written correspondence, once you leave Brass? . . . I promise that your letters won't end up in the 'unopened' pile."

# 14

# The Supper Club

After such a heartening—and slightly embarrassing, but mostly heart-warming—conversation with my old mentor, I left my orders with Nessalee and hurried back to the city center. Evening was falling quickly, and I had to hustle to catch a wagon that would deliver me to dinner in time.

Fortunately, the "supper club" Officer Thorn had gotten us all invited to was centrally located. Apparently, for its special Yule dinner, the club had rented out the dining hall of a swanky hotel along the main street. I'd never been there myself, but I was fairly certain I remembered where to go. I hopped off the supply wagon when we reached the central square, and from there I walked the last few blocks. The wind had picked up, racing along the road, bringing tiny little snowflakes with it; but it wasn't the weather that buffeted me around. The sidewalks were full of merry shoppers—shoppers too merry to get out of the way! I nearly missed the hotel's hanging sign and covered entrance because I was too distracted trying to disentangle myself from an extended family of raucous giants. From the smell of them, they'd already dipped into some seasonal mulled wine.

Stepping into the hotel, then, was a sigh of relief. As soon as the old wooden doors closed behind me, I was in a three-story lobby, decorated with potted evergreens trimmed in tasteful, magical tinsel. The noise of the street was eclipsed by the soft sounds of a piano player in the far corner dreamily performing holiday tunes.

My wide eyes as I took in the immaculate tiled floor and curving banisters must have given me away. The clerk behind the counter to my left knew I wasn't there to rent a room. "The dining hall's straight through that door," he called, gesturing across the lobby with a sweeping motion. I felt vaguely like I was being cleared out of the way for more important guests.

*Well, not everyone's impressed by my potion belt and thick cloak,* I thought with good humor. With a grateful nod at the clerk, I did as I was bid.

I'd thought I'd made good time, but the hotel's dining hall, it turned out, was already full of folks. The room was as long as the lobby, but the ceiling was lower; the same evergreens stood sentinel in the corners and near pillars. Along the exterior wall, a bank of what *had* to be enchanted windows opened up onto an idyllic, snowy sunset scene (*not* the bustle of the city and the brick sides of neighboring buildings). To one side, a polished bar stretched along the wall; this seemed to be the preferred spot to sit, so I walked over, keeping an eye out for my friends.

Unfortunately, I got caught trying to sneak in undercover. A chipper woman in a fuzzy red jumpsuit appeared from nowhere, cutting off my progress. "Hi! Are you new here? Do you need a place to sit?"

"Um, I'm here to meet friends," I said, glancing at the tables around us with a sudden fear. *She's not going to try to sit me with a bunch of strangers, is she?* Investigation or no, I hated these kinds of events, where everyone has to scramble for a seat and then be stuck there all evening. In my experience, it only ever worked out for the people who already knew—or thought they knew—everyone present. "I'm sure we'll find somewhere. It's fine."

"It's so nice to see newcomers," the woman continued, as though I hadn't said anything. "I'm the acting secretary, you can call me Bryn. You probably know Katerina, I bet, or over there is Boa, he's always very helpful for new people. I'm new too, you know. Fred and Theo, over there, invited me only this fall. It's such a *meaningful* group, don't you think?"

"Uh huh," I said, noncommittally. I was barely able to follow her as she singled people out in the crowd, and I was certain I wouldn't be able to remember their names. Katerina seemed to be an orange-haired young woman simpering and grinning at us while Bryn talked, and Bryn herself reminded me of someone, but I couldn't think who . . . I was fast becoming overwhelmed.

"Red, you beat me," a welcome voice behind me said.

I turned, my strained smile flooding with relief as I spotted Luca coming in from the main door. "Thorn and William will be here in just a minute," he added as he gave me a quick side hug. "They just wanted to chat with the hotel clerk. I met them coming in." He turned his attention to the woman watching us, still beaming positive energy. "Hi! I'm Luca. You could probably tell this is our first time here?"

"*Someone's* in conference mode," I murmured to Luca as Bryn launched into her welcome speech once more.

"And someone else probably has a lot on her mind after visiting the old stomping grounds," he murmured back, making way for Officer Thorn and William to join us. Bryn was talking quietly to Katerina, who disappeared. Luca went on, "I want to hear all about it. But I figured we have to make a good impression first."

"Ugh. Fine," I agreed, grinning despite my exaggerated resistance.

Fortunately, Thorn—who had conspicuously dropped her title "officer," which she usually wore like a second skin—took over from there. She soon freed us from the secretary and stationed us at the end of the bar, where we could observe the club members and have a quick chat before dinner began at the waiting tables.

"Let's not be downers," was the very first thing she said—and she said it directly to me. "Bakis is trying to keep the case low-profile, so most of the rank and file here won't even know about it. It's the top brass we're really interested in. Get it?" she asked William, nudging him so that he almost slipped off his stool.

"I'm never coming with you to Brass again," he muttered.

"I'm not a downer," I protested, meanwhile. "But Bricky and Sweep were both members here. Wouldn't the club want to do something to observe their passing?"

"After the holidays," Officer Thorn said with confidence, as though she herself ran five of these clubs back home. "No good stirring things up now. This is their annual Yule get-together, you know."

"I wonder if that has something to do with the timing of the murders," Luca said thoughtfully.

"Regardless, we don't want people putting up their guard,"

Officer Thorn reminded us. After an authoritative signal to the bartender, she distributed glasses of spiced apple juice to each of us, adding, "But I expect each of *you* to be on your guard at all times. No alcohol. Got it?"

"That's fine," Luca said, answering for all of us. "After my day at the conference, I'd probably just fall asleep if I had too much mulled wine."

"You two are one team," Officer Thorn decided, pointing at Luca and me. "William and I will be on our own teams. That way we can check out three separate tables."

I raised an eyebrow. "Did canvassing the neighborhood not go well?"

"It went perfectly well," William sniffed. "That's why Thorn and I know we can each handle ourselves."

I made a *can you believe this?* face at Luca, but he just chuckled. Seeing his amusement made me relax about it. It *would* be nice to have a teammate for all this socializing, and I'd hardly gotten to spend time with Luca at all on this trip.

"You two keep each other sharp," Thorn admonished us, before sending us out to take seats at a table she pointed out.

As we made our way to our assignment, I realized two things: first, that everyone else was slowly making their way to their chairs for dinner too, and second, that the "Lost Rabbit Supper Club" was much bigger than I'd expected. From the way everyone had been talking about Bricky's friends, I'd assumed the dinner club was a group of three or four people who liked to talk politics. But the dining hall was filled with people. Given that each table sat six, there had to be at least forty or fifty members present.

Luca noticed my trepidation when I followed close behind him and immediately claimed the chair next to his. "Don't worry, Red," he said, leaning over. "This is nothing."

"Feeling shy, are we?" One of the diners asked. I had to look up, and even farther up, to see his face. I found myself squinting into one dark eye set deep into a trollish face. The other eye was covered by a leather patch that looked like it could have served as a body shield for a mouse. Trolls, by and large, could be seven or eight feet tall and built like small houses. This one was no exception. His pale skin was covered in tattoos, which peeked out from underneath a sweater that stretched uncomfortably across a barrel-like chest. Straw-like hair seemed like it might fly off his head at any moment. But his grin was friendly—if also rather toothy.

"Um," I said, only proving his point.

"We're new," Luca said, coming to my rescue. "I guess that's pretty obvious, huh?"

"You can say that again!" The stranger looked Luca up and down, grinned again, and promptly took the seat next to him. "But you've come to the right place. Name's Boa."

"Boa?" I repeated uncertainly as Luca and I sat. *Why does that sound familiar?*

"Nickname. Never mind about the real thing, no one can pronounce it—not even me," he added with a loud laugh. "So, what brings the two of you here?"

As Luca made introductions and explained our presence in the vaguest possible of terms, I snuck a quick glance around. Officer Thorn was seated at a table with someone I was willing to bet was the club president; a bright red sash ran across their front. William was across the room, seated at a table with Bryn, the enthusiastic secretary. Suddenly, I remembered where I'd heard Boa's name before. *Bryn mentioned he was helpful for new people, I think,* I recalled. *So that must be why Officer Thorn meant for us to bump into him. Looks like she's got us all at tables with important—or at least talkative—members of the group.*

"Always glad to see new faces here," Boa declared, recapturing my attention. "You'll not find a better place for company. Or for a meal! No one's ever hungry or lonely at the Lost Rabbit Supper Club. You can be certain of that."

"Now, those are two aims I can get on board with," Luca told him, smiling.

"Hey, you scholarly types are smart folk, you know?" Boa replied, truly beaming as he rocked back in his chair—a chair, I noticed now, which was specially reinforced.

"Thank you," said Luca, responding to the good-natured ribbing with grace. "So, how did you come to be part of the club?"

"Oh, one way and another, you know. I get around," Boa said as the salad course made its way to us.

I did my best not to see any menace in the words—at least, no more menace than was there already. Boa's attitude was entirely friendly, and it was possible that he'd lost one eye in some completely peaceable manner, and that those tattoos of swords and bleeding hearts were only metaphorical . . . but it was also possible that he was being *over*-friendly because he was actually some kind of bouncer for the club.

*And if he was, he'd be pretty high on the list of suspects who might have dealt with Bricky and Sweep in a time of trouble.*

As we tucked into spinach salad with cranberries and toasted almonds, I decided to take a more active role in the investigation. "So, Boa, is this how most meetings go?"

"This one's special, for Yule," he said, his salad disappearing rapidly. "You came at a good time. No better introduction to the club. That's not to say the usual meetings are anything to sneeze at, you know. No, there's always a good meal. And then, with dessert, an *improving talk,* you know."

He elbowed Luca in a jocular manner. The reverberation nearly knocked Luca right into me.

"How interesting! What kinds of topics do they talk about?" Luca asked, recovering gamely.

"Oh, the usual. Someone gets up first to give us the policy updates and calls to action. Then there's the presentation. Most are from members of the club. Keeping us up to date with the news, dangers of city life, the like."

"Dangers?" I repeated.

"Sure. Isn't that why you came? Because you want to be in the know? Don't tell me you aren't planning to vote on the city's near-life forms proposal coming up."

Boa was giving me a very earnest look, but I wasn't sure I bought it. *What about "magical near-life forms" would an eight foot troll find dangerous?*

*Maybe it's the* magic *part,* I realized, remembering how Mix had said that Bricky, too, was skeptical about magic in general. *Maybe magic is the* only *thing an eight foot troll with a missing eye finds dangerous.*

Before I could think of anything to say, though, Boa had turned to Luca again. "We all look after each other, that's why," he said confidentially. "Specially now that crime's on the rise."

"I think that's nice," Luca assured him. (I wondered how long this evening could go before Luca ran out of positive adjectives, myself.) "I'd be happy to talk, if there was anything I could say that'd be useful for everyone."

If I hadn't already been in love with my boyfriend, I could have fallen for him all over again right there. It was perfect. And turned out it was *exactly* what Boa had wanted to hear.

"You're the type to know plenty," he said at once, pushing his empty salad bowl aside. "We'd be lucky to hear from you. Easiest thing in the world. We'll put in a word for you with the president, and make sure Bryn has your details so she can fit you in the schedule. You give her a little summary of what you want to say, and just like that, you're on."

"How neat, very easy, just like you said," Luca agreed. "I'm looking forward to seeing the one tonight, to see what they're like."

"Ah, that." For the first time, Boa pulled back, scratching at his chin. "I'm not sure *what* they put on the schedule. I'm sure they came up with something."

"Is it hard to find someone who wants to talk at the Yule meeting, since it's such a big one?" I hazarded a guess.

"Oh, no. People're dying to talk at this one, believe me," Boa said. He might have seen my reaction—I tried to hide it behind my water glass, but still, the words sounded ominous. But Boa laughed it off, nudging Luca again. "Just a bit of bleak humor, you know. Picked it up in the trade."

"Oh, really? What trade?" Luca asked, managing to sound more intrigued than alarmed.

"Carpentry," Boa said, with the innocence of a babe.

"I didn't realize carpentry was so bleak," I couldn't help but observe.

Luca gave me a look, like, *are we doing "good cop bad cop" right now, or are you just provoking him?*

But again, Boa tipped back his head and laughed. "There's a lot of things alchemists don't know, I bet."

I frowned. This was becoming so routine it was frustrating. Yes, goggles, but *still,* what was it with everyone and pointing out my profession? "How did you know I—"

The rest of my words were drowned out with a splintering crash.

# 15

# Ill-Weather Friends

I glanced toward the noise, alarmed. The last time I'd looked at William, he'd been deep in conversation with Bryn, the secretary. But now, their entire table was in disarray.

"What happened?" Luca asked at my shoulder, concerned.

"I think everyone's okay," I answered, thinking aloud, "but it looks like . . ."

"Someone's gone and broken a soup tureen," said Boa, who'd stood up for a better look. He towered over our table. "Now, who'd do something like that?"

*Who indeed,* I wondered. While it might have been strange that Boa would immediately assume that someone was at fault, the noise had been so loud that the tureen must have been huge. Hard to spill on accident.

But Luca, of course, was willing to be friendly. "Oh, I'm sure they couldn't have meant to. Do they need help?"

"The waitstaff has it covered," Boa answered. "Them and Kat. Trust Kat to be on top of things."

I was still watching William, just in case. It looked like the person beside him had been the one to receive the brunt of the spill. As they hurried away into the waiting arms of another club member, William continued talking intently to Bryn.

*Trust* him *to be the most focused of all of us,* I mused.

Meanwhile, Luca, too, was intent on our interviewee. "Is Kat the president?"

"No, no," Boa said with a guffaw. He dropped back into place, making our table shake. "Kat's the vice president. It's always them that does all the work, eh? But she's very quick on her feet. Always knows just what to do in a crisis, too."

"Sounds like a handy person to have around," I said.

"Sure is," Boa said briskly. "Now, let's see if we can handle our own soup without spilling it, eh? Show the rest of them how it's done!"

He took the tureen a passing waiter offered and plopped it into the center of the table, directing the rest of our dinner mates to fill their bowls in turn. Luca went first. As it turned out, the soup was a very thick—and very hot—squash chili.

"I worry for whoever got spilled on," Luca murmured to me as I took my turn.

"I wonder how bad it was," I agreed quietly.

"Maybe they'll come back, and we'll be able to get some idea," he suggested.

The soup course passed without another peep about the incident, however. Boa started introducing us to the other club members at the table, performing conversational icebreakers with a gusto that could not be denied—nor diverted with careful, curious questions (on Luca's part) or straight-up reluctance to participate (on my part). Eventually, we resigned ourselves to being social. Luca even poked me, as though to say, *it could be good to meet the other members—just wait and see!*

I had my doubts, though. There were too many people in this hall for us to hope to meet every single one, and I certainly didn't need to know anyone's favorite flavor of ice cream or where they'd lived when they were eight or when they'd first realized that magic was dangerous. No; Bricky *and* Sweep had been involved in this club, and it stood to reason that if their murderer was here, then that person would be acting suspicious. Not hoping to make new friends.

As chili gave way to a truly delicious creamy pasta, I kept scanning the room, looking for anyone acting strangely. Officer Thorn was happily chatting up her table, and William seemed to maintain his focus, too. I did my best to help Luca out with the meet-and-greet going on at our table as well, but Boa was trying my patience.

"Well," Luca whispered to me when there was a brief lull, "I could spill pasta on you, if you wanted to get out?"

"No, thanks, but I appreciate the gesture," I said, knowing that he was teasing. But the idea did strike a nerve. *Maybe the person who had to leave because of the broken tureen is less innocent than we thought?*

"You've got to stop treating them all like murderers," Luca added, his voice low enough that only I could hear.

"I'm not sure treating them like themselves is much better," I muttered back. "Doesn't this strike you as too much friendliness? I mean, I know it's *you* I'm talking to, not William, but still—"

But Luca was already nodding. "Love-spelling. I just heard a paper on it today."

"Excuse me?" I'd never heard that term before.

Unfortunately, before Luca could explain, Boa noticed that we were whispering and immediately proposed a new game:

everyone at the table had to share when they met the love of their life.

Now, not only was I annoyed, but my cheeks were on fire.

*Bricky and Sweep* liked *this?* I couldn't help but think.

Fortunately, the waitstaff intervened, cleaning away the dinner plates. As tea and coffee were passed around, Bryn got up and made her way to a dais in front of the magical windows.

"Hello, and welcome, everyone!" she called. Rather than use a magical microphone or speech spell, she spoke through an old-fashioned megaphone, like some kind of sports announcer. Her nails flashed dimly in the sparkling lights, and I realized for the first time that she had a gray, lion-like tail, too. "Wasn't that an excellent holiday dinner? Who's ready for some chocolate torte?"

A cheer went up, which Bryn seemed to absorb the way a flower soaks in sunlight. In a brief moment of shuffling and scraping, everyone turned their chairs toward her. Apparently, the "informative" portion of the evening had begun.

"For those who just met me, I'm Bryn, the acting secretary," she went on. "This is my first Yule party with you all, and I'm so excited! Now, we just have a few notices before we can begin our presentation . . ."

"Not bad for an 'acting' secretary," Luca leaned forward to whisper in my ear as Bryn read out member accolades and life updates.

"Some people are born for this kind of thing," I said, giving him a pointed look over my shoulder.

He chuckled. "It's the conference. It pulls it out of you. Don't worry, when we get back to Belville I'm going to hide in the bookstore for a full week, I think."

"We'll be sure to send in provisions," I teased. "Now come on, we have to listen to see if she says anything." *Anything about Bricky and Sweep,* I meant, but I knew I didn't have to spell it out for Luca.

She didn't, though. After an exhaustive list of new official members, a message from the president, a warning about "recent efforts amongst magic sympathizers to disrupt our new law," and detailed instructions on how to participate in the "secret Yuletide helper" gift exchange, Bryn finally cleared her throat and announced, "I'm afraid our scheduled presenter had to leave early. I know, it's so very sad! But don't you worry, everyone. We always have a few back up plans in place to take care of you. So, without further ado . . . I'll be sharing with you the tragic tale of the besieged sorcerer!"

"Good, you're in for a treat," Boa said not-too-quietly to Luca and me. "Bryn's filled in for a presenter before, and she's great. Really relatable."

"That's wonderful. But I feel bad for the other presenters! Was it stage fright?" Luca asked, much more sympathetically than I would have—it was on the tip of my tongue to say *how often do your presenters or members go missing?*

"Aye, with that one," Boa confirmed. "Tonight was just an accident, probably, like you said."

*The person who was spilled on?* I wondered. *Was it really an accident, then? Or did Bryn really want to talk to us about a "besieged sorcerer"? I don't think I've ever heard any story by that name, anyway.*

But before I could get any further in my musings, the party was interrupted by two sets of rapid footsteps and yet another crash.

# 16

# Tangled Strings

Once more that evening, William was at the center of a commotion.

While Bryn had been setting up her presentation—one of the windows was now a large screen, filled with an image of a very sad-looking old man in a purple pointy hat—William must have spotted and chased someone in the crowd. His chair was on its back, empty, and several people leaned over their tables as if someone had just run behind them and knocked them over. *Two* someones. They had run right behind the table where Luca and I sat.

But I could see at once where William had gone. He'd darted out the door at the back of the dining hall. I could see his familiar blue glow coming from the other side—the kitchen. While club members around us murmured and gasped at the interruption of the presentation, I didn't hesitate. I sprinted for the back of the room.

I reached the doorway but made it no farther: I could see that William was okay. It was what I *heard* that gave me cause for concern.

"*How DARE you?!*" William shouted, his voice nearly a howl.

He had his back to me. The kitchen was huge, but it was nearly empty: some servers cowered at the far end, and a swinging door in the corner indicated that any club members or other staff had beat a hasty retreat. Instead, William was yelling at a ragged stranger, a tall, bent man pinned against a bank of magical freezers.

"You don't understand," the man was saying. "Let me explain . . ."

*Explain what?* I wondered. *And why does he sound like he knows William? I've never seen him before . . .*

But that wasn't entirely true. I had to peer around a rack of hanging pots between myself and the stranger, but even still, something about him *did* look familiar. It was his posture, maybe; or his voluminous dark winter cloak, which he wore even inside the warm hotel; or maybe it was that colorless gray gaze?

*The man who's been tailing us,* I realized in an instant. For a split second I was relieved: *I really doubt he could be working for the alchemists!* But concern took over once more as William continued yelling.

"You don't need to explain anything to me! I already know *exactly* what's going on!"

"What is it?" Luca whispered at my shoulder. Like me, he'd stopped against the door frame. "Officer Thorn's redirecting the presentation. One of the waitstaff put a kind of glamour between us and the diners, so at least they won't be disturbed. Still, Thorn said to keep a lid on this—whatever this is."

"Of course a hotel like this would have that kind of spell just lying around. But this isn't a time for kitchen-themed puns," I whispered back, furious in my confusion. "Luca, I think William knows that man."

"Th-things have changed," the stranger was saying—was pleading, in fact, still cowering before a glowing William. "You have to let me go—you don't understand—"

"I UNDERSTAND ENOUGH!" William roared. "I SAW YOU USING MAGIC!"

"Is that the person who's been following you? Do you think we should interrupt?" Luca asked me, under the din.

"I don't know," I murmured, torn, my fingers digging into the carved wood of the door frame. All my thoughts of the Lost Rabbit Supper Club and its suspicious members were gone. I'd never seen William so angry before. "I mean, yes, that's the man. But I'm not sure—"

"I *am* allowed," the stranger protested to William, trying to straighten himself up.

"NO, YOU'RE NOT, AND ESPECIALLY NOT AROUND FAMILIARS!"

"Oh my gods," I hissed to Luca. I didn't even care that I sounded like Nessalee. "What does he mean? Isn't William the only familiar here? What was he doing?"

Luca's hand came down on my shoulder as the stranger began glowing too, a violent black-streaked purple. "Red, that man is a sorcerer. I don't think it's a good idea to go in there after all. We need to think of a way to distract him, from here, so that William can get out."

"I don't think William wants to get out," I protested.

As if to prove my point, the magic around William began sparking, flashing white and gold in answer to the stranger's display. Every bit of fur on his body seemed to be standing on end. He went on, "You've gotten lazy. You've gotten sloppy. What, you think the rules don't apply to you any more?! You think no one is paying attention?"

"I'm not—breaking—any—*rules,*" the stranger insisted, sending a wave of frothy shadow through the room.

But William's starlight shine broke through the shadow, revealing the kitchen unharmed. "You're not *welcome here!*"

"You're the one—who came—back!" the sorcerer retorted.

"*That's because you don't scare me any more!*"

There was another blast, another explosion of magic, and this time the white counter tops all around them were slightly singed and sizzling. I could hear both of them panting. My heart was in my throat. I couldn't speak.

The sorcerer looked down at William with a strange and ominous grin. "You were never scared."

"Come within eyesight of me or anyone I know again and *you'll* be the scared one," William growled. The magic around him crackled.

But something had changed; the sorcerer lifted his chin. "You know that's not how this works. You may be strong but you'll *never* be as strong as that."

"I don't need to be," William rumbled. "You've gotten weak."

From across the room, I could see the strangers' shoulders tense. I could see the hand he kept back, a pulsing ball of blood red magic floating over his palm, strengthening. I didn't need to know anything about magic to know it was bad.

"I'll show you," the sorcerer hissed.

I finally found my voice again. "*William!*"

Three things happened at once: William's ears perked up. Luca's hand on my shoulder tightened, almost painful. And the sorcerer threw his ball of magic straight up into the air.

"*WILLIAM!*" I repeated, flinging myself forward.

I crashed into him, sending us both onto the kitchen tile.

Luca threw himself over William's other side, so together we blocked him entirely. The room was chaos. The air smelled like sulfur, and there was light from every angle, and there was a sound so loud I could hardly hear it—instead, I felt it reverberating through my spine. I pressed my nose into William's fur and held on.

And then—it was over, just as suddenly. No one was moving, and the sorcerer was gone.

"You know," said William, in a small, muffled voice, "he was only trying to create a diversion so he could run away. Like he *always* does."

"We didn't want to take that chance," Luca said.

"He had a fireball," I agreed, lifting my head. "Or something. It looked awful. I thought he was going to . . . but I guess he threw it into the ceiling?"

"Like I said, a diversion," William grumbled. "Are either of you going to let me up?"

I sat back onto my butt, the room spinning. Swirls of smoke drifted around us. Or maybe that was my own vision, going blurry?

"You could say thank you," I told him thickly.

William scrambled up and looked at me solemnly for a moment. Then he looked at Luca, who didn't seem to be faring much better. Of the three of us, William was certainly the most composed. "I would have been fine."

"William," Luca said softly, his robe askew, "we care about you."

"Yeah. Well." For the first time, William's composure broke, and his voice was heavy. "Thanks."

I shook my head, going over the events in my mind once more, trying to piece things together. "You knew that man?

The one who's been following us? He was here?"

"Posing as a waiter," William rumbled. "Not that he was ever any good at disguises. I *knew* something was off all evening. I could sense he was hiding."

This didn't answer hardly any of my questions; in fact, it left me with *more*. But just one seemed to matter. "Have you known him all along?"

"You could say that." William heaved a sigh. "You just almost met Orlix. The sorcerer who created me."

# 17

# A Helping Hand

Even after a night of sleeping on it, I was still reeling. After handily glossing over the mess at the meeting with a story about a holiday dessert gone wrong, Officer Thorn had lectured us all the way home. She then informed us that we were to "take the morning off to get your act together" and to "remember, we don't have days and days to solve this one: the conference will be over soon, and Bakis is counting on us!" Needless to say, this added pressure did not improve anyone's morale. Luca at least had been sympathetic when he left to attend his morning sessions. Which just left William and me . . . alone, and still very much confused.

The nice thing, though, was that as soon as Luca left for his (ridiculously early) first meeting, William had hopped up on the bed with me.

"Hey," I said, as silence filled the little room.

"Hey," he returned, looking more at the frosty window than at me.

"I'm getting that you don't really want to talk about it," I said, a little awkwardly.

William huffed. "I know it doesn't make much sense."

"Oh. Well. I appreciate you understanding that much, at least." I even smiled a little as I said it, because honestly, I was buoyed by even this admission. If he could admit that, then maybe he wasn't super mad at me—he was just taking time to process things. And I for one could never begrudge anyone processing time. After all, hadn't my friends given me so much grace over the years?

At that thought, I had an idea. I sat up a little straighter. "Remember how you and Officer Thorn were able to have a magical 'call' when we were at Seaside?"

If William was unsettled by this abrupt change of topic, he didn't show it. Instead, his beady eyes glanced at me speculatively. "Yeah. Why?"

"Well, do you think you could do it again?"

"Sure. If it was someone I knew."

"That's kind of what I was thinking," I admitted, smiling in earnest now. "How about giving someone at home a call? Maybe Dusty, or Sakura? We could probably benefit from an outside perspective about now."

William tilted his head, giving this thought. "Okay," he decided. "But I'm not involving that shadow witch. We'll try calling Dusty."

I had to chuckle a little at his reluctance to seek Saki's advice, but it was about what I had expected. Dusty and William had been best buddies since the moment they met.

We shifted to sit side by side on the bed, and William proceeded without explanation. I didn't mind the silence as much now, though. First, a glowing circle appeared before us, and it grew until it was porthole-sized. Then an image of a floppy cap and a bag of trail mix filled the ghostly screen—

things William associated with Dusty, I guessed. It made me smile, because I instantly recognized Dusty from those items, too. A gnome and local carpenter-plumber-emergency-fix-it service, Dusty often appeared in the potions shop in between jobs. And he was *never* without his cap, denim overalls, and a snack of some kind.

I could intuit that William was drawing on his emotional connection to Dusty in order to perform the spell. After a moment, it seemed to work: within the glowing blue frame, a brownish sort of cave appeared, and in front of it, a round brown-skinned face with smushed nose and blue eyes.

"What're y'doin' now?" Dusty asked, peering around at what must have appeared as a strange floating picture out of nowhere. "William?"

"We want to talk," William said. "Where are you, under a sink? Come out from there."

Dusty did so—not without a few bumps and clangs. Instantly, the picture brightened.

"Is now a good time?" I asked. "We aren't in an emergency here; we can call back later."

"Naw, it's fine," Dusty said as he straightened himself out. "Just the old school plumbing actin' up again. We were just talking about you, actually. So, how's Brass?"

"Cold, and a little more dramatic than expected," I chipped in before letting William take the lead.

"You heard Thorn got a case," William said, by way of preamble. It wasn't a question. Dusty and William together were probably the two biggest gossips in all of Belville, and Officer Thorn had been so loud that morning at the Pomegranate that it stood to reason that Dusty had heard the news.

"All kinds of rumors 'bout that," Dusty commented by way of agreement. He swung himself up to sit on the counter he'd just been underneath. His little boots swished through empty air as he fished a bag of apple chips out of his pocket and began, thoughtfully, to snack. "Word at the tavern was it was some big political scandal. But Trent told me it was somethin' magical, all very hush-hush. Must've been important for them to bring you and the Officer in though, huh?"

I glanced at William, who sneezed. "As usual, no one's quite wrong, but no one's got it quite right either. There were two victims, and one was a familiar, like me. But the other was a gnome who seems to've been mixed up in a weird political club."

"You don't say?" Dusty set aside his apple chips. "Magic and politics—nothing *I*'d want to be mixed up in, myself. How'd it happen?"

"Crime of passion, it looks like," William said. There was more energy in his voice now than in the past several days put together. As far as I was concerned, this call had already done its job. He went on, "Both victims were in the gnome's apartment and seem to have been caught unaware, in the kitchen. The weapon was just a knife from the counter. But nothing else was taken."

I hadn't realized we knew that for certain—*this must have been part of what William and Officer Thorn talked about yesterday,* I decided. But my confidence in the matter was shaken when Dusty snorted.

"Yeah, but, what would the police know about that?" he remarked rather cheerfully.

"Presumably a lot, wouldn't they?" I asked, baffled. "I mean, that's one of the first things they look at."

"Not if it was in a *gnome's* apartment," Dusty said with certainty. "Gnomes are great at hiding stuff. 'Specially from you bigger folk. No offense."

I took none, of course, but was busy thinking this over. "But—"

"But," William said, at the same time, "it wasn't a traditional gnome home, though, Dusty. They were renting out rooms in an old converted house—both the victim, and some of his family next door."

"If there were two of them there, that just makes me more sure," said Dusty. "Listen, there's an old saying, 'your land is your wealth.' Gnomes take that seriously. They keep everything in their house. I mean *everything*. And most of 'em have a lot more than you'd think."

Given Dusty's uncanny ability to come up with the exact part that he needed, no matter what he was trying to fix or how old it was, I could certainly believe that last bit. I'd never seen his home in Belville, but I shuddered to imagine how full it might be of "helpful" mechanical items.

"That could give us a motive. And it does fit with something else we've found," William said, meanwhile. "There's someone in the neighborhood trying to buy the property out from under them. But they're doing it without revealing themselves or why they're interested in the house."

Dusty leaned back, scratching at his cap. "If you buy the house, then it's yours to search, I figure. Otherwise I don't see much sense in it."

"But *we* could probably search it again right now," I broke in. "Dusty, is there anything you'd suggest we look for?"

"I could," he said, glancing around the empty room on his end, "but you'd have to promise it stays between us three."

I exchanged a glance with William. It amused me how secretive gnome culture could be, given that most gnomes I'd interacted with—like Dusty or Mix—were usually open and honest to a fault. But at the same time, if it was important to Dusty, I had no qualms keeping this secret.

"We promise," William said, for both of us.

Dusty nodded. "You got your alchemy doodads, Red?"

I stifled a grin. "Yes, Dusty, I do."

"And they keep getting her into trouble," William muttered.

If the conversation had been less serious, I would have asked how he'd known that. But as it was, I didn't get a chance. Dusty went on at once: "You can do a test for 'em, then."

"For 'them'?" I asked. "Them what?"

"The markers," he said, simply. "Everyone knows you don't want to be like a squirrel who buried its food and can't remember where. So lots of people mark where they hid something for later. We've got a special kind of string for it."

"A special kind of . . . string," I echoed, feeling like a parrot. But at the same time, I could see a kind of genius in the idea.

"Real thin, like," Dusty continued, "and sometimes it comes with iron threads, kind of like a wire almost, to ward off any pixies. But it'll always be coated in cinnabar powder."

"Cinnabar powder?" I repeated once more, alarmed this time. "Dusty, that can be very toxic if it's inhaled!"

"They aren't inhaling it, they're using it to tint their special string," William pointed out, coming to his friend's defense.

I was not amused. Cinnabar might be my namesake, but it was no joke. "Even so, you'd have to be very careful—"

"We've been at this a long time, Red," Dusty said, grinning. "The gnomes who make it know what they're doing."

"And yet apparently they don't feel the need to make sure

their local police know about it," I surmised, shaking my head. A string treated with cinnabar would be bright red. It ought to be a distinctive and relatively easy-to-find marker—*if* anyone other than an informed gnome knew to look for it.

"You're just jealous they never taught you to make something like that at alchemy school," William told me.

"I'm just saying, this is like the time Thorn arrested Dusty because he wouldn't prove himself innocent. It'd save a lot of time—"

"You're forgetting," William interrupted, "that Bricky and the others chose to move *out* of the usual gnome district. It may be that the police stations in areas where more gnomes live *do* know this kind of stuff."

"They prob'ly do," Dusty piped up. "And anyway it's just one of those things that's an old tradition. The kind of thing you never think you'll have to explain to someone."

I sighed away my frustration and smiled at Dusty. "Well, thank *you* for explaining it. Believe it or not, we didn't call just to put you on the spot."

"I figured the Officer put you up to it," Dusty said with a lopsided grin. "Everyone's on the spot when she's investigating. Even those of us that aren't there!"

"You're not wrong, that's for sure. But actually . . ." I glanced down at William, wondering how much he wanted to say.

Finally, he huffed and leaned toward the magical circle. "Red's worried about me because of all the magic involved here," he confided.

That wasn't *entirely* true, but I bit my tongue.

"Serves you right," Dusty told William, promptly. "You're always running around thinking you know better than us. Why shouldn't she know better than you from time to time?"

*But I don't know anything about this case at all.* It was on the tip of my tongue to say—and then I caught a glimmer of Dusty's meaning. *I do know enough to be careful, though. And to keep in mind my priorities.*

"I wouldn't have called you if I knew you were just going to gang up on me," William retorted primly. But he seemed a little more relaxed now, too, like maybe that reminder had been what he needed to hear.

"And give you work to do," Dusty reminded us. "Go and search the place, will you? Let me get back to my sink."

This was, as always, imminently practical. We gratefully said our goodbyes and set out.

# 18

# Hidden Gems

Refreshed with not only a friend's perspective but new knowledge as well, William and I were markedly more cheerful as we left the university. We had no trouble convincing the police officer stationed at Bricky's apartment to let us in, either—although once we were alone in the little home, I realized how strange the whole affair was.

"I get that they have more officers here than in Belville, so they can take more precautions," I murmured to William, "but doesn't it seem a *little* excessive that someone's still here, guarding the scene? It isn't even much of a scene, and I'm sure Chief Bakis already had the professionals in here."

"*We* are some of those professionals, and we aren't done with our exams," William pointed out. The door behind us was safely closed, and he obviously felt we wouldn't be overheard, because he added, "From what Thorn was telling me yesterday, guarding the scene and any tangible evidence seems about as far as any of Bakis's officers are willing to go. Especially after the whole mistake at the beginning of the case."

"Not listening to Meteor, you mean. But in that case, you'd

141

think they'd want to be *more* proactive, in order to make up for that," I mused. William was sniffing around the living room, so I began a visual inspection of my own. I wasn't really sure we'd find some red string that everyone else had missed, but it seemed best to look for obvious clues before we started more invasive search methods.

"You've been spoiled by Officer Thorn," William called from his investigation of the sofa.

I opened the drawers of a side table and stepped back as an explosion of threads, bobbins, tiny scissors, rolls of tape, balls of twine, and who knows what else popped out. *Hoarding,* I thought, remembering Dusty's explanation with a smile. Unfortunately, the thread seemed to be completely ordinary. As I cleaned up my mess, I thought about William's point. "You might actually be right, much as I hate to admit it. For all her faults, she *is* an extremely capable investigator—and never afraid of facing a mistake. But I suppose, for the officers here, we can at least say that if Bricky *did* have a valuable cache, they've kept it safe!"

"Even from his heirs, probably," William huffed. He was now sniffing the doorways and along the floor.

"Though if Bricky used this traditional gnome marker, they probably know how to find it when the time comes," I said. Though it seemed a reasonable assumption, I realized as I crawled around the living room that it was actually much harder to visually locate a red thread than I'd thought. The 'marker' could be a tiny little knot on the underside of something, even. After all, Bricky had had a much different perspective than mine! But I tried to focus on practical matters, like wills and motives. "I guess that's assuming Mix and Shades are his heirs."

"They are. Whatever we find is theirs, don't forget," William reminded me.

I snorted. "You know better than to think I'd pocket it!"

"More like run tests on it and end up melting it or something," he muttered.

"No, I don't much care what the cache actually *is*—just what everyone else thought it was. And if they found it or not." I stood, blowing stray strands of hair out of my face. "The only test I had in mind was how to *find* it, actually."

William sniffed at the bedroom, and plopped down with a sigh. "Looking is going to take ages, I admit. But you can't test something you don't have. And I can't find something just going off of vague ideas of 'special cinnabar thread.' In order to do a searching spell, I'd have to actually have experience with what I'm looking for."

"Right. But you can amplify things, right?" I asked, crossing over to him.

He looked up at me suspiciously. "What do you have in mind?"

"Exactly what Dusty intended." I held up a vial from my belt and a lightstick in each hand. "How about we mix up a little science with your magic?"

* * *

William took some convincing—and he insisted on sniffing around the rest of the apartment, just in case the marker was staring us in the face. But soon enough, we were huddled on the floor in the dining room, just outside the kitchen, like two kids up to no good at a slumber party.

"Okay, so this" I held up my vial "will react with cinnabar.

Since Dusty was so confident that the marker thread would have cinnabar pigment, and there's really no reason anything else in the apartment would, I think we can rely on this to show us a cache. But I don't have enough to coat every room with it, and anyway, that'd create a terrible mess. However, if you could somehow use your magic to spread around just the *essence* of the potion . . ."

"We should get the same effect, without the physical mess," William concluded. "You know, Red, that idea's not half bad."

"Thanks, I—"

"Especially for someone who's terrified of magic."

"I am not!" I paused, abashed. I couldn't help but think of the Lost Rabbit diners, sharing stories about "evil" magic encounters. "Look, I know my reaction to the sorcerer—Orlix—last night was extreme. But what Luca and then Dusty said was exactly it. We were worried about you. If anything had happened—"

"Well, it didn't," William sniffed. "So let's get on with your experiment."

I sighed. I wasn't sure why he was still avoiding this subject with me—he'd seemed okay talking to Dusty about it, albeit vaguely. *But experiments require focus,* I reminded myself. And William wasn't wrong to be so single-minded. After all, who knew when we'd have uninterrupted access to Bricky's apartment again?

I pulled a palm-sized ceramic dish from its holder on my belt. That would serve as the surface for my "experiment," since I didn't want to risk messing up any of Bricky's furniture—or floor. I pulled my goggles down over my face, set aside my cloak and outer layers, and activated my gloves so that they were no longer fingerless but instead coated the end of each finger in a thin but sturdy protective layer. My gloves are the kind often called "griffon talon tips," specifically because of that capability; messing with them made me think of something—just briefly—something I'd seen the day before, but I soon forgot it entirely.

The potion I'd decided to use had originally been devised to test materials for toxicity by creating a flameless heat reaction. Some substances, cinnabar included, are most toxic when heated up, or ground and inhaled. So the potion would encounter a substance, create heat, and then flare yellow if toxicity was detected.

That was the theory, anyway. I was actually excited to see how well it would respond to William's amplification. If the magic worked, then it was a good way to make the potion even safer to use, since we could be on the other side of the room while it did its thing.

At my request, William covered the windows and turned off any lights. This made the apartment dark enough that we'd see even a small flare of light. Of course, it also made it a little tough to see my hands, but fortunately my goggles could adjust for low light! We had the lightsticks too, for backup, but I wanted to delay using them as long as possible. I didn't want anything to interfere with the experiment.

I uncorked the first vial and poured it on to the dish, to give William a little more to work with. He settled next to me and leaned in. For a moment he glowed blue, the brightest light in the apartment. In the next, all his light poured in a steady stream down into the golden puddle of potion on the dish. When the two mixed, a wave of sparkly yellow mist rolled out over the floor around us.

"I didn't think how dense it might be," I murmured, dismayed that our little cloud of magic-potion only seemed to reach about one foot high.

"Probably for the best," William said. "You don't want to be inhaling all that, do you?"

"The potion itself isn't poisonous," I protested, although he *did* have a point. If I had done something like this at the institute, Paracelsus would have reprimanded me for not wearing a mask.

"Less talking, more looking," William decided. "I'm not sure how long the spell will last."

The yellow mist had covered the dining room floor and was spreading into the kitchen and living room. I weighed our options. "Might be best to split up and cover more ground, just in case."

"I call the kitchen and dining room." William stood and began walking through the mist, scanning the corners and furniture where it clung and swirled.

"I guess that's fair, since it was my idea," I sighed to myself. The living room and bedroom would be harder to search—there were so many things to keep an eye on. But, there was no use delaying now. I got up carefully, trying not to disturb anything too much, and headed out into the living room first.

Sparkly yellow fog had coated the carpet and rolled right through the doorway into the bedroom beyond. I sank down lower, trying to look everywhere at once. There *were* little flares, here or there, but nothing like the candle's-flame-light I'd expect from a reaction with cinnabar. *Did we use enough? Or did the magic thin the potion out?* I worried as I moved carefully through the room. *Or is the string and the cache behind it just so well hidden that we'd have to coat the apartment to find it?*

I moved into the bedroom, mindful of our limited time. This

was the darkest room by far; I could only make out shadowy shapes of a small bed and dressers lining the room. Another doorway led to the bathroom, squished between the bedroom and kitchen walls. I paused in the bedroom, though. *This does seem like a likely place to hide something valuable; you'd want to keep it close, wouldn't you?*

As I tried to look over every dark surface, Dusty's comment came back to me. *If you bought the house, you'd have time to search it.*

The thought made me grin wryly to myself. If that was what our mystery buyers were after, I couldn't blame them for wanting to take their time.

There was a flicker by the bedstand—a false alarm. I'd just finished inspecting it when a light bloomed behind me. I'd expected a candle's worth of light, but this was a veritable bonfire.

# 19

# Treasures and Troves

"What's it now?" Officer Thorn called cheerfully. "Looking for a clue in a smokestack?"

The bright light I'd been so worried about—of course—was the officer opening the front door. As I ran out to face her, so did the results of our experiment, spilling into the hallway and dissipating.

"Trying to follow up a lead," I said, trying not to sound *too* exasperated. *So much for guards at the door* . . . "Looking for a bit of string tinted with cinnabar."

"They found it already," Officer Thorn said, as though *I* was the strange one.

I gaped. "What? Red string, in the apartment?"

"Not red. It was pretty well blackened," she answered, more thoughtfully. "On his wrist, like a bracelet. They think it got snapped in the attack."

"Oh. Well, that's probably not what we were looking for, anyway," I said, tugging my hand through my ponytail as I processed the turn of events.

Officer Thorn glanced around the apartment, which was

dim but otherwise untouched. "Doesn't look like the search came to much. Ah, well, don't worry. You can explain it all to me on the way."

"On the way to what?" William asked as he skidded around the corner from the kitchen.

"Lunch," the officer declared, "and a council of war."

I sighed. *I can't believe we did all that, and it came to nothing.* But Officer Thorn was already on her way out, with William hot on her heels. I let him take over explaining the experiment while also somehow keeping Dusty's secret. In the meantime, I gathered up my vial and dish and prepared for another phase of the investigation.

* * *

The sun peered at us through heavy clouds as we may our way down the street. For a brief moment, the world was bright— though it was still cold. I caught myself looking wistfully into the window display of a hat shop as we passed, my brain lingering on thoughts of knitted caps and felted berets instead of Officer Thorn's latest findings.

This changed abruptly when she reached out and poked my arm.

"Hey," I protested. "You're lucky the streets aren't icy. I could have fallen over, you know."

"*You're* lucky your feet are still on the ground at all, with your head in the clouds like that," she replied briskly.

"I'd rather my head was wrapped in something warm," I muttered, but I made a greater effort to pay attention. "What'd I miss?"

"Nothing," Officer Thorn replied, more cheerful by the

minute. "What, did you think we were discussing details of an open case out here on the open road? By all that's just, Red. We might as well have just left you at the conference."

"I helped you with a lead once already today, and it isn't *my* conference," I retorted. "What about you? Weren't you supposed to be presenting to the scholars?"

"Tomorrow," she informed me. "So don't get too excited. Today, we work. I want to wrap this up as soon as possible. Wouldn't that be a nice holiday present for Meteor?"

The rebellious streak in me wanted to point out that *not being involved in a murder case* would be a better present for the kid—but I had to admit, Thorn did have a point. In all my musings on magic and alchemy, I'd lost sight of the human element in the case.

Well, human and magic-human, too.

By this point we'd reached the station, and Officer Thorn was bounding in, practically licking her lips. The scent of lunch—cheesy marinara subs, from the smell of it—drifted through the open door. But William had been suspiciously quiet, so I paused and looked down at him.

"Been keeping an eye out?" I guessed.

William shook himself, tiny blue sparks flying from his black fur. "Nothing. He's given up—for now."

"For now," I agreed, because I had an uneasy feeling that there were too many unanswered questions left regarding Orlix. "But either way we'll be alright, William. We're staying safe, and staying together."

"You say that without having heard Thorn's plans," he reminded me ominously as he passed me on the way into the station. But his voice was a little less tense than it had been; he appreciated my point—at least a little.

I followed my friends into the old building, and then followed my nose down the hall to the lunch room. There, I found Thorn already sitting with the Chief at a round table in the back corner. A holly-festooned window framed their heads, making them look like a holiday tableau for just a moment. Smiling to myself, I shook my head, grabbed a plate and half a sandwich, and then crossed between other tables and diners to join them.

"See, now, Red," said Officer Thorn as I sat, "*here* we can have a safe discussion."

Next to me, William glowed blue, then fell silent. It seemed he agreed.

"I was just about to invite Officer Thorn to compare notes with me," Chief Bakis added more politely.

"We have a few things to chip in too," I said. The Chief's mild attitude was welcome, and I warmed from the inside out as I shed my coat. "There's a lot going on here, for sure, but we *are* making progress. I think."

"No chips, just sandwiches," Officer Thorn said, over her foot-long sub. It was already halfway gone. "And more confidence, Red. It always gets messier before it gets cleaner."

"Country wisdom?" Chief Bakis lifted an eyebrow as they addressed Thorn, and it took me a moment to recognize a tease.

I chuckled, while Officer Thorn just tossed her hair back and launched right into her report. "All the backstories from the club members check out, with the exception of the vice president—one Katerina. I checked with the city register, too, and all the paperwork for the club itself is above board— as far as we can tell. However, some of the things in their announcements last night were *not* true."

"Announcements?" I repeated, trying to remember what had been said before William had run off into the kitchen and I had followed.

"Welcoming newcomers and holiday gift exchanges," William rumbled, reminding me.

"Those parts were fine," Officer Thorn said, swallowing another bite of sandwich. "It was the bit in the middle, the warnings about a 'familiars' movement.' I wasn't able to verify that there *is* any such thing. Strictly speaking, no 'pro magical near-life forms' clubs are registered with the city, and no one's proposed legislation to oppose the new law codifying who's a 'near-life form' and who's not. There have been a few neighborhood protests here and there just saying to vote 'no' on the new definition system, but that's it so far."

"At the Blue Fairy School?" I guessed, musing.

"Yes, but organized by the parents, not Adam," Thorn replied. "Carla told me about it yesterday, though I didn't think much of it at the time—she said Bricky wasn't there. And yes, I know," she said, interrupting herself to talk over Chief Bakis, who had raised a hand. "You could have had your officers do all that legwork. But I didn't want to tip them off. I still have a feeling there's something funny going on with the Lost Rabbits."

"It's a political club. Of course there's petty things going on," William said, bristling.

"Be that as it may," Bakis put in, "we have also completed our checks into the school and the parents. We have not found any connections or discrepancies so far, although it remains true that Bricky was involved in some school activities."

"Nothing about Sweep, though?" I asked.

Chief Bakis shook their head. "Nothing as of yet. Familiars

are incredibly difficult to trace, even for our officers who do use magic. It's part of why they've become a . . . *touchy* subject, not only in the political sphere, but in law enforcement. Unless—?"

We all followed the chief's glance at William.

"Sure," he said calmly, as though the unspoken question in the air was *would you like another sandwich?* "If I had seen Sweep myself, I could have picked up a signature. A scent, even," he added, with a look at Thorn. "And if I knew the sorcerer who'd made Sweep, or came across them later, I could recognize the trace of their magic. It's basic. I expected you to ask me as soon as we landed."

*You can* what? I kept my mouth shut, but my thoughts reeled. Of course, I *had* seen William do similar things in the past—*I should have put it together,* I thought. *I wonder if that's why he decided to come along? He thought he could be especially useful?*

"But nothing remains of Sweep," Chief Bakis said, doubtfully.

"Familiars disappear when attacked like that," Officer Thorn added, making me wince.

"After a moment or two for the spell to dissipate," William agreed.

I could tell he was holding something back, and it was killing me. I nudged him. "But?"

"Most sorcerers make animal familiars," William said. "Animals are more useful. Brooms don't even have *hands.* Besides, a broom familiar could easily be confused with a plain old *animated broom.* And that's Witch stuff."

This was not the answer I had expected, but I had a feeling he would come around to a point. And I could recognize that sorcerer-vs-witch animosity: I'd seen it play out between William and Trent, the local Witch back in Belville. In fact,

I'd also seen Trent animate a series of brooms over the years, with varying results . . . *William does have a point about the limited usefulness of a magic broom,* I realized.

"Any sorcerer who'd make a *broom* familiar either doesn't care about being confused with a witch, or actually *wants* their activity to pass for witchcraft. And Brass is where all the *serious* sorcerers come to show off. There's only one here who would fall into either of those categories," William concluded.

My stomach plummeted. "Are you saying it was Orlix?"

# 20

# Perils of Mentorship

Officer Thorn glanced at me sharply. "It was Orlix who what? How do *you* know about this?"

"We met him last night. He's been following us. He's the one who made that commotion at the club," I said, my gaze straying to the top of William's head. "We, um, we didn't tell you his name at the time because . . . well . . . it was pretty emotional."

"Explain," she demanded.

William cleared his throat. "Orlix is the sorcerer who made *me*."

This was met by momentary silence—confused and torn on my part, surprised and speculative on the part of the police officers.

"And yes, Red," William added quietly. "I do think he's the one who made Sweep, too."

"You've thought so from the beginning," I realized.

"*This* is why you were so fired up to come along?" Officer Thorn guessed.

Chief Bakis shifted, leaning forward. "Just to make sure I'm following this. You've recognized a sorcerer here in Brass, hanging around the scene of the crime, who has connections with your past. And you think this Orlix made Sweep because—?"

"Because he's disgraced," William said. Some of the residual stress in his voice finally dropped away as he explained, "Orlix got in trouble years ago. I was still a familiar, here, in the city. I was there when it all happened. He got in trouble with the other sorcerers for going too far. Sorcerers act like they have no rules, but they actually do. There's a whole system of rules, almost like scholars have. And when one of them breaks the rules, they get cast out. They're not supposed to do magic any more in certain circumstances, or at all. It all depends. But it's a *really* big deal in the sorcerer world."

This was a heaping helping of news to me. William had always insinuated that he left his sorcerer because he got *bored*. This sounded like the opposite. But given what William had yelled last night, and if Orlix was breaking rules—*maybe he didn't want to talk about it all, and relive it*, I thought. *Maybe it was easier to let me assume he set out on his own.* My heart broke for William; even gruff and self-sufficient as he seemed to be, he was still my little buddy, too. I wrapped an arm around him, burying my fingers in his fur.

Meanwhile, of course, Chief Bakis kept us on point. "And the rule Orlix broke?"

William hesitated. For just a split second, he leaned into me. Then he leaned away, lifting his head up. "Sorcerers have three rules: don't mess with love, don't mess with riches, and don't mess with life. Orlix was reported for the third one. He was . . . getting *too greedy*. That's what they called it."

My heart twisted as I thought of Adam, and then squeezed

into a teeny, tight ball as I thought of the children at Meteor's school.

Officer Thorn let out a low whistle. "And this is the person who's been following us?"

William was silent, so I nodded and said, "Luca and I saw him last night. But not up close. Still, William said it was him, and I know he's right."

Chief Bakis glanced around the table gravely. "I think it is time to move this conversation into my office. This lead merits some very thorough and *careful* investigation."

* * *

"Now," said Chief Bakis, as we settled into a sparse office, the main accent color—a deep maroon—vaguely reminiscent of coffins out of ancient vampire myth. "I'm sure it will come as no surprise that a sorcerer, even a potentially disgraced one, is still a citizen of some repute in Brass. Before we proceed, I must ask: have anyone else's investigations led them to such illustrious names?"

William and I were seated on a bench along the wall, while Officer Thorn paced the velvety rug in front of the chief's desk. Both of them turned to look at me.

"Um," I said. "I apprenticed with the alchemists' institute here, on the other side of the city. With Paracelsus. He's a big name in alchemy, but—"

Chief Bakis's face said plainly that he was a big name elsewhere, too. Eyebrows delicately arched, they asked, "You think alchemists are involved as well?"

"Not exactly. It was more like a lead I had to cross off the list," I said. "I went and visited the institute yesterday, and they didn't know much about it—aside from the fact that your officers had checked up on my background, apparently."

"Ah. Yes. Our aim in this case is to cover all angles," Chief Bakis said. It wasn't an apology, just a statement of fact.

"So careful you're forgetting connections because you've found too many," Officer Thorn ribbed her old friend good-naturedly.

"That's why I have you here," they replied, unruffled. "And at the moment, these sorcery connections are most promising."

"But you can't just go confront him," William put in. "That's what you're about to say, isn't it? This is why I didn't say anything at the beginning."

"Admittedly, true. Though I would have preferred to know your suspicions earlier," the chief said.

"Same here," Thorn said, focusing on William. For a moment, she looked almost hurt.

But even so, I didn't like how they were ganging up on him. "What's done is done, and we know what we need to now," I interrupted. "The real question is, what are we going to do about it? Chief Bakis, it seems like you have some plan?"

The chief considered me, steepling their hands, resting their elbows on the dark desk. "My plan is to have the three of you devise a plan."

*Uh oh.* I glanced at Thorn. I had a feeling I knew where this was headed.

"This is why we're here, Red," she confirmed.

"But Orlix knows us," I protested. "We can't pull some kind of covert operation when he clearly knows William, and . . ."

"And," Officer Thorn took over, "he's only seen the rest of us from a distance. Me, of course, I'm recognizable. But you go everywhere covered in five hats and a pile of cloaks, Red."

"It's cold in Brass this time of year!" I reminded the room in general.

But the officer persisted. "What I'm saying is, he might not recognize *you*. Especially if you turn up in full alchemist getup."

"Saying that you're an emissary of Paracelsus, which you very well could be," Chief Bakis added. Apparently, they were entirely on board with this nonsense.

"What exactly do you people think 'full alchemist getup' is?" I asked, querulous. "Long robes and a beaked mask? It's not going to be enough to change what I look like."

My comment was meant as facetious, but Officer Thorn was giving me a very serious look. "Come on, Red. If you lose the cloak, display your belt of doodads—"

"Pull your goggles down over your face," the chief suggested.

"—and wear your lab gloves, not mittens—I know you brought both. I bet you even brought a lab coat along, just in case," Thorn continued.

I turned to William, expecting him to pipe up and say that this was all silly. But he, too, looked solemn. "He probably never gave you a second glance," he said. "You don't have any magic, so he wouldn't have been interested. My guess is he showed up because he sensed something happen to Sweep, and then afterward he was following *me*. He hasn't been around since last night."

"Great. So I go in alone, and then what?" I asked, despairing.

"You won't be alone. William and I'll be right nearby," Thorn said, like this was reassuring.

*Now* William injected some sense into the conversation. "We won't be able to get too close, because there'll definitely be wards up around his property. Magical sensors, at the very least."

"So I go in *alone*," I repeated for emphasis, "and then what? What will that get us?"

"Say that the alchemists are concerned with the murder. Because of the school," Chief Bakis suggested. As my eyes met theirs, I realized that the Maplehouse police had definitely uncovered Adam's past during their investigations.

"Say that you believe Sweep was the real target, not Bricky," William added slowly.

I turned back to him, my voice coming out in a squeak. "Go in alone and accuse a powerful sorcerer of *murder?*"

"No," William replied, forcefully. "Tell him you're worried about him. The other sorcerers won't care if he's in trouble . . ."

"But another powerful group could offer protection," Officer Thorn said, pouncing on the idea. "On the condition he tells you everything he knows."

"And then what?" I frowned at her. "What if Orlix actually *does* need protection?"

"He doesn't," William muttered. I was inclined to agree, but I hated the thought of making false promises.

But Officer Thorn ignored this. "If he does, we can set something up. Tell him arrangements are still being made and that you'll come back tomorrow."

"Be sure to make it clear that your entire guild—Paracelsus included—knows what's going on and where you are," Chief Bakis added, in a belated show of concern.

I sighed. It was clear that this train was already on its track: there would be no rerouting now. "I'll do it, but I'm going to need you both to watch the house like it's your firstborn child while I'm in there. And I want a handheld radio. That's something police guilds have, right?"

Chief Bakis and Officer Thorn looked surprised, like somehow I'd caught them out in a secret. But William seemed to get it. He stirred. "Not a bad idea, Red," he said, grudgingly. "He'll have wards to sense any magic, but he'd probably never think of needing to protect himself against magitech."

"I suppose you could pass it off as a new tool the alchemists are using," Officer Thorn said thoughtfully, stroking her chin.

"And I suppose you'd rather I'd say I was a lion tamer and show up with a real live lion, since the show is so much more important than safety," I muttered, rolling my eyes. I loved Thorn dearly, but sometimes she forgot that everyone else was *not* an over-six-feet-tall, excessively-muscled half-orc.

"What was that?" she asked.

"Oh, nothing. I also want to stop by the university to pick up the elements of my 'disguise,'" I told her.

"You mean 'pick up your nerd gear,'" she corrected, flipping her hair back with a grin. "That's the best part of this, Red. You don't have to pretend to be a lion tamer in order to pull it off."

## 21

# The Rule of Three

It was only just after lunch when we left the Maplehouse police station, but the clouds had won back the sky: shadow and a brisk, mischievous breeze ruled. Officer Thorn, who never seemed to mind the weather no matter *what* it was, opted to stay outside the dormitory while William and I ran in to grab my things. If she was hoping to guilt us into moving more quickly, her hopes were misplaced. The moment we were back in our shared room, I sat on the bed and stared at William.

"Hey. Are you really okay with all this?"

He huffed, long and hard, like the Big Bad Wolf trying to blow down the university from the inside. "Of *course* not, Red."

After all his avoidance, I was honestly a little surprised by his—well, honesty. I kept staring, waiting.

Eventually he flopped onto the floor. "This is exactly why I didn't say anything at the beginning. Because I *knew* this would happen."

"'This' being . . ." I hesitated.

"They couldn't send *me* to see him," William growled. "And

they can't send Thorn. She's so obviously a police officer, and no sorcerer's going to talk to the police—unless they think they've been wronged."

"So," I said, putting the pieces together, "you've been worried all along that *I* would be the one to face him?"

William actually covered his snout with his paws, something I had only ever seen him do in jest. Little blue shivers of magic skated over his fur. It took me a moment, but then I realized—*I think this is him crying.*

Instantly I was on the floor, half laying across him, half hugging him as best as I could.

"It's *not fair*," he said. His voice was harsh and muffled. "You're just a stranger who met me on the side of the road. You shouldn't have anything to do with him. You shouldn't have to be the one to make this stand."

"Hey, I may have been a stranger years ago, but I'm not any more," I protested, smiling into William's fluffy shoulder. "I get your point, but still. You have to know I'd do anything for you."

"But why do you have to be the one to do *this*? All the time!"

I'd been about to answer, but *all the time* stopped me in my tracks. I could understand what he meant. "I don't think it's a bad thing. I mean, so maybe I stood up for Gloria—"

"And me," a dark spot near the door interrupted. The shadow shimmered, and Luca came into focus. "I'm sorry, I didn't mean to sneak up on you both. I just heard voices as I came up the hall, and I got spooked, and—anyway, William's right. You did the same for me, Red. And Gloria, yes, and Saki, and Taiwo, and—"

"This isn't about me," I protested. "It's about William."

"It's about *you*," William growled, still prone in the middle of the room. "Why do you keep attracting these kinds of situations?"

I shifted; my leg was falling asleep on the hardwood floor. "It's not like I volunteered to go face down Orlix. And for all we know, he could be perfectly reasonable. To me, I mean, in this particular circumstance."

"You're going to see Orlix?" Luca walked over to us, a little hesitantly, and dropped into a cross-legged position by William's head. "I do think there's a reason it's you, Red. William's right. You do attract these things. I think it has to do with your guardian," he added softly.

My head jerked up of its own accord. I hadn't heard anyone use that word, in that context, since I left my remote family of Seers behind. *But of course Luca would know it. He always knew . . .* I bit my lip, thinking of a conversation I'd once had with Jade. Little more than a spirit at that time, he'd haunted a library with tomes on Seers and their customs.

It was a tradition—something I respected, but had never been on easy terms with. I'd never had a gift for Seeing the future. Everyone else in my extended family, everyone I grew up with, had an ability for divination; they were renowned for it. My own inability had been part of the reason I left to study alchemy. Every person in my clan, in addition to having magical Sight, also had a guardian spirit . . . something I knew I did have, though I'd never given it much thought. I'd seen it, just once, when poison gas nearly killed me and my friends in Seaside; but then I'd confused it with Luca, because he also had a horn. But usually, that was hidden. The same way I hid traces of my heritage.

I'd never really let myself think about the fact that Luca was afflicted with a dark unicorn curse, while I supposedly had a light unicorn looking after me. It was all a bit *magical* for my taste. But apparently, Luca had not had similar reservations.

"And your nickname," he added.

I scoffed. "There's nothing about 'Red' that says—"

"Little Red Riding Hood," said William, lifting his head, "is the archetypal victim. Your mothers wanted you to remember."

"Because they could See your strengths," Luca agreed. Then he broke the meditative, revelatory atmosphere by adding, "I mean, that's what I can only assume. Since you haven't invited us to *meet* your family . . ."

I recognized that he was teasing me and I smiled, though all this was way beyond me. Shaking my head, I said, "Well, there's no remembering necessary here. William, you're my best friend. That's all that really matters to me, and it counts just as much when you're in trouble as when we're safe at home in Belville."

"'Trouble' is one way to put it," he snorted. But his words were lighter, and I knew—as I always did—that we'd turned a corner for now.

"Trouble is exactly why I'm coming along," Luca added, his voice unusually firm. I looked up at him but he was ready for my protest. "Don't bother arguing. I was already planning on taking the afternoon session off, anyway. He doesn't even have to know I'm there. But I will be."

*Of course.* Luca, when he tapped into the residual curse left behind—the aspect of him that was "Jade"—could fade into shadow like the spookiest of ghosts. In all my worries about precautions going into Orlix's home, I'd entirely forgotten this. The look on Luca's face told me I'd be hearing about that later.

William perked up a little at this. "You're not technically cursed any more, and you weren't magic to begin with. You're just an echo of what happened," he said, tilting his head as he looked at Luca. Though I half-gasped, half-laughed at this harsh appraisal, he added pointedly, "That means Orlix may not sense you at all."

"I'll get in through a loophole," Luca summarized. I had a feeling that, loophole or not, he'd get in one way or another. "Good. The three of us can handle this, no problem. When are we leaving?"

* * *

Of course, it was actually *four* of us—although Officer Thorn informed me that she nearly abandoned us and went to see Orlix herself, since we took so long. But I just smiled at her, and I never bothered correcting Luca. It had been so sweet to see him and William in perfect accord.

Even if we *were* about to confront some kind of evil sorcerer.

It was well into the afternoon by the time we got to the right neighborhood, a fancy area north of downtown that the locals called "Aspens." Apparently, sorcerers had no need of accessible trolley lines—and they certainly didn't believe in sharing space. William led our little group down a street lined with mansions, each more palatial than the next. Sorcerers might not have been allowed to directly manipulate gold with their magic, but they'd certainly learned how to accrue it as a result of their spells.

*That, or they're very good at illusions,* I thought. I could practically hear my mother's voice in my head: *there are always more sides to the story, Cinnabar.*

*And did you tell me that because you knew I'd end up here?* I wondered.

But wondering about destiny gave me the willies. As an alchemist, I'd learned to focus on the task at hand, never to leap to the end of an experiment. I glanced around with renewed vigor, shivering in only my woolen coat and lab outfit. To our left was a house at least four stories high, seemingly carved out of living marble; to our right, a stately roof peeked out over a veritable maze of topiary. But what really caught my eye was a house farther down the block. While all its neighbors went for limited color schemes or tasteful building materials, this one screamed for attention. In fact, it screamed *holiday*: the yard was full to the brim with larger-than-life Yuletide characters, magical icicles dripping from eaves, and even a theme song playing along to flashing lights.

"Well, I guess we know which house the angry old sorcerer *doesn't* live in," I quipped.

William turned on the sidewalk to give me a look. "Actually . . ."

As one, the four of us stopped and considered the holiday display. It was such a confusion of sound, light, and color that I could barely make sense of the house behind it.

Officer Thorn tugged at her ear. "You're serious?"

"Deadly serious. In fact, I think we shouldn't get any closer. Sorcerer etiquette says that you only put up wards as far as your own yard, but every sorcerer breaks the rule," William said.

"If you say so," Thorn shrugged. "We'll cross the street and find a nice bench, then. I've got my radio. Anywhere on this block should be within range. Red and Mister Shadow, looks like you're in the spotlight."

"Har har," I said dryly. I hated it when she called Luca silly names like that—although, to be fair, it didn't happen very often. *Because we don't rely on him as often as maybe we could.* Normally I would have thought of that as a *good* thing. But from the determination in Luca's eyes now, I could see how much it meant to him to be able to help.

"Don't worry," Luca said—whether to Thorn or to me, or perhaps to William, I wasn't sure. "We'll figure this out."

William whined. "That's what I'm afraid of."

"It'll be okay," I promised him, squaring my shoulders. "He had the jump on us when we first got here, and yesterday at the meeting. But the tables have turned."

As our two groups parted ways, I looked up at Orlix's mansion and thought to myself, *third time's the charm.*

# 22

# A Wintry Caller

As I passed the neighboring house, Luca disappeared beside me. I'd never seen him do this in daylight; one moment he was beside me, and the next, his robes seemed to crumple into themselves, as if he was falling into his own shadow. Then there was nothing, except a sort of wispiness in every dark patch of space, just at the corner of my eye.

*"I'm still here,"* he whispered over my shoulder, as though he could tell what I was thinking. *"I'm not leaving your side."*

Luca at my shoulder, then, and Officer Thorn on the little magitech radio buried in my pocket, and William in danger of barging the doors down at any moment. No matter what he said about wards and precautions, I *knew* he was still using a tiny piece of his magic to monitor me. He always had, almost since the day we met. After all, protection was William's strength.

*I guess I really am not going in alone after all,* I thought to myself wryly. With that, there was nothing left to do but pick my way between Orlix's holiday decorations as normally as possible.

Behind all the glitz and Yuletide cheer, the front door was a little disconcerting. It was just a *door.* The wreath above the doorbell seemed entirely average, and there were no fireworks or alarms when I stood on the welcome mat and announced my presence with a rapid knock.

And there was no magic housekeeper or familiar, either. The door opened to reveal Orlix himself. I recognized him at once: he wore the same long robes, though up close—and relaxed— his face appeared much less mysterious. Light silver eyes regarded me with suspicion, while the wrinkles and gray hair pulled back into a low ponytail bespoke relatable weariness. He was taller than me, but he was also rail-thin: all magitech and shadows and alchemical vials of goo aside, I still would have put money on myself over him in a fight.

Except, of course, for the magic. It sparkled in his eyes and down his sleeves as he looked at me. I knew from my witchy friend Sakura that this was purely a magic-user's intimidation tactic, the sorcerer's equivalent of a dog baring its teeth. No doubt if Saki'd been there, she would have been rolling her eyes. But I was a *little* intimidated, nonetheless. After all, I'd seen what his magic could do.

"Who are you, and why have you come?" Orlix asked. He might have been going for ominous, but he mostly sounded kind of . . . sad.

"I'm a representative of the alchemists' institute," I said, being careful not to lie outright. With a silent apology to my newest friend, I went on, "You can call me Nessalee. I run errands and the like for Paracelsus. We're concerned about a recent crime in Maplehouse."

Though I'd been intentionally vague, the way I figured

any diplomatic professional might be, I saw Orlix's interest immediately. He gave up on the magic tricks and leaned forward, lowering his voice. "Paracelsus is . . . concerned?"

"He prefers to remain discreet, of course," I said, thinking on my feet. None of my preparation on the journey here had been of any use; it fell away the instant I'd knocked on the door. But in its wake, I found new inspiration. "But we believe there is reason to suspect danger from . . . uncontrollable elements. In light of that fact, we have a proposition you might find helpful."

"You certainly talk like an alchemist. And smell like one," Orlix said, leaning back with a sniff. I tried not to cringe, wondering if somehow his sense of scent was magically enhanced—like William's—or if he was just strange. Or trying to unnerve me. *Or do I actually smell? That potion earlier shouldn't have left any residue!*

"Of course, my message is supposed to be delivered in private," I added, a little desperately.

Around me, a sudden winter wind picked up. Orlix pulled back from the swirling leaves and chill; in that moment he seemed to make his decision. "I'll hear what you have to say. I'm not saying I'll agree, mind you. But you might as well come in."

As I followed Orlix into the house, a bit of shadow slipped ahead of the closing door. I wondered if it was Luca who had made that breeze—in fact, I had to stop myself mouthing *thank you.* But it might not have mattered if I had, because Orlix wasn't paying attention. He led the way down a dim hall without once glancing back.

Inside, the house was the absolute opposite of its glaringly cheerful yard. The hallway stretched on and on, into the bowels of the house, and the rooms we passed on either side were dark, the furniture shrouded. That's when the doors were open for me to peer in, which more often than not, they weren't. Only the warmth and a vague smell of garlic convinced me that Orlix actually *lived* here.

He went on until we reached the back of the house—the kitchen. This was the only room lit. A stone hearth at one end crackled with a normal, non-magical fire, its flames so large they coated the flagstone floor with ash. A wooden table, the kind which might once have been in a fancy dining room, clearly served as counter space and dining space. The counters themselves were covered in an assortment of books, tea mugs, mixing bowls, half-empty ingredient bottles, and even a crumpled robe or two. The cabinets above them looked like they might not be much better, their doors hanging at angles or uncomfortably propped open, like something slightly too large had been stuffed inside. The sink was dripping, and above it, the room's one window was dusty with soot.

*The one good thing about being here,* I thought, looking at the flickering magical lights in their sconces on the wall, *is that there's plenty of shadow for Luca to hide in.*

And then, *William would never, ever put up with living like this now.*

"Go on, then," said Orlix, gesturing carelessly at the table. "Deliver your message."

I stepped gingerly forward, and found that there was a mismatched bench tucked beneath the table. I chose to remain standing. *It's probably more fitting for an apprentice-messenger, anyway,* I decided. Aloud, I said, "We've been investigating the murder of Sweep—"

"Gnome," Orlix interrupted. As I gave him a bewildered

look, he waved one hand in the air. "The murder victim. A gnome. It was the gnome's fault."

"But can you be sure of that?" I asked.

By now, the sorcerer had dropped onto a stool at his one-size-fits-all-activity table, and he leaned over it, his arms flat amid the various stains and burns. He seemed to be focused on a nearby forgotten wine glass, not on my words. But my gut feeling was telling me that he was thinking this over very quickly.

When he didn't respond, I took a chance. "We believe it may have had more to do with Sweep."

Orlix's frail shoulders twitched. He didn't look up. "That's why you've tracked me down."

"We think you might be in danger," I said, gaining confidence now. "If you're willing to share what you know, we may be able to offer you protection."

"And why should you care?" His eyes, when they snapped up to meet mine, seemed to have been drained of what little color they'd had.

"We have a . . ." I hesitated. "Local interest."

"The school." Orlix nodded. He was looking at the table again. I risked a glance around the room, searching for comforting shadows. So far, he seemed to be buying my story . . . and a soft, tiny breeze at my back seemed to agree.

At the last moment, I just hadn't been able to mention Adam or the kids in this sorry excuse for a kitchen. But Orlix must have pieced things together on his own, maybe when he'd followed William there yesterday. I wasn't too surprised he would have figured it out—not when he was such a powerful magic user.

*Not that he's using his magic to clean . . .*

173

A muffled burst of static from my radio interrupted my musing, sending a trill of panic down my spine. I shuffled to cover the noise. Fortunately, Orlix seemed lost in his own world. Clearing my throat, I asked, "What can you share about Sweep?"

This got his attention again. "I made it, of course. It was mine." His voice held absolutely no trace of irony or self-awareness. "I . . . sent it away . . . it, and its amulet, too . . . I can't do anything now. It's out of my hands."

"So you're saying you have nothing to do with this at all?" I asked. The shadows pressed at my back, and I added, "You don't believe you're in any danger?"

"I can take care of myself."

This wasn't an answer, and even *I* could tell that it was a lie. "When did you last see Sweep?"

Silence.

I took a risk. "Have there been any other attacks on your familiars?"

"Why?" Orlix looked up again, and I almost recoiled. His eyes truly were drained of color now, and hollow, almost hungry. "Why would anyone destroy Sweep?"

*"Destroy." Not "murder."* My stomach twisted. Without being able to voice exactly why, I *hated* this man. But that wasn't very diplomatic. Taking a very deep breath, I opened my mouth—

And realized that in all our planning, we hadn't considered *motive.* What popped out was pure, unadulterated improvisation. "You may be familiar with the Lost Rabbit Supper Club?"

Orlix jerked back, the biggest reaction he'd had yet. It was as if I'd shot him. *But why should he be so scared? I wondered. Unless—that's what he secretly suspects, too?*

"They're nothing," he whispered.

This only confirmed my suspicions. "My superiors disagree."

"A misguided cult," Orlix insisted.

*Cult?* That seemed like strong language, even from him. Just as I took a breath to ask about it, my radio buzzed again, and I froze. Orlix was looking right at me this time: he couldn't have missed it. My mind raced with possible explanations. Nothing fit. I was drawing a blank—

Until a log sizzled and broke on the fire. The sound was so reminiscent of the radio that both Orlix and I breathed covert sighs of relief.

"A dangerous one, though," I said, regaining my composure.

"No more dangerous than the sorcerer's rule," he seemed to say.

I hadn't heard of such an expression. I hesitated. "Excuse me?"

Orlix rose, very slowly, unsteadily. "There's nothing you or Paracelsus can do."

True fear flooded my veins. In my coat pocket, I clutched my radio so tightly it vibrated with static again. But Orlix wasn't listening.

"There's nothing anyone can do," he went on, looking straight through me. "I am condemned. This is what comes of ambition! This is how low greatness tumbles! Let them come and get me; let them finish their work; I have fallen but I will cower no longer. I will take what is mi—"

Just as Orlix was gaining steam, glowing black and red, the window over the sink flared so brightly blue I had to cover my eyes.

<h1 style="text-align:center">23</h1>

<h1 style="text-align:center">Broken Promises</h1>

The kitchen was full of glass.

Before I could make sense of it, I was falling. Instead of hitting the floor, though, I collided with something soft. Luca. His arms were wrapped around me, no longer shadowy. He'd pulled me to the floor to avoid the explosion.

But it wasn't an explosion, not exactly. It was William. *William.*

He crashed through the table in the middle of the room. Half of the tabletop fell backward, sheltering Luca and me. I could hear splinters and the tinkle of glass hitting the walls.

*Red.* I didn't hear the question, but I could feel it, almost as though William was reaching out with his magic, searching the room.

*We're okay,* I thought back, unable to make my voice heard amid the chaos.

Somehow, it must have got through. When William spoke, it wasn't to us. "You *coward.*"

"Why? Why do you do this to me?" Orlix's voice, laced with self-pity, came from the back wall. He must have been thrown

176

backward by William's dramatic entrance.

I shook my head, ready to rise, but Luca's arms tightened around me. *"Wait and see,"* he whispered. *"I don't think Orlix is as strong as we thought. Let William have his say."*

"You've been *waiting for this day,*" William barked. Even hiding on the floor behind half a table, I could hear how his voice was still crackling, still full of magic. It wasn't some empty intimidation show. *Maybe Luca has a point.*

"I—I don't know what you mean," Orlix whined.

"You *knew* one of them would be found," William said. "You were tried, sentenced, and outlawed, but you never stopped. I left thinking you would stop. But you never did. You've been making them for *years* when you knew it was *wrong* and you've just been *waiting* for someone to find them. And it isn't you who's paid the price!"

"But I don't *know* why Sweep was ended," Orlix said piteously. "That's why I went to see! But nobody knows!"

"YOU KNOW WHY," William roared. "You put Sweep in a dangerous position as an unsanctioned familiar. Something like this was always bound to happen because of *your* irresponsible actions!"

"But I *can't* make them sanctioned!" From the sound of it, Orlix wasn't trying any counterattacks. In fact, his voice was still coming from floor level, like he'd remained slumped against the wall.

"That's the *point,*" William retorted. "Do you remember what I told you when I left? Do you?"

"But I didn't know—I didn't know—"

"TELL ME WHAT I SAID."

"It was a good thing I was sentenced," Orlix muttered brokenly. "Because I was making beings for myself and never thinking of *them*. I was making things knowing there wasn't a place for them in the world. Lives without homes."

*William said that to him?* The words struck right through my heart, and I buried my head against Luca's neck. He shifted, his hand running through my hair, his cheek on mine.

"But they *did* have homes," Orlix added pathetically. "Most of them. These days."

"The magic children." I could hear the bristle in William's voice.

*The magic children. Meteor.*

"The families wanted them," Orlix insisted. "They paid for them."

"And this is how you make a living?" William demanded. "Doing the one thing you were forbidden ever from doing?"

"They came to *me!*"

"I don't want to hear about how you're the victim here!" William's voice rose, and he was glowing so fiercely that even Luca and I were cast in a bluish shadow. "You could have stopped at any time! *You were told to stop!*"

"Those children were nothing like you and Sweep!"

"Then you should thank your gods damned lucky stars," William growled. "Maybe they'll have a chance to do some good. They won't have to live their lives running from *you*."

The blue light crackled and exploded again, sailing over our heads, assailing the walls. Tea cups rattled and the fire winked out, but other than that, there was no harm done.

As the silence and the cold crept in, Orlix mumbled, "But why? Why did you run? Why did you leave me?"

It was a long moment before William spoke—so long that I almost lifted my head to see if he was okay. Finally, quietly, he said, "Because you never could see that it was agony for me to stay."

My gaze met Luca's, through unshed tears. As we struggled to sit up and look over the table, Luca wiped at his eyes with his sleeve.

"William," I said gently.

He turned his back on Orlix and bounded over to us, still glowing, clearly checking us over for injury. "You were scared," he said, an accusation—whether against me or Orlix, I wasn't sure. But I knew it was also an explanation. He had sensed my fear, and that was why he'd burst in.

"I was," I agreed. "But I don't think we have anything to fear right now."

One glance at Orlix was enough to confirm this. The man was broken—not so much by anything I or even William had said, but by his own shredded nerves, it seemed. He was still unmoving, slumped next to his empty hearth.

"Tie him up anyway," William growled. "He's not who we're looking for. But he still needs to answer for what he's done."

"Agreed," Luca said, with a tight fierceness in his voice that I'd never heard before. He was already picking up rope from a nearby shelf.

I moved over to the hearth with Luca, ready to help in tying up our host. Orlix offered no resistance—he didn't even ask where Luca had come from. I, however, noticed the displaced fire poker near the hearth, and nodded to myself. *Luca was the one who broke that log. Looks like I'm not the only one who can improvise.*

We had to help Orlix rise, and as we did, he met my eyes. My defiance flared. "I love William," I told him. "As far as I'm concerned, he's a person. And so was Sweep. Familiars aren't *ended.* They're *murdered.* They're human," I added, even though I knew it didn't make technical sense. "Somewhere underneath it all, maybe you are too."

Luca's green eyes were uncharacteristically hard.

We marched down the hallway to find Thorn and a gaggle of other officers waiting. As they took Orlix away, the three of us stood, a little forlorn, on that cold front step.

William sat heavily next to me and leaned into my leg. I buried my head in the fur atop his head. "I do owe him thanks for one thing," I said softly, watching Orlix being taken away. "For making William."

"We owe him nothing," Luca said flatly. "*William* has made the William we know and love."

Surprised, I glanced down at him—at my best friend. He was panting, a doggy smile.

"Of course I did," said William. "And don't you ever forget it."

## 24

# Behind the Scenes

Officer Thorn saw the officers and Orlix off at the end of the yard, and then turned back and gestured to us. As we caught up with her, she began explaining. Or at least, that's what I was expecting her to do. Instead, the first words out of her mouth were a reproach.

"Cinnabar Sunset, *why* did you not respond to your radio?" she chastised, her tone decimating the holiday cheer surrounding us.

My hand went to the radio in my pocket. Had I broken it? I pulled it out and looked it over. "It was making funny noises. Was that you trying to call? Why would you call me when Orlix wasn't supposed to know I had a radio at all?"

"The *point* of a radio is calling," Officer Thorn said, plucking the device from my palm as though I'd proven myself unworthy of such technology.

"Yes, but in this case it was just for me to call *you*," I retorted. "You almost blew my cover! Luca had to distract Orlix so he wouldn't notice."

"We were worried," William interjected, quite calmly. "You

181

went too far into the house."

"I think he's only been living in the kitchen," I protested, but more weakly this time. *I was right all along: William was monitoring me. Even though it was a risk.*

"We might not want to talk about it on the street," Luca said, glancing around us. His arm was still around my shoulder, as though he was protecting me from the Yule decorations behind us—or, more likely, the curious faces that had started appearing in the doors and gateways of the other mansions.

"Leave them to speculate," William agreed, his voice rumbling. "I bet you not a one of them did anything to stop him breaking the rules *again*, even though I'm sure there was plenty of gossip about how he made his living."

This last bit was added quite loudly, actually, and while I could sympathize with William's frustration, I was glad when Officer Thorn shepherded us all down the sidewalk.

For a few minutes, we walked in silence. The icy air was a welcome relief.

"The good thing is, at least *one* of us knows how to use her radio," Officer Thorn remarked as we left the sorcerers' neighborhood, Aspens. She walked right behind Luca, William, and me, her voice as light as if she was discussing the upcoming holiday. "I was able to get some back up from the local station. That's who came and picked Orlix up, if you're wondering."

"Will they take him to Maplehouse?" I asked. Luca and William were conspicuously silent.

"City of this size, there's probably a main hub downtown where suspects are held for interviews prior to being charged," Thorn informed me. "But even if they don't take him there, it's unlikely he'd end up at the Maplehouse station. Aside from stalking, intimidation, and disturbing the peace, his main crimes are based in this area, so the Aspens station will take care of it. Assuming you're *certain* he wasn't involved in our case, of course."

"I really think he was just as confused as we are. And consumed in his own guilt about Sweep," I said, thinking back through our interview. "William, what do you think?"

"You're giving him too much credit," William growled. "As usual. All he wanted to do was protect his own skin."

"And manipulate everyone else into feeling sorry for him," Luca agreed.

I glanced from one to the other. *Owl,* I realized. *Orlix did act kind of like him. Maybe that's part of why Luca is so . . . angry.* Not that his anger was unjustified; it just wasn't common for Luca to get so worked up.

"Looks like it worked on Red," Thorn prodded. "I agree she's too soft, by the way."

"It's not that it *worked,* exactly," I protested. "It's just that— well, this whole thing is complicated." I debated telling them about Paracelsus's trouble with Vincenzo, but that might have led to spilling Adam's secret, so in the end I kept quiet.

"It's not that complicated," Luca said, eyes straight ahead as we followed the uneven sidewalk. "It's about intentions."

"It's about intentions and *owning what you've done,*" William added. "Not even his peers putting him on trial could ever get him to take any responsibility whatsoever for his actions. You heard him in there. Someone says 'hey, did you make that familiar or that magic child, even after we told you to stop creating life forms?' and all he could say is 'the parents paid me.'"

"Hold up," Officer Thorn said. "Are you saying Orlix made Meteor? When was someone going to tell *me* that? I'm lead investigator here, you know!"

Recalling the scene had riled William up; the fur along his shoulders stood on end, making him look more wolf-like than ever. He rumbled, "We're telling you now. Yes, he made Meteor. He made a lot of the kids at the school."

"You could tell," I realized, thinking back to William's unusual assertiveness ( even for *him*) on Adam's tour.

"Of course I could tell. And I know what you're going to say, Red. Those kids are well-loved and in a safe community. That's as it may be, but it was still wrong for *Orlix* to be the one who made them. None of them were over eight years old, and that's when his trial was."

"You think that's how he's been keeping the house, the appearances, everything?" Luca speculated. "Ever since the trial, he's been supporting himself this way?"

I swallowed. My throat was tight. "Giovanni did hint that there was a sort of back-alley person who was 'helping' families get children. He seemed to think it was a good thing. Mostly."

"The end result is good for the families and the kids, too, but they were still being taken advantage of," William argued. "The children are fine. Orlix is not. That's the point here. You know why he got that reputation for 'gifting' families children? I bet it's because he was doing it on the cheap, without any of the due diligence or precautions anyone else would take. He didn't care who he was creating a child for, he just needed some money—any money. And of course he would never think of actually *working*.

"And," William added, before anyone could respond, "he was doing it *poorly*. A *really* powerful magic would be able to create a child who is wholly a child. They'd still be magic to some degree, like me, but there wouldn't be any of this *you have to prove you're worthy of being a person* hoops to jump through. The *child* wouldn't be responsible for completing its own creation."

The light went on in my head. This *is the problem,* I thought. *This is what's been making William mad.*

"That's not normal for magic children?" Officer Thorn asked.

"It isn't," Luca confirmed. "I wondered about that, when Red told me about Meteor. Often in the past all magical or unexplained children were called 'snow children.' The term comes from old traditions where the child is created from literally a wish, some powerful magic, and snow. And while they're usually documented as having some defining characteristics—very white skin, for example, or a tolerance for cold, if they were made with snow—they aren't always made from snow; they could be made from wood, or rock, like Meteor. But they usually do not have to prove to anyone that they are alive. There is no question, for example, of a moral *test* to determine their worthiness."

Thorn whistled, long and low, the noise lost in the increasing clamor from the street. "Are you telling me there could be a direct connection between the city's recent confusion over magical life forms and Orlix's reputation for creating more and more of these kids?"

"I don't think we can make that leap without more information," I said, pulling my coat tighter.

"Come on, Red. It's obviously all related," William said. "I'll admit it might not be *all* his fault, but I doubt it's coincidence. Familiars have been living in Brass for centuries now, and suddenly it's some big problem everyone cares about?"

"It may have been an underlying issue that's only recently

been brought to the forefront," Luca agreed solemnly. The darkness was falling fast around us, and he looked more like Jade with every step.

"All that said, those are things the Aspens Station will sort out," Officer Thorn cut in. "I'm sure they'll be reporting him to his fellow sorcerers, as well."

Luca's response was mild, but still tinged with bitterness. "What good will it do? They couldn't stop him the first time."

"It'd do more good to put them *all* on trial," William rumbled. This was unexpected; he'd been vitriolic about Orlix, but rarely about sorcerers as a group. The three of us looked down at him in surprise as he went on, "They *did* do something the first time, but if you ask me, it only made them more complicit. Sorcerer punishments are usually a form of binding curse. Basically, they cursed Orlix so that if he *did* dabble in creating life forms again, his magical power would suffer. But it obviously didn't suffer enough."

"Instead of creating a reason for him to stop doing those spells, it actually allowed him to, with the only drawback that the spells were weaker . . . which is why the children have to 'complete their own creation'?" I hypothesized.

"And you could sense that, too," Luca added, to William. "That's how you knew you could take him on. His punishment and continued practice weakened him."

"I'd have confronted him anyway," William said darkly. "It was time. But yes. I could tell. Any sorcerer should have been able to tell, if only they'd get their heads out of the sand."

Behind us, Officer Thorn cleared her throat. "All valuable information, which I'll pass along to the other officers. But for now . . . let's not pass up a chance to visit that bar over there, eh?"

* * *

Honestly, at first I thought all the talk about magical rule-breaking had driven Officer Thorn to drink. But she quickly relieved me of that notion.

The establishment she'd pointed out was nowhere near as dingy or dive-y as the bar William had taken us to on our first night, but it had a similar secrecy to it. It was housed in an old bank, the white facade and pillars still looming over the other storefronts on the street. A sign slung over the old grand entrance read *The Vault.* Once inside, we found out why: much of the old bank furniture and, indeed, the vaults, had been kept. Private rooms lined the back wall, and tables were made of old tellers' booths. The bar itself stretched along one side, painted to look as though it was propped up on piles of gold bricks. Though the ceiling was high, the lighting was low, and most of the patrons turned to look as we came in.

"You sure about this?" I asked Officer Thorn from the corner of my mouth.

"Absolutely. It came recommended," was all she said at first.

She shepherded us to one corner of the bar, where she could stand and look around the entire room. As we shuffled coats and cloaks onto a nearby coat rack, she explained a little more, surreptitiously: it turned out, some of the supper club members had mentioned to her that this bar was a favorite haunt of the Lost Rabbit officers.

*And here I thought we were going home after a long day,* I thought, wryly. *Trust Thorn to have a few more sites on the to-see list. And while the rest of us were distracted talking over Orlix, she got us to walk straight here without a second thought!*

That said, the bartenders were friendly and efficient—and I

*was* excited to finally have a taste of some of that mulled wine that was so popular in Brass this time of year. Officer Thorn could say what she liked about "keeping your mind clear for investigation." I'd taken point with Orlix; someone else could take over now, I decided, cradling the warm mug between my hands and savoring its spicy scent.

"At last, huh?" Luca said over my shoulder, grinning. Though the place wasn't jam-packed, it was popular, and our little group had to stand huddled beside the bar.

"At last," I agreed, grinning at him. Officer Thorn and William could watch the door all they liked. I was going to relax for a moment.

Luca clinked mugs with me, then took a sip of his own wine before turning thoughtful. "Hey, Red. About what happened earlier . . ."

"I'm sorry," I blurted out preemptively. When Luca stopped, looking surprised, I added, "I'm sorry I didn't think to ask you to help us out. I know you have insight, and you're quick on your feet, and well, basically invisible. And that's all great for investigating. It's not like last year—I wasn't trying to keep you out. Only . . . everything's happening so fast, and . . ."

"And I'm supposed to be busy with my conference?" he suggested, smiling. "It's okay, love. As long as you know that I *am* willing to help out. That's all I wanted to say."

"I know. But your conference is important too," I insisted. Officer Thorn and William were preoccupied with scanning the crowd and trying to casually peer into the open vaults.

"It is. And it's been really neat to meet new friends, and catch up with Rachel and hear all about Seaside, and to hear all the latest research, too," Luca admitted. "But safety comes first, right? And there's safety in numbers."

"Try telling that to these wacky police we're surrounded by," I told him, chuckling. "You sound like my conscience."

"Maybe I should be their conscience instead, huh?" Luca sidled closer, laughing too as we both looked at a seemingly-oblivious Officer Thorn. "I could probably haunt her."

"Good luck," I told him, chortling now. "She told me once she doesn't believe in hauntings."

"I didn't say that," she protested, her facade breaking. "I said I'd never *been* haunted. There's a difference."

"Please. Belville Station's probably crawling with ghosts," William observed without turning around.

The four of us laughed, and I sipped my wine, and for a moment everything was cozy and warm.

# 25

# Tied Up in Knots

Of course, in a murder investigation, moments of levity are often fleeting.  Before I could make a further comment about the kinds of ghosts that probably hung around Officer Thorn's police station back home, my friend perked up and shushed the three of us.

"There he is," she said, her excitement purely businesslike now.  "Red, Luca, did you make friends with him like I told you to?"

This made absolutely no sense to me until I followed her gaze across the bank-turned-bar. In the room farthest from us, I caught a glimpse of an oversized shoulder and a patch of straw-like hair.

"Do you mean Boa?" Luca asked, catching on a little quicker than I had. "I think anyone could make friends with him, as long as they showed interest in the Lost Rabbit Supper Club. He's here?"

"In that corner," I told him, trying my best to be discreet. "But I don't see anyone else from the club. Was he one of the officers?"

"In as much as an 'enforcer' is an officer," William observed dryly.

"I got that impression too, but was it ever explicitly said? And why would a dinner club need an enforcer, anyway? He didn't do much when Orlix interrupted the dinner, did he?" I asked, realizing in that moment how little thought I'd actually given to Boa's position.

"Why don't we go ask him about it?" Officer Thorn said, a grin spreading across her face. She caught the look on mine and added, "Oh, don't be a wet blanket, Red. I'll ask *nicely*. You can come too."

"Thanks so much," I muttered.

"You can introduce us," she went on confidently, already starting across the crowded floor.

I glanced back at Luca and William. "We'll hold down the fort here," my boyfriend promised.

"And keep an eye out for more of them," William said.

I sighed. "Alright, then. Here goes."

By clutching my wine to my chest and weaving through tables like a champion barrel-racer, I was able to catch up with Thorn just as she reached the far room. It was more a cubicle or closet than a room—vault-size, appropriately enough. A private booth and table fit comfortably within, but no more. The whole thing was raised a step up from the main floor, so Boa sat looking us straight in the eye as we approached.

He *was* alone, though, and he waved at me in a friendly manner. So I put my best foot forward and made some introductions. "Boa, hi! You remember me and my boyfriend, Luca, from the other night? This is a friend of mine—Thorn. You might have seen her there that night, too."

"Officer Thorn," Boa confirmed. So Thorn's surreptitious—

and very heavy—stomp on my foot had been ineffective! She'd no doubt done it so that I would introduce her without her title, but her uniform had given her away, anyway. I was tempted to make a face at her but managed to hold it in by a supreme effort of will.

"Off duty," she said gracefully, ignoring my ire. "Someone at my table last night recommended we check this place out, and as you can see, Red couldn't resist."

Fortunately, Boa seemed entirely unfazed by it all. He grinned at my drink and lifted his in a "cheers" gesture. Apparently, Officer Thorn had left hers behind, seeing as she was so professional. *Or maybe she'd finished it already.*

Even so, it was doubtful that one glass of mulled wine would have much effect on someone as large as Officer Thorn, and she proved as much by handing the conversation deftly. "That was some scene at the dinner, though, wasn't it? That kind of thing happen often?"

"You can go home but you can't clock out, eh?" Boa gave her an appraising grin, then waved us both into the booth. As we slid into the bench opposite him, he went on, "You got security concerns, you're right to bring them to me. You stepped in pretty handily, though. Can't imagine you're all that concerned about a little kitchen mishap, are you?"

"I didn't mean to step on your toes," Officer Thorn said easily. She didn't sound taken aback to be called out; actually, so far, she and Boa seemed to have a healthy respect for one another. "As you say, it's difficult to leave the officer mindset behind sometimes. With a group of that size, security must always be a concern."

"Sure. Especially once the wine starts flowing," Boa said, lifting his mug again. "Wouldn't be the annual Yule party without *some* kind of mishap. It's the biggest event of the year—regular meetings are handled on a neighborhood chapter basis. But don't you go getting carried away. We've never had any kind of violence with the Lost Rabbits. Most likely it was just another broken dish. No harm done. Unless the hotel staff said something to you?"

It struck me dimly that Boa had an angle in asking Officer Thorn that question; he'd invited us to sit down not only to reassure her, but to see how much we knew. But I didn't give it much more thought than that, because I was distracted by something else he'd said. "Boa, did you say there are neighborhood chapters? I thought last night you said everyone meets together."

"You must be remembering wrong," he said effortlessly. "It was a big night. Lots going on."

"But—there *are* chapters?" I pressed. Something here didn't sit right with me. I'd assumed at the party that there were so many people in the club that Bricky and Sweep had been effectively invisible. But that wouldn't be the case in a smaller neighborhood chapter at all.

"Of course there are," Boa said, his mouth momentarily hidden behind his mug as he took a drink. "It's one of the new initiatives. Why hog all the fun to just ourselves in only one part of the city?"

"Red's right, though," Officer Thorn said. "No one at the Yule party mentioned it. Not even for the secret gift helper. Wouldn't it make more sense to organize things like that by neighborhood?"

"There you go with that Guild mentality," Boa said, looking at her almost pityingly. "Always *organized.* We at the Rabbits are a people-first outfit. The aim is bringing people together.

We want people to mix between the different chapters as much as possible. To rely on each other."

"'We'?" I asked, tentatively.

Boa's light eyes snapped to mine, though his voice remained friendly. "We officers run the place as a team. Really, *all* the members have a say in the direction. That's the whole point."

This only made me more confused. "Do you have votes and all, then?"

"Sure. You looking to run?" Boa held my gaze.

I stuttered, and Officer Thorn came to my rescue. "Do you have any open positions?" she asked, leaning in. "Red here might get tongue-tied, but I like a bit of leadership."

"The Rabbits are led from the ground up," Boa said, and as he said it there was no doubt it was a company line. It sounded rehearsed. "That said, we *could* use a capable set of hands. Matter of fact, the treasurer position is open right now." He glanced at me again as he added, "Might be a minute before they instate someone new, though. Normally the position has an assistant, but—"

*But what?* I wondered why he abruptly stopped talking.

Officer Thorn, however, wasn't one to leave a gap in conversation for long. "What's the application process?"

"Well, you'd have to talk to the secretary, of course," Boa said, shifting back. "Fill out some paperwork, no doubt. Then she'd give it all a going-over and get back to you at the next meeting."

"And the vote would be at that meeting?" Officer Thorn pressed.

"Eh? Oh, that. Sure," said Boa.

"Pretty quick turnaround for a group of that size," Thorn observed. "I would've thought I'd need to make a speech or campaign or something."

"We don't waste our time with things like that," Boa said. "Matter of fact, that's why I like the Rabbits so much. No runaround or taking up time with nonsense fluff. Just getting down to the important stuff."

"And what is that?" I asked. When Boa looked at me again, hard, I coughed. "You see, Luca and I missed the talk, and I was really curious . . . about the besieged sorcerer?"

"Oh, that," Boa said again, but this time he chuckled. "An old tale. You didn't miss too much, really. A sort of 'cautionary tale,' they call it. An old sorcerer who thought he'd make life easier for himself by setting up a bunch of *magical* help, if you catch my drift. Well, you can guess how that turned out for him. No time at all, his help has gone wild, and he's out of a house and home. Just more proof to show you can't trust magic. It can't be controlled. It's *chaos*."

I stared at him. Three thoughts ran through my brain.

First, the tale *did* sound familiar. It sounded like the story of the Sorcerer's Apprentice—told from the sorcerer's point of view, leaving out the actual apprentice.

Second, it reminded me uncomfortably of Orlix. Of course, he'd been creating familiars and snow children for money, not to help him with household chores, but still . . .

Third was most baffling of all. During the course of his story, Boa had drained his drink. And before he'd finished talking, a broom had appeared at his side, tendrils of silver magic extending from its bristles and clustering around a fresh, full mug.

Boa took the refill without a second glance and immediately, the broom was gone. But Officer Thorn and I were still staring at him.

"My 'lost rabbit,'" he told us with a wink, gesturing to where the broom familiar had been a moment ago. "Once you're high up enough, and have proven you've got a good head on your shoulders, they let you look after one. Make sure it doesn't get up to no harm, see."

I suddenly found it difficult not to snarl. "Once you get high enough . . . in an organization that is led from the ground up?"

"That's the way," Boa said, cheerfully oblivious to the subtext of rage in my voice.

"Fascinating," said Officer Thorn, landing her elbow in my ribs in what probably looked like an accident. "Where do they come from in the first place?"

"Oh, they ain't stolen, don't worry, officer," Boa said, grinning. "We've got all the papers you could need. Come by and see them any time."

"I was only curious," Thorn said carelessly, "since it seems to me they're out of favor these days."

"And rightly so, isn't it?" Boa's grin melted into a satisfied smirk. "The club's got a supplier, see. In fact, once you're an officer, maybe you *will* see. Just a little friendly deal we made. Keeps 'em off the streets, doesn't it?"

"Does it?" I ground out. If the club was *commissioning* familiars, that seemed counterproductive to their overall goal to me. "Isn't the point of the new law defining 'magical life forms' to make the first step in getting *rid* of them?"

I would never have said something so blunt or confrontational if I hadn't been mad. But it *was* true. And Boa did not seem affronted in the least.

"Got it in one," he told me, winking with his one eye. "You're sharp. Stick around and maybe you'll be drafted to help write the next bill. We've all got to *act* to keep our society out of chaos."

I don't think I could have come up with words to say to save my life.

"You know, it strikes me that I've heard someone say that before," Officer Thorn chipped in. "Who was it? . . . Must've been a gnome I met, a while back, in Maplehouse . . ."

"Bricky," Boa said calmly. "Real shame what happened."

"Oh?" Thorn leaned heavily over the table. "I hadn't heard anything happened to him."

"Lost control of his assistant," Boa told us, his face entirely straight, as though he was passing on gospel. "Went wild and killed him right in his kitchen. Just like the besieged sorcerer, eh?"

26

# Final Exam

It took absolutely everything in me to end the conversation with Boa like a normal person and walk across the room like nothing had happened.

By the last few steps, everything in me gave out. I half-ran, half-fell into Luca where he stood next to William's stool at the corner of the bar. *"You will never believe it,"* I hissed, slamming my empty wine mug onto the counter between them.

"What? What happened? Are you alright, Red?" Luca's arm was around my waist, steadying me.

"Obviously she's not," William rumbled next to me. "Would you give her a second to say why?"

"No scenes," Officer Thorn declared as she caught up with me. "If you can't hold it together, Red, you're off the case."

"Boa's whole thing this entire time has been 'oh familiars are bad and magic is dangerous' but it turns out he has a familiar and he just keeps it hidden somehow and it's a broom exactly like Sweep," I said in one breath, thinking, *Fine, then, just try and take me off the case now!*

Luca blinked. "So—he's hiding it from the other members

of the club?"

"Worse than that," Officer Thorn admitted, lowering her voice. "Sounds to me like all the club officers have 'em."

"He said it was like taking them off the streets and you get one as soon as you prove yourself and Luca you should have heard it it was *awful*," I rambled again before closing my mouth with a snap. My arms went around William, who was tolerating the hug with far more grace than usual.

"Hypocritical, at the very least," Luca agreed, eyes wide. "The familiar—was it alright?"

"We only saw it for a moment," Officer Thorn admitted. "Seemed like he could summon it somehow. Just before it showed up, he waved one wrist, like, and a bracelet he had on seemed to sparkle. Mean anything to either of you?"

She gestured as she spoke, imitating a flip of the wrist that did look vaguely like something Boa had done. Clearly, Thorn was better at staying focused during interviews than I was; *score one for Guild training*, I thought, grateful that she had been there with me.

"Yes, there's lots of magical theory out there about making familiars 'portable' or 'invisible' or even binding them to objects like lamps, dolls, or jewelry," Luca said, glancing down at William in the center of our huddle.

For his part, William nodded. "Anyone can be cursed or bound into a physical object, if you have enough magic and enough time to set up the spell. Since familiars don't have a lasting physical form, it's even easier. It was all the rage among sorcerers for a while."

"Bricky's string," I blurted out as the thought found its way up through the turmoil in my mind. "Thorn, you said among Bricky's personal items was a string, like a string bracelet, you said, but it seemed to be broken or burnt . . ."

"I did," she acknowledged grimly. "William, 'sat sound like something that might happen if a familiar's bound to an object and then the familiar's killed?"

"The object would suffer, too," William confirmed. "Because the object and familiar would be bound together at that point. It goes both ways."

Luca set aside his own empty glass. "Wait. Are we saying Sweep *was* Bricky's familiar?"

"Evidence doesn't lie," Officer Thorn shrugged.

"But no one we've spoken to has said anything about it," I said, thinking aloud. "And I still think William's reasoning at the beginning makes sense. I don't think Bricky ever viewed Sweep as *his* familiar, exactly. He was hiding Sweep instead. Boa said something about assistants, didn't he? What if Bricky saw Sweep as an assistant purely for club matters, and not as an actual familiar in his day-to-day life?"

William rumbled. "'Club matters'?"

"It's looking like Bricky was the group's treasurer," Thorn told him and Luca. "Position's suddenly open, apparently, and as Red says, word is it comes with an 'assistant.'"

"'Assistant' being Boa's euphemism for familiar, I assume?" Luca thought. "How in Beyond is the club acquiring 'assistants' when they're actively campaigning against all sources of magical beings?"

"Who *cares* when the real danger is that this *club* is actually most likely a *cult*, exactly like Orlix said?" I burst. Immediately regretting it, I went on, "I didn't mean that, not exactly, I'm sorry, Luca. I do worry for the familiars who have been roped into working for the officers, and I agree the whole thing's incredibly hypocritical. But the worst part of it all is that they are *lying,* lying through their smiling teeth! They've been lying to us from the very beginning, every last one of them. And there's absolutely no reason to think any of them will stop. They're just going to cover the entire thing up. There's no way we can get them to talk to us honestly or answer our questions or even admit what they've done, because they have this whole group of people who hangs on their every word and will happily accept their lies and lie for them!"

I was panting, winded. My hands were clenched. *So much for acting normal.* Fortunately, the bar was boisterous all around us, and it didn't seem like anyone but my friends had noticed my outburst.

"You're overlooking something, Red," Officer Thorn said, after gesturing to the bartender and shuffling our little circle closer together. "Didn't you wonder why my friend Bakis is already Chief of Maplehouse?"

"Vampires could be any age," I muttered rebelliously. "They could have been at that station for centuries already."

"Not if they were going to meet me in training," Thorn replied cheerfully. "No, Bakis has only been out a few years, same as me. But their first major case was a game-changer for the Guild. They started up a whole new protocol . . . for dealing with the victims, that is to say the members, of cults."

William startled, brushing against me as he straightened on his stool. "That's a bit of a coincidence, don't you think?"

"Maybe not," Luca said slowly. "We just had a session on this at my conference this morning. Not on cults, I mean, but on recognizing when you're too close to a certain topic, to the point where you're making all the facts fit your theory instead of letting your theory fit your facts. Or just focusing on what you want to be there, sort of like the saying 'when you have a hammer, everything looks like a nail.' I haven't actually met Chief Bakis, so I don't want to put words in their mouth, but is it possible that this is a secondary reason they asked for you all to help with the investigation? Maybe they wanted someone to evaluate the cult angle from a fresh perspective and corroborate their suspicions."

I didn't process this suggestion at all, at first—I was struck by a sudden fondness for my scholarly boyfriend and his four-syllable words at a time like this. But William shook his ears and spoke up in agreement. "Actually, that first day, Bakis did say something along those lines. Not about the Lost Rabbits specifically, but about the whole feeling around familiars. 'Shadowy forces,' those were the words they used."

"So Maplehouse Station has experience with cults," I said, my impatience returning. "That's good for the average member of the Lost Rabbits, but how does it get us closer to solving Bricky's murder? The fact remains that it was probably one of the officers who came after him, and they're *never* going to give themselves up. Why would they?"

"I'm thinking you're too close already, Red," Officer Thorn declared. "You're letting them make you angry. You're taking on too much responsibility for the case."

"I am not—"

"You are," she continued, overriding my protest, "a very good *helper*. You are not the single investigator here who has to run down every single lead and cover every angle of the case. You hear me?"

For a moment, I gaped like a fish. Then I sagged, leaning against William's back. "Okay, yes, you're not wrong. I hear you, that I'm getting too wrapped up in things, and that in order to catch the murderer we're going to have to work together. With the officers from Maplehouse and wherever else, too."

"I think what you're hearing is actually, *take a step back, have another drink, and relax a little,*" Luca corrected, handing me a refilled mug of mulled wine with a kind smile. "Although your summary of our situation sounds good, too."

"Course it does, that's half the reason we keep her around," Officer Thorn agreed affably. She held out her own refilled mug and momentarily, we were silent, clinking our four glasses together; apparently, that gesture to the bartender earlier had been a request for a new round. I decided I wasn't one to complain. *Although I'm definitely going to need some dinner soon if we keep drinking!*

As usual, Luca was way ahead of me. He put in an order for cheesy fries and pickle chips, then turned back to us and winked. "Since we're going to be here a little longer," he said.

"We are," Officer Thorn agreed. "I want to see if anyone else joins our friend in the corner. And besides, as Red has been so passionately pointing out, we don't have any kind of plan for our next step yet."

I swallowed an admittedly calming sip of mulled wine and observed, "It's too bad we can't just do some kind of test on them. Like what William and I were doing for the string." *Was that really just this morning? It feels so long ago!*

"Maybe we can," Luca said, his eyes lighting up. He'd been filled in on our antics this morning, of course, and very interested in the combination of alchemy and magic. Now, that scholarly light was returning to his eyes.

"You can't just go and throw goop all over them," Officer Thorn said uncertainly. "What's that going to prove?"

"Not on *them,*" Luca told her, grinning now. "On the crime

scene. It's classic. Right?"

"What he *means,*" William interrupted, "is that all you have to do is tell your new best friend Boa over there that the Maplehouse police are planning to perform some new test on Bricky's apartment, something bound to turn up solid evidence. Then sit back and wait to see which Rabbit returns to the scene of the crime."

"It *is* classic," Thorn said thoughtfully, downing some more of her wine. "But what test could they do that'd be sure to turn up evidence? We have to say something specific in order to get the murderer worried enough to turn up."

I was watching Luca, thinking of his four-syllable conference language earlier. "Maybe we don't need to get that specific, though. I mean, how much do any of you follow me when I start rambling about esoteric alchemy? We just have to say enough to make them worried. Something about familiars . . ."

"Something about a new way to trace familiar magic," Luca suggested.

"Something about a new way to resurrect familiars," William said. "Tell him we have a potion that we can pour on the spot where Sweep died, and it'll make a shade of Sweep appear and tell us exactly what happened."

"Ghost evidence?" Officer Thorn clarified, still looking a little skeptical. As the food arrived, she swiped three pickle chips and made them disappear.

"It's perfect, actually," I said as I turned the idea over in my mind. "Think about it. If the murderer *is* one of the Lost Rabbit officers, then what will they fear more than the truth? A familiar. Every single meeting, they talk about how familiars will mislead you or betray you or fill your home with mopwater or whatever. Even if *we* know that ghostly testimony is questionable in a court of law, they'll probably be so worried already about familiars that they'll think it's worth interfering."

"Just be vague about how long the resurrection will last. Make it seem like Sweep could come back for good, even. Chances are they don't know very much about familiar magic either," Luca added.

Officer Thorn glanced at the three of us, busily chewing on some cheesy fries. "Okay, I'm on board. But why are you all talking like *I*'m going to be the one delivering the news?"

"You're the one who would know," I reminded her. "Tell Boa you just got some intel from your friends at the station, or maybe that you're going to go meet them to help them set it up."

"But that you're worried, because *familiars* are involved," William added. "Frame it like something the club should be aware of. Then he'll *definitely* go tell the others."

"And don't mention that Red will do the test," Luca put in quickly. "There's no need to, right? They don't know she's involved in the investigation."

"But whoever comes will recognize me when they show up tomorrow. Assuming we do this tomorrow," I said, glancing at Thorn.

"Tomorrow," she confirmed. "Sooner the better. As for them recognizing you, maybe that's a good thing. Throw them off guard, like. If they storm in the room only to say 'it's you, you're the one who's investigating me for the murder that I'm not supposed to know about?' then we've got them where we want them."

"Or even if they assume you're there like them, on club business," William suggested.

"Regardless, no one is actually thinking Red will be there *alone*, of course?" Luca asked, looking worried now.

"Course not," Officer Thorn said, pushing the half-empty plate of fries in his direction. "We'll all be there. *After* my presentation, of course. Good old-fashioned ambush, eh?"

"Tell them it'll happen at noon," I said, still thinking over how the experiment might work. "Tell him some nonsense about an anti-witching hour when science is at its strongest. That way we know when they'll be there."

"Science at its strongest," Officer Thorn repeated, chortling. "Alright, I'll go tell him. Be ready, because afterwards we'll have to leave, if we want to keep up the charade."

In her wake, the full amount of the nonsense we'd just put together hit me. I drained my mug. "Wow. I hope they really do buy all that."

"Don't worry about the specifics, Red. It's a game of magitech phone," William said. "Boa relaying a message that Thorn relayed that someone else supposedly relayed."

"The important thing is exactly what you said, that we hit on whatever the murderer fears most," Luca told me, smiling at me as though he was proud. "I think it's worth noting that your 'strong science' comes with a lot of insight, as well."

The praise made me blush, not least because it made me think of my time at the alchemists' institute the day before. But I couldn't help feel a little hypocritical myself, too. Here I was so angry at the Lost Rabbits for lying . . . and I had just concocted quite the lie to try to lure one of them in.

# 27

# Come Away

Officer Thorn had a strange kind of luck. She'd hardly been gone a minute, only barely disappeared into the booth with Boa, before her spot was taken—by a person in a red sash.

At first I apologized vaguely for having bumped into them. But the bright red caught my eye, and I looked again, flabbergasted. It was the person Officer Thorn had been chatting up at the Lost Rabbits supper—the club president!

Luca must have seen my open-mouthed stare, because he leapt into action at once. "Oh, hello!" he called amiably through the noise of the bar. "You were at the meeting last night, weren't you? Or running it, I should say!"

The president turned to Luca with an indulgent smile, which he then cast across William and myself, too. He looked like an entirely nondescript man in his sixties or seventies, white hair, pale eyes and skin. His smile was thin and wide. "Ah, our newest members!"

My mouth opened to say *not yet,* but fortunately, William beat me to the punch. "Would you like to join us?"

"I would, I would!  But duty calls, you know," he said, gesturing behind him. Through the crowd, I caught a glimpse of Bryn and someone else—Katerina, the "very effective" vice president—moving toward the booth in the corner. Watching them from behind, I realized they both had tails.  Katerina had pointy ears poking out above her unruly orange ponytail, too, suggesting she was "catkin"—that is, a person with some catlike characteristics. It was, I realized, the first time I had seen her.

"They put you on drink duty, huh?" I asked the president, wondering what they would make of Officer Thorn. And her news.

"A president lives to serve," was the rather grandiose response.

"You could have our space at the bar if you like," Luca said. "Just because, it seems like there aren't very many of you, and we're leaving soon. It does make it easier to get drinks!"

"Oh, we like our routine," the president said, smoothly sidestepping Luca's prying about the number of officers present—or missing. "But it was lovely to see you, you two, and your . . . talking dog," he added, glancing down at William and wavering for just one moment before slipping back into benevolence. He collected a tray of drinks from the bartender and was gone.

"'Talking dog,'" William snorted. "That guy wouldn't know magic if it bit his ear."

"So there's definitely a chance they'll fall for it," Luca said quietly, triumphantly.

But I was distracted.  While the busy bartender was still nearby, I decided to take a risk.  I leaned over William and called, "Hey, can I ask you something? We're just getting to know them," I said, gesturing to where the president had been, "and I'm curious. Didn't there used to be a gnome in their group?"

The bartender, a young woman in an oversized holiday sweater, seemed grateful for a chance to pause. She wiped her brow, pushing bright pink bangs back over her slightly orangey forehead as she peered in the direction of the corner booth. "There was," she agreed. "Used to come every night, but I haven't seen him lately. It's for the best, I guess."

"Why would you say that?" I asked, leaning in (despite William's "oof!" of protest).

"He and the catkin girl were at it last week," she informed me, leaning over the bar to grab our empties. "Just the two of them. Sounded like he wanted her to join in on some side project he had going. Funny how many friend groups split because of something like that."

With this sage observation, she disappeared, and I was left staring at Luca and William. *Katerina. Katerina knew Bricky was up to something . . . Bricky was treasurer . . . was it something in the club finances? What was he going to do?*

* * *

Our night ended with a long trip back to Maplehouse—interrupted with several snack stops along the way. There were no more chance encounters, which was probably for the best: my head was already spinning as it was.

The next morning, we were still talking it over. Luca was finishing up his final sessions of the conference, but Thorn's presentation had been among the first of the morning, leaving her free. Now Officer Thorn, William, and I had Bricky's apartment all to ourselves. Chief Bakis had apparently given the entire plan the go-ahead.

"They're on standby at the station," Officer Thorn said as she patrolled the dining room, ostensibly looking for any previous-missed exits or secret doors. "But we decided not to post an officer outside—want to make it as welcoming as possible."

"Yeah, 'one bed one bath, one recently committed murder, looking for owner with yet more murderous intent," William quipped. He sat squarely in the center of the living room, glowing faintly blue as he set up a ward of his own around the apartment.

"Speaking of buyers," I began.

"One lead at a time, Red," Officer Thorn interrupted.

I frowned at her over my alchemical set, which I was setting up on the table to add some credence to our story. "I was just going to say, what if whichever officer of the club is the murderer is *also* the one trying to secretly buy the apartment?"

""Possible," she agreed, without apology. "Bakis was saying how there comes a point in most cults' evolution where they start looking for property to set up a 'retreat' or 'stronghold.'"

"I don't think half of an old mansion in Maplehouse is really going to serve anyone as a fortress," William said dryly from the other room.

"They have to start somewhere," I said reasonably.

"It's not even half the house, since there's that upper floor," Officer Thorn chipped in. It was clear whose side she was taking. I let the point slide as she said, "So, who do we think we're going to catch?"

I protested. "That's hardly very scientific at this point—"

"—but it could be helpful in making us more prepared," she countered.

"Luca thinks it's Bryn," William called. "I think it's Boa."

"Boa's too obvious," I said, exasperated. "And Bryn's still new. *Katerina* is the one who was seen talking to Bricky in the bar. And when did you talk to Luca?"

"This morning," William said smugly. "While you were getting your beauty sleep. We both agreed that sometimes the obvious answer is obvious for a good reason. She *does* have a lot of energy."

"Boa'd be the obvious chance to send if it was the whole club behind the murder," Thorn put in.

I looked up at her. "You don't think that's the case?"

"Could well be. Or it could have been a personal vendetta related to the club. These cults, they stir up that kind of vitriol," she said easily, sticking her head into the little kitchen pantry as if it hadn't already been searched five times before. "So if it *is* him, we'll have to make sure to evaluate his confession."

"Assuming he confesses," I murmured. I was still plagued by the complete, impassive obliviousness in Boa's manner. With an attitude like that, he could be found with a bloody knife in his hands and still insist on his innocence.

"Another obvious thing," William said, still glowing. "The president is just a figurehead."

"That, I'll put money on," Officer Thorn agreed. "And I'm the one who talked to him at that dinner. I sat next to him all evening and I'll eat my hat if he said two useful words put together the entire time. Everything was 'we'll check with the treasurer' and 'that's something Boa handles' and 'have more soup!'"

"So," I reasoned, "you think that either the officers—aside from the president—are working together and ordered Boa to carry out the murder, or one of them acted alone."

"That's what we're saying, isn't it?" William's light flared, and went out. He stood up and shook himself. "My spell's set. I'll notice when they come in, and if they try to run, I should be able to trip them up."

"We'll catch them," Officer Thorn said with confidence. "Red, try to get whoever it is to talk a little first."

"Classic," I muttered, repeating Luca's word for the setup the night before. "While you two do what? Watch from the shadows?"

"Don't look so nervous," Officer Thorn said, sticking her hands in her pockets, her survey done. "People love talking to you."

"Boa seemed to like talking to *you*," I argued.

"That makes one of us," was her prompt response. "If it *is* him, don't worry, we'll come out of the shadows."

"No matter who it is, we'll have to look out for their familiar, too," I said, remembering the bracelet Boa wore. "William, can your ward do anything about that?"

"Maybe if I had another day to work on it. But as it stands, it's not that strong," he informed me.

Officer Thorn was watching him speculatively. "You've said that you *can* identify and trace familiars when you see them, though. Does the same go for objects that familiars are bound to?"

"No. Not unless I can get really up close with the object. What do you people think I am, a sorcerer in my own right?"

"Well, you *are* very capable," I pointed out, grinning.

"What I'm hearing is that we *could*, in a pinch, do a search for a familiar if it was missing," Officer Thorn said, still thoughtful. "Let's list out the officers. Were they all wearing bracelets? Is that the standard way they cart their familiar around?"

"We know for sure Boa does, and we think Bricky did," I said, ticking them off on my fingers. "I didn't notice the president's hands . . ."

"He did have a bracelet too," William affirmed. "I didn't sense anything from it, but I also wasn't fixating on it."

"Leaving Katerina and Bryn," I concluded. "I never really met Kat. We just saw her briefly at the dinner. I remember noticing Bryn's nails, but no jewelry—I could be wrong though."

"Sphinxkin," Officer Thorn said knowledgeably. "President told me."

"And she told me herself," William added. "Remember, *I* was the one who talked to Bryn that night. And Kat was supposed to sit at our table, but she was late sitting down, and then the soup incident—"

"She was gone all night after that," I realized, thinking it over. "Which seems a little extreme, don't you think, for some spilled soup?"

"Could she have been colluding with Orlix in any way?" Thorn asked, glancing at William.

He tilted his head, thinking about it. "There wasn't anyone else with him."

"We certainly didn't see her in the kitchen," I confirmed.

"That said, though," William added, "there *is* something—"

Unfortunately, we didn't get time to hear what the *something* was.

## 28

# Return to the Scene

The front door opened, and immediately, it was "go" time.

"Hello? Is anyone in here?"

Frantically, I shooed Officer Thorn and William into the tiny kitchen closet. They didn't remotely fit. In fact, they were smushed together like puzzle pieces.

"Hello?" It was a vaguely familiar voice—a woman's voice.

"Back here!" I said, as I shoved the door shut on my friends. I turned and leaned my back against it, panting, as I watched my visitor come around the corner.

"You," she said, stopping in surprise. "I didn't know *you* would be here."

*Katerina.* For a moment I stopped worrying about our trap and just stared at her in surprise. *Is it possible Thorn and William were right?*

"Hey, Katerina," I said aloud, so Officer Thorn and William could hear me. Probably. If their ears weren't blocked by bags of pasta or stray limbs. "I don't think we've officially met. I'm Red. What brings you here?"

"Well, Boa said the police were testing a new familiar technology here, and when he told us all at the officers' meeting, well, we figured that it'd be good for the club to know exactly what's going on," Kat told me. "You know, in case it's something to be worried about in the future."

"Oh," I said, stalling for time. Katerina didn't look threatening in any way. She was, however, starting to look a little suspicious. Of me.

"Why are *you* here? Where are the police?" she asked, looking around.

"I'm an alchemist," I said, feeling at a loss to have to explain this to someone when it seemed like everyone in Brass had known it at first glance. "I'm the one running the tests for the police. Their normal consultant was—uh—busy at the institute, and these things take a lot of time to set up."

"The potions, you mean? Is that what you're doing in that pantry?" she asked, her eyes straying to the door behind me.

"Um, yes," I said, thinking fast. "I'm using it as a sort of temporary lab. There's some fumes in there right now from the potion. It's in its final reaction stage. I just wouldn't want you to get too close—it could be poisonous right now."

From somewhere around my waist, a bump and rustle occurred.

Fortunately, Kat didn't seem too familiar with alchemical processes. "Wow, so, you've already started your tests?" she asked. "What have you found?"

I hesitated. *Does she really think I would test for Sweep's presence in the pantry?*

*Maybe she's never been here and doesn't know how big the pantry is,* I thought. *Well, aside from possibly having come here to commit the murder, of course.*

The bottom edge of the door shuddered. I pressed it back into place with my foot.

Katerina's eyes widened. "Some reaction, huh?"

"Yeah. Some reaction," I said. Pressing the door into place had reminded me of something: when William and I had first looked at the crime scene, the pantry door had been wide open. "Say, Katerina, did Boa happen to tell you what test I'm running, exactly? And how it works?"

"Oh, you know me," she said, waving an airy hand. "I'm just the vice president. If it doesn't have to do with event planning, I don't really get it."

The doorknob by my elbow rattled. *What is* with *them? Can't they get along in there for five minutes?* I gritted my teeth.

"So," I said, trying to keep my line of questioning in mind, "you don't know, for example, *what* I'm testing, or what I might find?" *William was right to call our plan a game of "magitech phone" if she didn't even get that much,* I thought.

"I'm really just the messenger," Katerina blinked. I straightened up, surprised. She added, "I was sent by—"

The door behind me burst open, knocking me forward.

"She's not the murderer!" William barked.

"Ahh! You! You can't see me!" Kat yelled back.

"Huh?" I stood between the two of them, my head spinning.

"I have to go. I just remembered," Kat babbled, leaping for the door.

"Oh no you don't!" Officer Thorn shot out of the pantry and tackled her.

In despair, I looked down at William. "What?"

"It wasn't her," he insisted.

"I figured that when I realized she didn't know the actual layout of the kitchen and pantry very well," I protested. In the hallway a few feet from us, Thorn and Katerina struggled on the floor. "But how do *you* know, and why did you have to burst out of hiding?"

"Because I could only sense it dimly from behind the door," William said, turning to look at Kat. "I had to come out to see for sure. She's a familiar."

"Ex*cuse* me? You can make 'people' familiars?" I asked, jaw dropped.

"I'm not—a—*human*," Kat shouted. Even though she was basically stuffed underneath Officer Thorn's wide shoulder at this point, her disdain was clear. "I'm—a—cat!"

"She's a . . . cat named Kat?" I rubbed my hand through my hair.

"*Get her!*" William cried.

But Kat the person was gone. A tabby cat squeezed out from under Officer Thorn and made a beeline for the door. In a streak of blue light, William was off—

And a moment later returned, holding the tabby aloft with blue magic. "Familiars usually have a strength," he said smugly. "Mine's protection and wards. Hers is probably changing shape."

"You don't know that for sure!" Kat protested, wriggling.

"Whereas you just found out you can't escape my spell," William retorted. "So I'd stop causing a scene if I was you."

"You weren't supposed to see me," she whined. "Whatever you have planned, I want no part of it! I wasn't doing anything wrong!"

"This must be why she was always suspiciously running away," I guessed, turning to Officer Thorn. She looked just as surprised by this turn of events as I did. We spoke in low tones in the kitchen as William and Kat continued to argue several paces away. "Like at dinner, when we left with the soup fiasco and never came back."

"That part makes sense now, I'll agree. But a cat?" Officer Thorn shook her head. "Maybe they didn't know she was a familiar when they let her into the Rabbits. Think she was infiltrating on purpose?"

"She seemed like she was really on the same page with everyone else just now," I mused, watching Kat struggle against William's magic. "And I doubt she'll say anything to us right now, either way. What's the other option? That they let her become an officer *knowing* she's a familiar?"

"Maybe not all the officers have *broom* familiars," Officer Thorn suggested.

I blanched. I'd blithely assumed that Kat might be a free familiar, sort of like William. But Thorn's idea implicated more people in the Lost Rabbits. "In that case, who does she work for?"

"I don't know, and I agree with you—in this setting, she's done talking. This is going to take some thinking over and a change of scene. I'll get our suspect to the station—maybe that'll help her calm down. She may not be our murderer, but she still knows more than she's telling right now. I want you to stay here in case anything else happens."

"One thing first though," I said. "How did William know she isn't the murderer? I mean, a familiar could still murder someone, right?"

"I heard that," William called. Apparently, his argument with Kat had run its course. "I knew she isn't who we're looking for because no one at the Lost Rabbits would send a familiar to do something important like deal with Bricky if they knew there'd be trouble. And she certainly wouldn't have been allowed to make the decision to kill him and Sweep on her own."

"So you think she is definitely working as one of their familiars, then?" I clarified.

Kat swung by a thick tendril of blue magic. "I'll die before I tell you who!"

"Great." Officer Thorn squared her shoulders. "Let's see if she feels more chatty at the station. You, stay here with Red. Assuming your little tussle is over?"

"Fine, then," William muttered, surrendering Kat into Officer Thorn's care. "Go ahead and take our credit."

* * *

"Well," I said to William, once the dust had settled and we had the kitchen to ourselves, "Credit or not, you've definitely been invaluable in this case."

"I'm invaluable in every case," William huffed. We sat side by side with our backs against the cabinets; I turned sideways to grin at him. But he was looking off into the distance, and his heart didn't seem to be in the boast like it usually was.

"So, Kat the cat and Sweep the broom," I observed casually. "Should I be calling you Dog? Or Big Bad Wolf? BBW, for short?"

"I prefer William," he said, his nose in the air.

"Uh huh. Well, that's good, because I'm not sure I could get used to anything else." I paused, glancing around the little kitchen. In a rush, it hit me: *this was our best chance to catch the murderer, and it's up in smoke. Every time we think we're close, we find another dead end.*

Officer Thorn might have chuckled at the pun, but I did not feel like laughing.

"You don't really think anything more will happen today, do you," I said eventually, when William also remained silent and pensive.

He shook his fluffy head and sneezed. "No. I don't. If the officer in question—whoever it was—sent Kat, no one else would feel the need to come."

"And us leaving tomorrow," I sighed. "I mean, I suppose we could change our travel arrangements—"

"You sound like Luca," William interrupted.

I tilted my head; at that moment, I felt *much* more despondent than Luca usually would. "Sorry?"

"When you say 'I mean.' You sound like Luca." William laid down, stretching his paws out across the tile. "You go everywhere together. You talk about everything together. Now you even *sound* like him."

If the cabinets hadn't been at my back, I might have fallen over. I just didn't see how this was relevant at all. *But if he's bringing it up, it must be important,* I reasoned. *In fact . . .* I cleared my throat. "William, is that—is that why you didn't really want to come along on this trip?"

"I always wanted to come along," he said, his voice skating low across the floor.

"But . . ."

"But you don't need me any more."

At this I sat bolt upright. "How could you say that? That's not true at all!"

"Even without my knowing about Orlix, you would have figured it out," he argued without looking up. "It's not like my information ended up being useful after all. We still won't catch the murderer."

"I'm not talking about the case," I snapped. "I'm talking about you. My *friend.*"

William sneezed again and finally sat up, looking back at me. "When I met you, your head was so full of science you barely had time for *friends.*"

"That's—probably true," I admitted, faltering. "But I'm not that way now. And it's—"

"You were lost," he continued, his words cutting through mine. "You needed someone to watch your back. You needed someone to cover for you while you found your way back home. But now you *have* found it. You *are* home."

My throat was closing up. "I don't—"

"Not *here,* obviously. In Belville," William went on. "You have your dream shop, and your friends, and Luca. You finally managed to open up to them. You don't need me to look after you anymore. You made it home."

"Oh my goodness, William." I dove for him, wrapping my arms around his neck, hiding my tears in his fur. "I had no idea you felt that way. That's not how I see it at all," I sobbed. "Of course you're right. I *was* lost. But I didn't go off and make a home all alone. *We* made a home, William. It's your home too."

"My, my," a new voice over my shoulder said. "This really is so *sweet.*"

# 29

# True Hearts

"What *heartwarming* examples for the familiars' movement you would make," Bryn added, a snide smile on her face as she stepped into the kitchen. "There *is* no familiars' movement," William retorted, as though by instinct.

I said nothing at first. For a moment I thought tears had blurred my vision. But no—I wiped my eyes and it was still Bryn standing there above us, striking in a bright crimson sweater-dress, her lion-like tail swishing behind her.

In that instant I realized who Bryn had reminded me of, the very first time I met her at the supper club. In old tales of Pinocchio, the puppet's first trial as a little boy is evading a nefarious predator and foxlike companion. Bryn's presence was incomplete without orange-haired Kat hovering behind her, simpering and agreeing with everything she said.

Apparently, however, Bryn wasn't feeling the loss. "Don't you think your very presence in Brass is evidence to the contrary?" She asked it in the same tone she'd asked us if we'd been to a meeting before, back at the Lost Rabbit dinner.

But now her eyes were hard as stone. She took a step toward us.

I scrambled up. "What's this all about, Bryn?"

"Kat's already been by to check on the investigation," William added, standing next to me. It was clear from his tone that he'd put two and two together: Katerina was most likely *Bryn's* familiar.

"It's a shame, isn't it, when the President has to do everything herself?" Bryn contemplated her fingernails. "I do so hate getting my hands dirty."

"President?" I sputtered, glancing down at William to see if he was following any of this. "I thought you were new. I thought the guy with the sash . . ."

"I really don't care what you thought, Red," Bryn said sweetly. "You've been thinking exactly what I wanted you to the entire time.

"You see," she went on, pacing a little closer, "that's the whole *point* of having a club, don't you think? So many people need to be told what to think. They *want* to be told. Thinking, holding opinions, solving riddles . . . it's all so *hard,* don't you think?"

William growled. "By 'club' you mean *cult.*"

"Semantics," Bryn replied with a wave of her hand.

"I'm still confused," I said, just in case anyone cared.

"Poor Red." Bryn smiled at me, her expression incredibly sphinx-like. "Too bad Bricky and his little puppet nephew weren't as slow on the uptake."

The penny dropped. "*You* killed Bricky and Sweep? Because—why? Weren't they helping you run the Lost Rabbits?"

"I've decided I'm running things on my own from here on

out," Bryn answered, stepping closer, just beyond arm's reach. "What's the point of having underlings? It's useful that the riffraff doesn't know *I'm* the one in charge, I'll grant you that. I have no patience for all the petty concerns they try to take to the 'president.' But there's really no benefit beyond that, when *I* end up having to do all the work because Kat and Boa are so hapless. And if it isn't *hapless* assistants, it's treacherous ones. *That* I will not stand!"

"Bricky was going to expose the cult, and Sweep was helping him," William surmised. His voice was low and he was glowing deep blue, preparing.

"And you only caught on to them that very night, at the officers' 'meeting' where he tried to talk to Kat," I added, thinking aloud. "He probably had no idea, like us, that she's a familiar. He would've told her too much."

"Because he was probably excited," William added, "about the presentation coming up. Be honest, Bryn: wasn't *Bricky* supposed to present at the Yule dinner? Wasn't he supposed to talk about how having a familiar makes a person susceptible to evil influences?"

I wasn't sure where William had come up with this—he must have overheard it at the Yule party itself. But I saw instantly where he was going. "Even if Bricky agreed to talk about that at first, he could have had a change of heart," I marveled. "Working with Sweep—and even with Meteor. He probably couldn't go through with it. So instead . . ."

"He very well could have outed you and the officers for having familiars yourselves," William concluded smugly. "And as soon as you realized that, you had to stop him and Sweep. Hence the very, very late night—early morning—murders . . ."

"Spare me your drivel and your demeaning guesses," Bryn

snapped. Though she'd been quiet while we reasoned it all out, she was vicious now. "It was *one* murder. Sweep never counted for anything. It was a *broom*. A broom *I* gave him!"

"Sweep was working for the Lost Rabbits," I pointed out, scandalized by her lack of empathy. "It must have believed in your group at one point, at least enough to stay on with Bricky!"

"And doesn't that just go to show you how useless it was? That *I* could get it to believe in a cause that literally said it had no worth?" Bryn inched closer, triumphant.

"*You* believe in the doctrine too," William said.

Bryn paused mid-step. "And what does that have to do with it?"

"You believe that magically-created beings shouldn't 'count,'" William told her, "but how much magic is too much? Is the magical heritage in *your* blood not enough to count?"

"You don't know anything!"

"Sphinxes are magical creatures," William went on, even louder. "They're not natural in the least. And in order to be part sphinx, somewhere along the line, one of your ancestors had to have made a pact with some kind of deity. A *magical oath* that turned that ancestor into a whole new person. How long ago was that, Bryn? Was it your grandparent, your great-grandparent? Or was it you yourself? Does it matter?"

"Stop!" Bryn commanded.

"And furthermore," said William, the magic crackling over his fur, "the reason you got familiars to believe in your *cult*—the reason *you* believe in your own nonsense cult—is because *everyone* is prone to doubting themselves. Especially if the people who create familiars are power-hungry, foolish sorcerers who know nothing about friendship or trust. Sweep never had a chance. Did you, Bryn?"

"*I said stop talking* now*!*"

Bryn was shaking, her voice taut with the effort of standing in place. She hadn't attacked, though, and I realized that she'd probably come to the apartment expecting to be able to steal a knife again. I started eyeing the counters, looking for weapons. We had no reason to expect Officer Thorn back any time soon.

"You don't know *anything*," Bryn repeated. "You don't know what I've done!"

That was patently untrue, since we'd already established that she was our murderer. But something in the sentence got my attention. "Speaking of, Bryn," I said casually, still scanning the room, "believing familiars are out to get you is fine and all, but why'd you make a *cult*, of all things? Why couldn't it have been just a club, as advertised?"

"It isn't a cult!" Bryn yelled.

"Oh, but we *are* out to get you?" William asked.

"It's just that *no one pays attention!*"

She was practically loud enough to be heard on the street. I risked a glance at William. *Is it too much to hope that we'll be overheard?*

In the meantime, Bryn seemed to have realized she was losing the upper hand. She took a breath and smoothed her hands down the front of her dress. In slightly more reasonable tones, she said, "People like *you* are exactly why I had to take over. All the elements were there, but no one was *doing* anything. No one was organized, no one else had vision."

"I think she just means people like *you*, Red," William said. It was unnecessarily needling our angry murderer, but he also had a point. And maybe if she lost control again, we could take advantage of an opening.

"I'm flattered," I said, keeping my eyes on Bryn now. "And I think I get it. The Lost Rabbits already existed. She just came in and slowly took over. She *is* a new member—she didn't lie about that."

"It's about the only thing she *didn't* lie about," William agreed, leaning against my leg.

"She probably didn't lie to them either, in the beginning," I mused. "Like you said, there are probably plenty of familiars in Brass who wonder about their worth, unfortunately. And we know Bricky had a history of not liking magical life. So everyone probably got along great at first . . ."

"Don't think I don't know what you're trying to do," Bryn interrupted, frowning. "Before you get all high and mighty, don't forget: you and your friends lied to *me* to get me here!"

She hit a sore spot, and I tried not to show it. I hesitated.

But William had an answer immediately. "We lied because we were worried about the people and familiars you hurt. *You* lied to get people to do your bidding. It comes down to what you want: friendship or power?"

Bryn looked like she was fit to burst. "If you think you're so smart, answer this: if magical life should *count,* then why do ragged little specimens like Sweep or Meteor have to *prove* that they're real?"

"I don't think they do," I said, slipping and getting angry myself. "I think the better question is, who is going around setting *tests* for people to prove their worth? Who gets to be the judge of that?"

"Judge and executioner," William added.

Bryn's eyes lit like they were on fire. "You know what I *do* know?" she said, glaring at him. "Red can't do magic. You let that little tidbit slip yourself."

And with that, she dove for William.

He'd finally gone just a little too far.

## 30

# Good Company

*ed can't do magic.* For a moment, the phrase echoed all through my soul, like my insides were hollow. *Red can't do magic.* The bane of my existence as a child. And it was so many thousands of times worse in that very instant, because what Bryn really meant was *if you die, William, Red can't bring you back.*

*"Get away from him you monster!"*

Bryn collided with William and I dropped like an anvil out of the sky on top of her. Any thoughts of kitchen utensils or frying pans went straight out of my head. I wrenched at her arms recklessly, not knowing if she had hidden a weapon. She reached over her shoulder and scratched at me with those rock-hard nails, and I pulled her backward all the harder. I lashed out and braced my foot on the nearby counter, trying to get some leverage, just before we were both thrown back.

William emerged from the bottom of the pile, fur standing on end, having used his magic to force us off him.

*"I* can do enough magic for the two of us," he declared.

229

*Oh, right.* I'd forgotten that part.

Bryn flailed against me, kicking across the hardwood floor. Apparently, the time for talking was over. I did my best to hold on to her arms while looking over her shoulder at William, waiting for a cue.

"And I know exactly how this ends," he added smugly above the sounds of the scuffle. Blue strings of magic rose from him and arched through the air before plucking Bryn out of my grip, twining around her and lifting her in the air . . .

. . . before dropping her right back into my lap.

"Um, William?" I grunted, as Bryn was now struggling twice as hard and it was difficult to avoid her nails.

"Might have . . . overdone things . . ." he panted.

*Shoot. He did already ward this place* and *catch Kat,* I thought, trying to remember when he'd last been able to charge up his magic.

"That's—what—comes—of—*vanity!*" Bryn howled, victoriously.

"I wouldn't go getting ahead of yourself," I told her, landing an elbow squarely against her side as she continued to fight.

"I could run and get someone?" William suggested.

I paused to look at him in disbelief.

"Right. Didn't go so well for Meteor . . . but if I can find Thorn . . ."

"You are *not* leaving me alone in here with her," I told him.

William huffed. "Well then what do you want to do? We can't just wait for whenever the officers finish up chatting!"

"Your—time—is—up!" Bryn yowled, still sideways across my legs.

I rolled my eyes at William, at a loss for words.

Amid all the bumps and protests, I hadn't heard anyone enter the house. But in that moment, the most wonderful comment of the day floated from the doorway:

"Wow. When you and Officer Thorn said you were going to set a trap here, I didn't think you were going to try to *physically* catch a murderer," Luca said. "Don't you have slime for that, Red?"

* * *

Of course, Luca was right. But since Bryn was firmly in place over my midsection—and therefore my toolbelt—it took some time to maneuver us all into a position where I could affix Bryn into place without also catching myself, William, or Luca.

Eventually, though, the three of us stood around a mostly-subdued murderer ensconced in a pile of bright green solidifying slime.

"Well. Uh. Am I the only one who feels like we should high five or something?" Luca asked sheepishly.

"Spare me your misplaced *friendship*!" Bryn shouted from the floor, one foot kicking helplessly from under the cement-like ooze.

Luca scratched thoughtfully at his head as he looked down. "Has she been like that the whole time?"

"Pretty much," William said. "Sunny dispositions and murder don't go hand-in-hand, I guess."

"So she *is* our murderer?" Luca asked, looking up to meet my gaze.

"You can't prove anything!" Bryn yelled.

"Sure seems like it," I told Luca over the noise. "She was really vehement about familiars—but it turns out Kat *is* her familiar, in disguise. And then she basically admitted to taking over the dinner club and turning it into a cult. Basically, she seemed to think no one around her had any agency of their own."

Bryn took issue with my summary, of course. "It's not a cult!"

William snorted at our captive. "You know, each time you say that, it becomes less and less believable."

"And either way, with all three of us as witnesses, we can definitely prove you assaulted Red and William," Luca reminded Bryn before looking up again. "Speaking of, where's Officer Thorn?"

This time I *did* hear the door to Bricky's apartment open, but it wasn't Thorn responding to her cue. Instead, a childlike voice called out from the living room. "Hello? Is something wrong?"

"Meteor," I said. With a quick glance at Luca and William to make sure they'd stand guard, I hurried out to meet him.

Even kneeling down, I was taller than the little rock child. "Hey, Meteor, do you remember me? My name's Red."

"I know you. You work for Chief Bakis." *Close enough,* I thought. Meteor's eyes strayed over my shoulder and he repeated, "Is something wrong? I heard noises when I was coming home to get my show-and-tell."

"Something *did* happen," I confirmed. "My friends and I have caught a dangerous person. Everything's okay right now, but it's probably better to go over to your place and stay there."

"Is it the person who killed my uncle?" Meteor asked, returning his attention to me.

I hesitated. It seemed like a gruesome subject for a child, but I didn't want to lie. Finally I told him, "Yes, we think so."

For reasons I didn't understand at first, Meteor brightened.

"Do you need the police?"

"Actually, we do. But I think our police officer friends should be here soon—"

"I could go get them," Meteor interrupted. And, just like that, he was gone.

I sat there for a moment, staring at the open door left in his wake. Then I felt a hand at my back, and Luca knelt next to me.

"Something to be said for childlike resilience, eh?" he observed, softly.

"I just hope it goes well this time," I replied uncertainly.

"Of course it will. Officer Thorn's on hand to see to that." Luca pulled me into a brief side hug, adding, "It's okay to trust each other. There's nothing 'misplaced' about our friendship."

"Yeah, but—but—if Thorn misses him—or earlier—if you were just a few minutes late—"

"Those are valid concerns," Luca told me, shifting to look directly into my eyes. "But we're all doing our best to look after each other. Can you see that?"

I thought of everything I'd just told William. I thought of William's efforts to save me, using magic until he couldn't any more. And I thought of the way Luca had been doing his utmost to support us *both* all along, from the sidelines, even when we were too wrapped up in our own trouble to notice. Doing puzzles with William on the balloon ride, staying up late to talk to me, taking William's side automatically when Orlix fought back. And always, always Officer Thorn would have our backs as well. She'd never let me down yet. None of my friends had.

"You know what? I can." I smiled at Luca, though my gaze was slightly watery.

And just at *that* moment, finally, a familiar ponderous step came up into the house.

"I hear you've all been having fun without me," Officer Thorn announced. From somewhere around her shinbone, Meteor mirrored her triumphant grin.

# 31

# Loose Ends

For the second time that day, Officer Thorn marched off to the station with a suspect tucked under her arm. Though I offered to stay and clean up, she informed me that some officers would be over to document the scene, and that I should "keep my paws off it until then."

So, instead, William, Luca, and I ended up hanging out with Meteor and his parents. After all the excitement there seemed to be little question of Meteor going back to school. The six of us clustered around their gnomish living room, eating sandwiches for lunch and listening to Meteor proudly recount his second trip to the police station.

"Officer Thorn said she'll give me a badge!" he informed us, probably for the fourth time, as he ran to and fro on the rug. While his father tried to get him to settle down and eat like the rest of us, I turned to Mix, who sat on the sofa at my elbow.

"I feel I should apologize," I told her quietly. "I really didn't mean to involve him, but—"

"Some things are meant to be," she said, her eyes shining as she watched her son.

"Well, I'm glad it all worked out, at least," I admitted, smiling too. William sat close next to me, and Luca was happily eating his second sandwich, racing Meteor to see who could eat their crust faster. "That said, Mix, I wanted to say—I mean, it's probably not my place, but—"

"Don't worry," she interrupted.

I paused. "What?"

"We don't care," she said, and went on to explain, "whether he stays like this forever, or maybe *does* one day pass a test and become a new version of himself. He did something heroic today, and that's that, no matter what comes of it. We think he's perfect just as he is."

"Oh, Mix," I murmured, my eyes watering for the second time that day. "Oh, goodness, that's not what I meant. We *did* learn about some of the magic children being tested like that, but—"

"That's not what you were talking about?" Mix looked up at me in surprise. "Then what?"

"Just—it seems a little silly now," I confessed, chuckling. "And I'm sure the police would rather tell you than me. But while we were poking around, we did find that some mysterious person—or people—is trying to buy this house. That's all. I just wanted to warn you."

"That!" The little gnome chortled. "That's nothing, dear, don't worry about it. Our landlady would *never* sell."

"But—they seemed awfully determined—well, we thought they might be after something Bricky had hidden, maybe."

"Our inheritance?" Mix asked, her smile both sad and knowing. "I can tell you right now what it is.

"Bricky was very good at his work, you see," she began, shifting to face me directly. "He'd been at it such a long time.

He didn't lay bricks any more; instead, he carved the gargoyles and statues that go on the buildings for protection. No one else could make them so lifelike. In fact, he gave us the statue that would become Meteor," she said, tears shining in her eyes as she glanced over at her boy. "He carved a little child for us, just as a consolation one year, and then we took it to the sorcerer later—he didn't know about it until we got home with our wish come true. Some people on Bricky's team, well, they just couldn't understand how he was so good at carving things so lifelike. And he'd always used the same set of tools, see, ever since he was just starting out. So there was a rumor going round. People said it was the tools that were magic, that made magic things.

"Truthfully, I think that's part of why he decided to come with us," Mix told me. "The rumors were getting to be too much back home. People would hound him all the time, asking for him to carve things, or for him to teach them. All he wanted was peace and quiet, he said, and that as long as everyone was safe he didn't see why anyone should bother him. But even though no one in this new neighborhood knew, the people at his work sites would still ask him. In fact, there were a few of his coworkers who even tried to get him fired as a way to get him to turn over his tools."

"And do you think those coworkers might be who we overhead?" I asked, putting the story together.

Mix nodded. "I'm sure they all thought he kept his tools hidden in the apartment. But he didn't. Ever since Meteor— well, something changed for him. Ever since then he'd have Shades look after the tools whenever he wasn't at work."

"So they were here all along," I mused. *And if Bricky's primary focus at work was protection, and he wanted safety and quiet so much, then it makes sense that the Lost Rabbits with their "informative talks" could have lured him in. Especially if he was conflicted about seeing his own carving come to life because of a mysterious sorcerer. Even though he loved Meteor, it must have been a shock at first, especially given the pressure from his coworkers.*

"Don't worry," Mix repeated, patting my hand. "We know how to stay safe."

"Hopefully this whole thing will be over, as of today," I agreed, smiling at her. "I hope you and Meteor and Shades are able to have a truly peaceful Yule, despite the sadness."

"Yes. That's the point, isn't it?" Mix said, her eyes on her son again. "Even in the darkest part of the year, there's always hope if you let it in."

* * *

That evening, after the final interviews, we were able to reconvene just in time to tag along with Luca to a farewell dinner amongst some of the scholars. It wasn't everyone who had been at the conference, by any stretch of the imagination, but there were perhaps a dozen of us clustered around one long table in a trendy restaurant in Maplehouse. The place was stuffed with so many evergreen boughs and sparkling trees that it smelled like the forest back in Belville. The roaring fire in the corner, too, made me think of Lavender's Tavern with a pang. But we'd be headed home in the morning, and in the meantime, everyone was in excellent spirits.

"What I can't figure," Officer Thorn yelled from one end of the table, "is how Luca called it beforehand. How'd you guess it was Bryn?"

The other scholars, who had been eager to hear all about our investigation, turned to hear the answer with rapt attention. Over piles of garlic bread and festive candles lining the center of the table, their faces shone bright. Though the spotlight was slightly unnerving, the sight of them all reminded me that *this* was the whole point of Yule: coming together and helping one another sort everything out. I smiled. I hadn't gone to any lectures, not even Thorn's, but maybe I *had* learned a little something.

"It was the keynote lecture on leadership in small towns, actually," Luca said, after overcoming his first impulse to hide behind my shoulder. Grinning, he explained, "The presenter said something about the best leadership coming from *behind*, like by encouraging everyone else instead of making everyone live up to your example, and I just thought, who in the Lost Rabbits is doing a lot of supportive work without wanting to be seen? And I figured that was probably pretty suspicious, given that the whole thing was definitely culty.

"That's also where I learned about love-spelling," he added to me, as everyone else turned to each other to discuss the crime. "I realized I never explained it to you. She listed it as something to look out for. Basically, a person or group makes you think you're the greatest thing ever, like they're under a love spell and you're their beloved, but then as soon as things go wrong—"

"They leave you out in the cold?" I speculated, thinking of how Kat had been abandoned in the police station earlier, amidst the interviews and hubbub. "I can definitely see that."

"It goes to what you were saying earlier about *agency*," Luca told me, grinning over his lasagna. "Whether someone is just manipulating you and trying to take your agency away, or actually listening to you and letting you make your own choices."

"Lectures or no, it did explain a few things," Thorn declared, her voice breaking through the various scholars debating things like the usefulness of the keynote speech or the definition of a cult. "Like why we never found the weapon. I should have thought of it, myself. Bakis was the one to put it together. Turns out, Bryn had just enough power from her sphinx blood to turn little things to stone. The knife is solid rock and at the bottom of some waterway—probably the one going round the university, if you ask me."

"Did she ever confess?" I asked, intrigued by this possibility.

"In bits and pieces," the officer confirmed. "They had her back in that interview room all day, and believe me, the interviewers got an earful from her. Most of it was ranting. But enough of it was self-incriminating that Bakis told me they feel confident taking it up to trial next month."

"Kat never did say anything," William added from my right. "I went and talked to the officers about her myself."

"A familiar who can take human shape," one of the scholars finally broke in edgewise, eyes gleaming. "Imagine!"

"Don't see the point, myself," William growled. "It's not like they'd be able to fool most magical people anyway. *She* certainly didn't."

"William," I asked quietly, thinking I might already know the answer, "were you able to tell where she came from?"

Hearing this, Officer Thorn stirred. "Whoever made Kat probably was supplying all the Lost Rabbit officers, and that means colluding with a cult."

"I *know*," William told her. "Like I told you, I already talked to the Maplehouse officers while you were all getting interviewed."

Luca peered around my shoulder. "It wasn't *him,* was it?"

William nodded.

I sat back, eyebrows raised. *Could Orlix just not help himself but get into trouble?* I had to wonder. But then again, he *did* seem to be the city's most active familiar- and magical child-provider. He'd been desperate for money, and had developed a reputation for himself. It made an unfortunate kind of sense.

"By 'him' you mean the sorcerer you helped apprehend, right?" asked another scholar—Rachel, a friend we'd made in Seaside, in fact. She was looking at Luca with that thoughtful look which I knew preceded a scholarly argument. When Luca confirmed the details for her, she said, "Then that proves precisely what I was trying to say earlier. What you have in this case isn't just *one* fairy tale, it's two."

My mouth fell open. "The *two* being—?"

"Pinocchio, and probably also the Sorcerer's Apprentice," Luca told me. "Even though in the Sorcerer's Apprentice, the apprentice is usually the one who creates the magic that gets out of hand. But at its heart, it's about messing with magic you don't understand, and hierarchies, too. I don't disagree, Rachel. In fact, we've often had cases where similar tales intertwine. Say, for example, Cinderella and Thousand Furs—"

I wasn't fully listening, I must admit. I know this was going to be way over my head. Instead, thinking of apprentices getting out of hand made me think of the alchemy institute—and Paracelsus, and Vincenzo. And Nessalee.

*What was it Paracelsus said?* I tried to remember. *"Apprentices must make their own choices"* . . . *and "your understanding has always been one of your strengths."* A far cry from being too involved in science to have friends, I thought wryly, despite feeling a pang over William and his recent troubles.

"But hear me out," Rachel was saying, putting up her hand. "That isn't my whole point.  My *point* is, it's the contrast between two similar tales that creates the tension and, to some extent, the mystery. Because while the tales are similar, they actually operate based on opposite assumptions."

I turned to William, looking for a sympathetic companion to share in my exasperation. *That's what we get for talking over cases with multiple scholars, at a conference,* I wanted to say. *"Contrast?" "Tension?" "Opposite assumptions?" What do any of those phrases really mean in context?*

But to my surprise, William was leaning over his plate. He was totally into it. "I think she's on to something."

*I wonder if he'd want to stay here with all these scholars,* I thought suddenly, irrationally. In the bustle of cleaning up a crime, he'd never really answered me about Belville being our home. But I tried to push that strange worry aside; it didn't seem fair, somehow.

"In Pinocchio, the woodcarver and the fairy who make the kid have good intentions," Officer Thorn said slowly. Apparently, even *she* was on board with this bit of philosophy. "Every assumption 'pulling the strings,' so to speak, is a good one."

"But in the Sorcerer's Apprentice . . ." Luca's voice trailed off.

". . . the intention when creating magical life is just to find a shortcut or personal gain," I concluded, finally catching on.

Rachel nodded in the background. "It's all about intention. See . . ."

She went on, but from there the conversation became *really* philosophical. I stopped following it entirely. Instead I kept musing about intentions, my focus on William.

*That's been what's bugged me all along,* I thought. *When talking to Adam, or Paracelsus, or Orlix. The creation of life, whether or not that life has a home—all of that comes down to intention. Orlix's intentions were selfish and short-sighted and led to a lot of trouble. But so many other people involved in this case—Mix and Shades, everyone at the school, even us—our intentions are just love.*

And that, I realized, was exactly what Mix had been trying to tell me about darkness and hope.

32

## Welcome Home

The next morning, as we were packing up to make the trip home, an unexpected visitor called.

Luca was busy trying to stuff robes into his luggage, and William was still groggy—it *was* before ten in the morning, after all—so when the bell rang, it fell for me to run down the stairs and see who it was. I emerged into the main lobby of the old dormitory and almost entirely ignored Chief Bakis, who stood solemn amid the post-conference bustle.

"Are you looking for Officer Thorn?" I asked them, once I realized they were looking at me. Around us, scholars carrying books and bags streamed in and out of the dorm. "I thought she was staying at the police station."

"Actually, I have something addressed to *you*, Red," the chief said. They held out a small package wrapped in brown paper.

I took it, curious. It was no bigger than my fist, and not very heavy. "Something for me? I already ran out and picked up all my orders from the alchemists earlier this morning. I didn't think I'd forgotten anything."

"It came from the Aspens station," Chief Bakis said politely.

"The sorcerer's neighborhood?" Instantly, I wondered about the wisdom of accepting the nondescript little gift.

"Not to worry. We had it checked over," Bakis said with a knowing smile. "Although, after the way you handled your latest case, I shouldn't imagine that anything they could think of would baffle you for long."

"Uh . . . thanks," I said, still vaguely worried. As Chief Bakis took their leave, William bounded up.

"You were gone forever," he announced. "What's taking you so long?"

"It's been a minute. Tops." Still, I showed him the little package. "What do you think?"

William's black nose twitched. "I think we should open it outside, just in case."

"Good idea." I pocketed the mystery gift, glad I'd kept my cloak on even in our room. Together, William and I slipped out the double front doors and found a quiet bench off to one side, in full view of the 'Puppetmaster' statue that had watched over the beginnings of our investigation. We had to pause to brush off a light dusting of snow before sitting and focusing once more on the delivery.

"Any idea what it is?" I asked William, hesitating.

"Nope," he said. "I can sense some magic, and it feels familiar, but . . ."

"Not familiar like a certain club seeking revenge?" I asked, mostly in jest.

"Not that kind of familiar," he grumbled back. "Just open it, Red."

"Alright, then. Here goes." I picked at the paper, and finally ripped it off, tugging a bit of twine along with it. A deep blue disc on a long chain fell into my hand, with a bit of parchment behind it. I picked up the paper and scanned it to make sure it wasn't a spell: William had taught me *that* much, at least. After a moment, I felt I could safely read it aloud. "'To Cinnabar,'" I began, choking slightly over the fact that someone—someone I was pretty sure was *not* Paracelsus—had used my real name, "'do not be alarmed. The police have seized all my effects, and this is the only thing of value I have left. But I think you and your friends will agree I have not proven myself worthy of it. I suspect—no, I *know* that you can do better. It is, as your actions at my home indicated, already rightfully yours.'

"Oh," I breathed, looking at the amulet again. Stars were inscribed on its shiny surface, and among those stars, the indigo outline of a dog. "William. Is it—?"

"It's true," he said, almost reluctantly. "He sent you the amulet that can re-summon me. I would have thought he lost it years ago."

"It's beautiful," I said, turning the disc over in my hands. Then, abruptly, I held it out to William. "It's yours."

"He sent it to *you*," William argued.

"But it's *yours*," I insisted. "William, this is your lifeline. With this, you could—you could go anywhere," I said, my voice cracking. "You can do anything."

For a long moment, William was silent, looking at the necklace swinging from my hands.

Then he swatted it back towards me with his nose. "That's stupid, Red. If *I* die and *I'm* the one with the amulet, how'm I supposed to use it to bring me back? That'd be like keeping your backup in the exact same place as the original, so when disaster strikes it hits them both."

"But . . ." I protested again, faintly.

"You take it," he said firmly. "It's yours. If something happens to me, then get that scholar or even that foolish Witch to help you use its magic and bring me back. Just not the shadow witch, *please.* I'd never hear the end of it. And if something happens to *both* of us," he added, lowering his voice, "then that's how it's supposed to end, and I don't want to be brought back. You are my home, Red. Even if you don't need me."

"I thought I'd made it plenty clear I *do* need you," I said, enveloping him in a huge hug, tears stinging at my eyes in the cold. "Not to look after me, but to be my friend."

***

When we hopped off the boat back in Belville that afternoon, the amulet was safely around my neck, nestled under my winter layers. As a necklace it was an unfamiliar size and weight, but it felt warm. Every time I noticed it again, I thought of William. It made me smile.

Naturally, Officer Thorn and Luca were full of energy. They chattered as we walked up the road towards Market Square. The light dusting of snow in Brass had been nothing: while we were gone, Belville had apparently gotten its first winter snowstorm, and each roof sported a fresh white blanket nearly a foot high. The roads were cleared, but slippery, and surprisingly empty . . .

. . . Because, as it turned out, all our friends were waiting in the Pomegranate for *us.*

Trent came out and met us as we reached the center of town. "Saki sent me," he admitted, after the initial spine-squishing hugs had been traded. "She says you're all to come to the café right now."

"What about our bags?" Luca asked, looking over his

shoulder as though he'd only just now realized that he'd walked right past the bookstore.

"Forget about them," Trent said, grinning. "We'll help you get everything settled later. For now, let's party!"

"Now *this* is a proper welcome," Officer Thorn agreed heartily. She clapped Trent on the back, nearly sending the scrawny Witch into a snowbank. The two of them led the way to Pomegranate Café.

"Wait, just a moment, both of you," Luca said, as William and I turned to follow. At first I thought he really did want to go back to the bookstore—no doubt the conference and unexpected brush with death had been tiring—but he looked, frankly, bashful. "I just wanted to say something before we're beset by, you know, *everyone*."

"Then hurry up," William told him. "I can smell the spiked cocoa from here."

"I will, I'll be quick, don't worry." Luca took a deep breath. "I just wanted to make sure I told you that I know that yesterday I could have lost you, like even if one speaker had answered an extra question and I'd been stuck at that conference one extra minute I could have really lost you, both of you, and that would have been unimaginable, and I know I was gone a lot at the conference while we were investigating so I never really got a chance to say that I'm on your side, Red, but also I'm on William's side, and I always will be, and I love you. *Both* of you."

For a moment we stood there, a little trio, dark figures in the snowy park. Glittery snowflakes had begun to float down around us. When Luca breathed, the mist billowed in front of his face.

"*Both* of us," I repeated slowly, looking down at William as a grin spread across my face. "You hear that? Looks like you're stuck with us . . . forever."

"No, that's not what I meant, not exactly," Luca protested. "I meant—William, to me, you *are* one of us."

William sat in the snow, pondering Luca, head to one side. When he spoke his voice was gruff, but I could see his tail wagging. "I'm not going to kiss you."

"That isn't what I meant either," Luca said, chuckling. "Maybe I did too much talking these past few days, and I can't make words work any more. I mean—"

"Don't bother," William interrupted. He jumped up and leapt over to Luca, rubbing against him, leaving trails of snow along his robe. "I know what you mean."

"All settled, then?" I asked. When two happy faces smiled back at me, I beamed back. "Great. Now can we please go to the café before we all become literal snow children?"

"She's been spending too much time with Officer Thorn," I overheard William confide to Luca as we set off.

"She really has," Luca agreed. "Obviously we wouldn't turn into snow children. For starters, you'd be an abominable snow creature."

"And you could be a yeti," William returned, with real affection.

I grinned. No matter what we were, it was good to be home.

# Epilogue

*A note from Paracelsus*

*To Cinnabar:*

The institute is happily wallowing in the post-holiday lull, and I find I have a quiet moment for catching up with my correspondence. You will be most interested, I think, to hear the results of the recent vote in the city. No proposal on the Yule ballot was as controversial, or indeed as meaningful, as the new legislation regarding magical beings. I'm told there was record turnout at the polls, despite a recent snowstorm. And in the end, the legislation was rejected. Many citizens interviewed by the press expressed concern for their magical neighbors, and alarm at the machinations of a certain supper club.

I write *in the end,* but of course, you and I both know that isn't entirely true. Life is the true never-ending experiment—not *creating* life, you understand, but living it. I am sure you *do* understand, Cinnabar, but one does have to be careful with words these days . . .

And on that note–that of living life–I hope you and your companions have settled back into Belville surrounded by peace and prosperity, with hopeful prospects for the new year. Do write, when you get a chance. And when next you consider traveling, bear in mind that I have not yet had the pleasure of meeting your scholarly beau or police officer friend.

All my best,
*Paracelsus*

# Recipes

The recipes included here have been submitted by the residents of Belville, collected (and at times translated) by the author. Mistakes might have been made at any part of the process, but with any luck, these will bring a bit of fun and inspiration to you, our readers! Always feel free to experiment with the recipes included. And if you do, reach out to info@elle hartford.com to let us know how it went!

That said, without further ado . . .

***

Red's Favorite (Non-Alcoholic) Mulled Wine

*Traditionally mulled wine is made with a fruity red wine and a splash of brandy or other liquor, but a detective needs to keep a clear head (most of the time!). Check out Red's adjustments to her favorite holiday recipe:*

Serves 4

Ingredients:

- 2 C pomegranate juice (preferably with no sugar added)
- 2 C cranberry juice (also preferably no or low sugar)
- 2 C water
- 8 cloves
- 1 cinnamon stick
- fresh fruit to taste: Red suggests a few orange slices, but you could also use some blackberries, sliced apple, or whatever fruit you prefer!
- brown sugar, to taste

1. Combine all ingredients in a large pot on the stove; bring to a simmer on medium heat.
2. Reduce heat to "low" and let simmer for 15 minutes, or up to 1 hour. This is a good time to taste a little and add more fruit, spice, or sugar as needed.
3. Remove from heat and strain into a pitcher or mugs.
4. Garnish with extra cinnamon or fruit, if you like. Then enjoy!

* * *

## Luca's Favorite Yuletide Cookies

*You may recall that Luca's family traditions included a fair amount of moon-gazing (more on that in* Beauty and the Alchemist!*). He has a special soft spot for these classic Yuletide treats, often called*

*Moon Cookies!*

Makes: varied, depending on size of cookie cutter (smaller cookies recommended)

Ingredients:

- 1 C butter (room temperature)
- 1¼ C sugar
- 2 tsp grated lemon peel
- ¼ tsp salt
- 1½ C flour
- 1½ C ground almonds
- 1 tsp vanilla
- (In place of icing: 1 C powdered sugar)

1. Cream the butter and sugar in a large bowl until light and fluffy.
2. Add in the remaining cookie ingredients (not the powdered sugar) and mix well.
3. Cover the dough and chill for an hour, or overnight.
4. When ready to bake, preheat oven to 325 degrees (F).
5. On a lightly floured counter, roll dough until it's ⅛ inch thick.  Cut out crescent moon shapes (a cookie cutter helps immensely!).
6. Transfer cookies to an ungreased baking sheet and bake for 8-10 minutes.
7. Sprinkle warm cookies with powdered sugar and enjoy!

* * *

# Sakura's Extra-Special Hot Chocolate

*What would a proper holiday party be without chocolate? Sakura delights in customizing this basic recipe for each of her friends. Get creative with it, and don't forget to share!*

Serves 4

Ingredients:

- 4 C milk (whole milk means extra creaminess, but any milk–including almond milk–works)
- ¼ C unsweetened cocoa powder
- ¼ C sugar (to taste)
- ½ C chocolate chips (Saki uses dark or bittersweet, but any chocolate is game!)
- ¼ tsp vanilla
- Additional add-ins, according to taste: chili powder, cinnamon, nutmeg, peppermint extract, caramel, coffee, or whatever you desire!

1. Combine milk, cocoa powder and sugar in a small saucepan. Set over medium heat, whisking often, until warm but not boiling.
2. Add chocolate chips and whisk constantly until the

chocolate is evenly distributed. This is a good time to taste for sweetness if you'd like to add more sugar.

3. Whisk in vanilla and any other mix-ins you like.
4. Serve warm and enjoy!

* * *

## William's Recipe for Peace of Mind: Lepus

*As usual, everyone's favorite magical familiar has his own unique twist on a "recipe." Enjoy!*

"Not many people know about this one," says William. "It may be hard to find if you're in a city full of lights. Do yourself a favor and find a quiet spot.

"In the Northern Hemisphere, during the winter, you can find Lepus right below another constellation we've talked about, Orion. Of course you remember that Orion is called 'the Hunter,' right? Lepus is a hare, or rabbit. (There's not a lot of puppets in the stars, but there *are* a lot of animals.)

"Lepus is small, and it looks like a rainbow leading to a piece of pie–with a pair of ears. You'll get the idea pretty quickly when you see it. They say it might be a rabbit running away from Orion, but after meeting some of the members of that supper club, I think Orion is the one who should worry. Either way, bundle up and spend some time outside this Yule!"

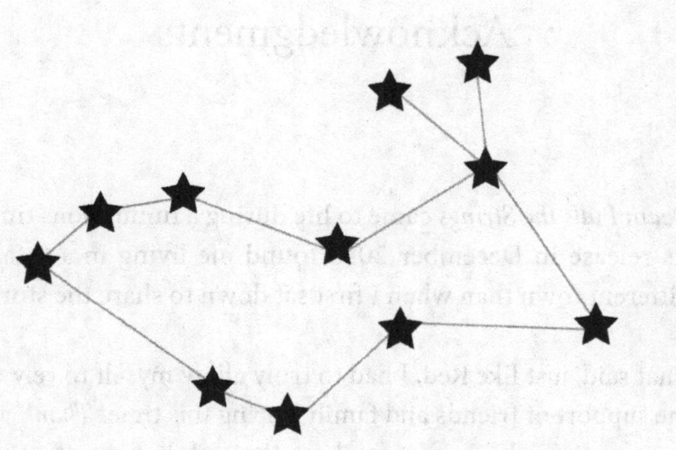

# Lepus
*the rabbit*

# Acknowledgments

*Death Pulls the Strings* came to life during a tumultuous time! Its release in December 2023 found me living in a totally different town than when I first sat down to share the story.

That said, just like Red, I had to truly allow myself to rely on the support of friends and family during this time. *Thank you* to everyone who encouraged me through low points, took an interest in the series and this particular volume, or even helped move a box (full of books, most likely!). And an extra special thank you to my partner, who let me tag along to a conference of his own. (Academic life may have inspired a few of Luca's references, and not a few jokes, but fortunately the murder investigation was completely fabricated!)

And finally, as always, a *massive* thank you to the other authors who have supported me from day one, the wonderful book community online, Sisters in Crime, the Cozy Mystery Tribe, and my intrepid ARC readers!

Most of all this holiday season, I'm very thankful to *you*. That means you, reading this! I hope your time with Red and her friends has been truly magical. And of course, if you find you have a little extra time on your hands . . . reviews are always an appropriate gift for a good book and its author! ;)

# About the Author

Elle adores cozy mysteries, fairy tales, and above all, learning new things. As a historian and educator, she believes in the value of stories as a mirror for complicated realities. She currently lives in New Jersey with a grumpy tortoise and a three-legged cat.

Find more stories of Red and her friends at ellehartford.com. And while you're there, sign up for Elle's newsletter to get bonus material, behind-the-scenes sneak peeks, and terrible jokes!

# Also by Elle Hartford

The Alchemical Tales
*Beauty and the Alchemist* (book 1)
*Cold as Snow* (book 2)
*Mermaid for Danger* (book 3)
*Cry Big Bad Wolf* (book 4)
*Cinders to Dust* (book 5)

Pomegranate Cafe Romance
*Worthy in Love* (book 1)
*A Tale of Rowan and Daisy* (book 1.5)
*Strong in Love* (book 2)